D1235494

PRINCE CHARMING

CD REISS

*everafter*ROMANCE

SOMERSET COUNTY LIBRARY
BRIDGEWATER. NJ 08807

EverAfter Romance
A Division of Diversion Publishing Corp.
443 Park Avenue South, Suite 1008
New York, New York 10016
www.EverAfterRomance.com

Prince Charming
Copyright © 2017-2018 - Flip City Media Inc.
All rights reserved.

No part of this book may be reproduced in any form or by any electronic
or mechanical means, including information storage and retrieval systems,
without written permission from the author, except for the use of
brief quotations in a book review.

For more information, email info@everafterromance.com

First EverAfter Romance edition February 2018.
Print ISBN: 978-1635760835

LSIEA/1801

SOMERSET COUNTY LIBRARY
BRIDGEWATER, NJ 08807

CHAPTER 1.

CASSIE

I trust men I'm attracted to about as far as I can throw them, which is surprisingly far if I have good leverage and mobility in my lower body, but not far enough to give them the time of day or half a chicken sandwich.

You don't have to like it, but I'm not going to argue with at least four generations of family history. Once I feel that little buzz in the sexual part of my brain, it's a four-alarm fire in there. Klaxons. Red flags. Lines in the sand. The guy can be a crown prince anointed by the good Lord himself and there's nothing he can do to get more than a few months out of me. It's not his fault. It's mine, and I'm all right with that. It's gotten me pretty far.

Then this morning happened.

We intercepted Keaton Bridge at a factory he's opening in the next town over and took him in for questioning. When he looked me in the eye, I went to DEFCON One. Code Red. My body began staging a bloodless coup while my mind lost its flank support.

He has the body and the eyes of a predator, silken movements and a churning, twisting mind that calculates ten steps ahead. I can feel it working, and it turns me on.

I don't know him. Nobody does. Trust isn't on the table, but I'm drawn in his direction as if the earth suddenly tilted and all the water of my attention is flowing downhill, toward him.

He's seen things, but no one has ever proven he's done anything. He knows things, but we don't know exactly what.

He's immune to bluffing apparently. We've had him in interrogation for two hours and he hasn't even asked for a lawyer.

Most black hat hackers have confidence deficits they cover in layers of bling and swagger. They compensate for social awkwardness with tough-sounding names and facility with numbers. Some have a talent for the long con until they have to look someone in the eye. Some are straight up sociopaths.

When we picked up Keaton Bridge—a.k.a. Alpha Wolf, though no one has proven it—I'd profiled him as the latter. He and his partner, Taylor Harden, are opening the first quantum-chip manufacturer in the world. The risk is enormous. Either his guts are made of stainless steel or he doesn't have a sliver of human emotion.

Then I met him. My name had barely passed my lips before I knew he wasn't a sociopath. He had emotions, tons of them, and they were complex, real, and intense.

I watch Ken interview him through the mirror. Both men are in profile.

Bridge waits two full seconds before answering any question. His hands rest flat on the table in front of him, and he's perfectly still. It's as if he knows any movement can be a tell, so he makes none at all.

Those emotions I sensed? He has control over them. His self-awareness is frightening and exhilarating. His voice has a British lilt that's masculine, confident, and educated without being snotty.

The dimples in his cheeks are a trick. The smile lines are a hoax. His voice, his looks, the leathery scent that filled the car on the way in; all of it is a long con game.

"I haven't a clue," he says over the speakers in the dark observation room.

"But you are Alpha Wolf?" Ken replies, referring to one of the three most powerful figures on the dark web.

One-Mississippi.

Google can't find the dark web. The only browser that will take you there hides your activity in so many layers of encryption, you can peel them like an onion and never find the center.

Criminals trade credit card data, guns, drugs, people.

The FBI has a presence there. We use it to speak to informants and assets. Journalists use it to contact anonymous whistleblowers.

Two-Mississippi.

"It's quite funny, that."

"That what?" Ken asks.

One-Mississippi.

There's no official or provable connection between Keaton Bridge and Alpha Wolf. But that's the thing about covered tracks. Cleanliness has its own stink.

Two-Mississippi.

"That stupid fucking assumption."

Between Ken and Keaton Bridge, one of them is a federal agent. One of them has the power in the relationship. And one of them is making stupid fucking assumptions.

"Are you the same Alpha Wolf who maintains a relationship with Keyser Kaos?"

One-Mississippi. Two-Mississippi.

"You're a very insistent chap."

Ken opens a folder. It looks like a complete dossier, but in fact, it contains cherry-picked items from a two-terabyte hard drive on Alpha Wolf and Kaos. "Is this you?"

One-Mississippi.

Bridge glances over the paper Ken hands him. It's not a photo of a person. It's a screenshot of a post on a dark web onion thread.

Two-Mississippi.

The screenshot Bridge looks over is a normal Keyser Kaos /Alpha Wolf chat about how much they'd charge to dox a female gamer. This is the least of their infractions, and he knows it.

It's proof of nothing, and he knows it.

Bridge puts the page down, then leans back. He and Ken share a moment in profile.

Three-Mississippi.

I'm in the observation room because I asked Ken for a change in strategy. I wasn't convinced I wouldn't be railroaded by my body's reaction to Bridge or that my mind's alarm bells wouldn't distract me. Now I'm not sure I did the right thing.

Four-Mississippi.

Though Keaton was intimidating at first sight, with his perfect suit, open collar, broad shoulders, and chiseled jaw, he wasn't cold. He saw me before he saw my badge, as if he'd whipped away my cloak of invisibility.

I hadn't felt naked. I'd felt noticed.

Then Keaton had glanced to my right, where Taylor Harden stood. Without saying a word, he apologized to his partner.

Fascinating. He was fascinating.

Five-Mississippi.

Through the mirror, Bridge turns and looks straight at me. His eyes are the color of the seven o'clock sky and they can't see me, but they do. He sees everything. He sees how I tap my fingers to count the seconds. He sees the lint on my jacket.

I can't move. I am sealed in my rigid skin. Joints locked. Muscles frozen. He sees the spit dry on my tongue, the callouses on my hands, the tightening of my jaw. He sees the nights I was up with firearm fist, and the mornings Mom counted my night's haul.

He hears the cacophony in my head.

Six-Mississippi.

He sees so deep into my loneliness that a *huh* escapes my throat, then he speaks.

"Won't you join us, Agent Grinstead?"

CHAPTER 2.

KEATON

Agent Rotter won't let it go. He thinks I spent sixteen years covering my tracks to be intimidated in a little room by a little fucking prat.

"You're a very insistent chap."

Rotter opens a folder and flips through the pages. It's all for show. I don't look at what he's flipping through because he has fuck-all on me.

He spins the folder to face me and taps the page he's found. "Is this you?"

I will not be rushed.

I will not be coerced.

I will not be strong-armed into risking QI4.

I don't care about the company itself. Don't give a flying fuck about quantum mechanics or changing the world blah, blah, blah. I don't even give a shit about money anymore. They can have it, the whole rotten lot of them.

I push away the folder. This entire drama's put me off my lunch. Agent Rotter's bloody smirk is going to get him a mouthful of fist one of these days.

But not today.

I promised Taylor I'd be there today, and I will be.

Taylor could have turned over on me a hundred times. But he didn't. And when I told him I was looking to go straight, he partnered with me, knowing I was a risk. He could have gotten plenty of investors.

I'm not going to be late thanks to the rotter here. But for the bird?

Where is Agent Bird?

Someone's on the other side of the mirror on my left, and if I'm any judge, the woman who helped drive me here from Barrington is watching five feet away, on the other side. She's distractingly beautiful and gloriously proud. As soon as I saw her, I had a vision of her atop a mountain, ruling the world, and a second vision quickly followed. Her under me, begging, with my name on her lips, over and over, pride shattered.

I feel her watching from the other side of the mirror. It's not an unpleasant feeling. It is, however, inadequate. I want to see her again. I want to see if I saw something that wasn't there. I want to regain control of the situation.

Turning to the mirror, I make my request. "Won't you join us, Agent Grinstead?"

Agent Rotter clears his throat. On the other side of the mirror, we hear a door open, then close.

Taylor's going to get on my arse for bringing the FBI calling. I'm going to have to convince him they were jagging off into their little files, trying to get me to turn on Keyser Kaos. They brought me all the way to Doverton to see if I have a death wish.

When the door opens and she comes into the interrogation room, I smell her perfume. It's lavender, calming, and I know the scent isn't to calm her but to lull me.

I'm not lulled. I'm physically aroused in a way I have no control over.

"Mr. Bridge." She stands astride the FBI action doll of a man.

No, I was right. She's proud, but not arrogant. Her accent's American. They could have flown her in from anywhere.

Thirty-ish. Five-eight.

Freckles on her nose the makeup doesn't cover.

Grew up outdoors.

A few grey hairs at the root.

Fingernails trimmed, clean, unpolished.

A bare left ring finger.

Does she have a lover?

That releases a flood of mental imagery I have no time for.

"Why hide behind a mirror, Agent Grinstead?"

She looks me in the eye without shame or fear. It's a frontal attack

I'm not ready for. Her hair is the black of silk sheets, and her eyes are the grey of London's early morning fog.

"We were giving you a little space."

She's blindsiding you.

It's true, but I'm not turning away. She can come at me all she wants.

I can tell there's no love lost between her and Agent Rotter. As soon as she's in the room, I know she cares a bloody ton more about this case than the Boy Scout.

Which is good. I can use that.

"That answer's beneath you."

"If you have someplace else to be," she says, tilting her chin toward the dossier, "you know the quickest way out of here."

I lean forward. My answer should shake her a little, but not too much. I think about her response two seconds and formulate my own. "We're in the middle of a promotional event. The mayor's there. The press. The Lord himself is looking down on the Barrington factory, and you expect me to believe you want to give me space."

"If you want less space, that can be arranged." Her voice is so crisp, it's seductive.

Walking confidently in six-inch heels, she steps from her position and gets behind me. Her calves are shaped for my hands. If I want to see her, I'll have to twist all the way around. If I face forward, she has the benefit of speaking without me watching her reactions. This puts me at a disadvantage, technically. But without seeing her, I don't have to be captivated like a schoolboy, getting me back a fraction of the leverage I've lost.

"Is this where you move from implications to accusations?" I say. "Maybe pull something else out of this little folder here? Reveal your narrative of crimes? Make a sincere but manageable threat, close the walls in on me, then show me a singular way out? Yes? A little Reid technique?"

Ken looks over my shoulder to her.

"A plea bargain. Maybe you want me to flip on someone?" I push the folder back toward Ken. "Keyser Kaos maybe? I read an article in the *Intercept* about him. Quite a character. According to the article, of the thousands of people on the dark web offering assassination services, he's the only one who can make good on them."

She speaks from behind me. "We have a trail that connects you and Alpha Wolf."

"No." I turn slightly, so her blur is in my peripheral vision. I can smell her with more clarity than I can see her. "No, you don't." I turn back toward Agent Rotter. Even in the corners of my vision, Grinstead is distracting. She takes up way too much room in my attention. "You could just tell me what you want."

Rotter's watch tick-tocks. The air conditioning snaps off. I hear Grinstead breathe. Otherwise she is immobile behind me. I know she and this plastic version of a man are talking with looks and hand signals.

"Two years ago, you invested in QI4," Ken says.

"My friend Taylor came to me with an opportunity I had the resources to take advantage of."

Such a flat answer for such a thick web of motivations. Taylor's a genius. I wasn't surprised when he cracked quantum computing. Anyone would have invested, but I did because it's the right way to thank him for his friendship and loyalty before the rest of my plans go into motion.

"You and Keyser Kaos have been partners for years," Rotter says. "We've tracked everything, and now you're claiming to be legit? How could we not follow up?"

He shrugs as if this is just procedure. He's going to be the good cop now. The role reversal is standard in Reid technique interrogations. I feel as though I'm the only audience for a play that's been put on every day for a generation.

"When did partnerships become illegal?" I ask.

"When their purpose is to launder money," Grinstead says, and I like her as the bad cop. She's got a slick competence for wickedness that intrigues me.

"Maybe not?" Rotter's like a teddy bear at this point. "Or maybe you never intended to finance QI4 with laundered cash and it's Kaos with the baggage. It's Kaos who lied to you. Maybe you're just getting caught up in his malfeasance."

I wait for her to go bad cop and say something refuting this soothing fairy tale, but she doesn't.

After a few breaths, I say, "I'm sure that you think you have something in that folder that proves I'm Alpha Wolf, or that I launder money through cybercurrencies. But I know you don't. There are no recordings, no screenshots, nothing of Kaos communicating with any persona you can prove is me. This is a parlor trick, and a particularly bad one."

I lean back, knowing I'm right. They have fuck-all. I know what exists in my world and I know what's been erased, and by whom.

"Thank you, Mr. Bridge," Grinstead says, coming back around the table. She's quite a sight, and I wonder why a woman that beautiful would want to be a federal agent. She must be ever so much more than she appears. "We'll spare you further exposure to our parlor tricks."

She walks out, taking the air out of the room with her.

CHAPTER 3.

CASSIE

"What were you thinking?" Ken's look of incredulity is cartoonish on his generic handsomeness. "He's not flipping."

We're in the lunchroom of our field office with our boss, Special Agent in Charge Cesar Orlando. His shaved head has flat parts, leaving a dark arc connecting his ears every few days. His tie is loose and his suit is too wide at the shoulders, but that's normal around here.

A black-and-white poster of our ten most wanted hangs on the fridge with a curling note taped to it:

> DON'T BE LIKE THESE GUYS.
> EAT ONLY WHAT YOU BRING.

By the side of the sink, mismatched mugs stand on their heads. Locked grey cabinets hide cleaning supplies. Crushed-cornered boxes of who-even-knows pile under the window.

"We have an established pattern of racketeering," I reply.

"Onion site chats aren't enough to bring him in," Ken argues. He's believable and passionate now. He's most animated when disagreeing.

Orlando stands against the counter with his arms crossed, silent until he has something to say. We're chasing a white supremacist cell, one of many across the country with plans to start a race war with coordinated, simultaneous attacks, if we could just find them past the chatter. This is Orlando's chance to validate the existence of our tiny office.

"This guy doesn't spook," I say, pointing out the door in the general area of the unflappable Keaton Bridge. "He's slipped past the cyber division a dozen times, and now he's trying to go straight. He's in transition between Alpha Wolf and…I don't know—"

"I agree," Ken adds. "We need real-life leads, not digital creeps behind a screen."

I continue without acknowledging the comment because it's the only way to be heard. "This QI4 thing he invested in? It's huge, and from everything we can trace, it's above board. If we don't flip him now, before he's too well-known to hide, we've lost him."

"He's not taking the bluff, and he's not a white supremacist. There's a slim chance he's useful."

"He knows every corner of the dark web. That's where they're organizing."

"I agree," Ken snaps, not agreeing at all. "If he's Alpha Wolf, he's useful."

I cross my arms. "Do you want to get into Third Psyche or not? Because I do. And I want to do it before they take up arms."

"They're not that organized." He shoots a look at Orlando. "Not yet."

I'm waiting for Orlando to chime in and agree with Ken. I'm waiting to be erased. But it doesn't happen. It's on me to convince him through Ken.

"Are you willing to be the guy who heard chatter about a synchronized multi-state armed takeover and didn't follow up?" I ask.

"We can follow up without that guy."

I'm about to answer when Orlando chimes in. "He's a good lead right on our doorstep. But Ken's right. He's not flipping, and odds are against him even having the intel."

I don't know why I don't buckle. Maybe because—for a second—when Bridge saw me, he really saw me. Maybe I want to feel that again. Or maybe I'm just sick of taking a backseat.

"Let him go, then give me half an hour," I say to Orlando before I turn to Ken, wishing I'd said forty minutes. "I'll have something. Maybe not enough to put into Delta, but something."

Orlando will say no, but I've said what needed saying. I'll fight another day.

"Take forty," Orlando says. I'm shocked, but I keep my composure. "You've got the best shot. I think he liked you."

CHAPTER 4.

KEATON

The air is thick as London's. Wet and foggy. A nip of cold. It's early evening, and though I have control over my appetite, my stomach grumbles.

That whole interview was a fishing expedition with a barbed hook. She must be their closer. I don't trust my attraction to her. It's coupled with a compulsion to speak to her, tell her things, break promises I made to myself.

I want to tell her how important that company it is to me and why. Not Agent Rotter, not the FBI, but her. I cross the car park, closing my jacket and knotting my scarf as I walk over the wet concrete. I can resist the compulsion to see her, but even as I deny it, the pressure vibrates the webbing of my thoughts. I want her to understand me.

Doverton's a small city about twenty miles from the two-horse town of Barrington, where I need to be. I stayed at the Doverton country club on a few previous visits, so I have the lay of the land, more or less. I'm not lost or disoriented. I'm just slightly angry, very impatient, and deeply concerned.

"Mr. Bridge!"

Her voice cuts the mist with the accompanying clap of her high heels. Even at a half-run, she's steady in them. Her hair is wet at the ends, and the grey corner of a laptop peeks out from the front of her coat. She cradles it to her chest as if it's a baby.

"I have to go," I say. "If you want to arrest me—"

"No." She stops short in front of me. "This isn't like that."

The misty rain is running the hell out of her mascara, enlarging the charcoal-colored ovals around her grey-fog eyes. Compared to how she came off in the interrogation room, this federal agent in front of me is the vulnerable version of herself. She's not broken, but bending.

Half-sodden, she's still captivating. What would it take to break a woman like her?

"What is it like?" I ask.

"Can we get out of the rain?"

I scan the car park. There's no quick shelter. I check my watch. I don't like being late, even for Taylor, but this version of Agent Grinstead in an uncontrolled environment is dangerous. I want to ask her what's wrong. What has she given up on to run out after me like this? It could take all freaking night. Late is late, but too late is too late.

"I don't have time." I walk, and she stays put.

"I need your help."

I turn and look at her. Is this the same person? "What's your game?"

"No game. My laptop's getting wet."

I let her get rained on, resisting the urge to hold my coat over her. "Your shoes are getting wet too."

"I have an extra pair in my desk." She indicates my feet. "Do you?"

I do not, and my shoes aren't built for standing in the rain.

She shivers once, quickly, then stills her body. That moment of vulnerability seals the deal. I figure Taylor can handle the pleasantries with Beaver.

"Ten minutes," I say.

"My car is over there," she says, turning and pointing at a black Buick without extending her arm enough to drop the computer.

"Your car or a company car?"

I'm not getting into an FBI fleet car. They'll record everything and collect DNA after.

"Mine."

"Show me the registration."

"It's in the glove compartment."

CHAPTER 5.

CASSIE

I'm already soaked through when I pluck the registration card out of the glove compartment. I hand it through the window. He unfolds it with his hands inside the car so it stays dry.

His hands are six inches from me. They're tendon and bone, calloused at the tips from hitting keys. They're the hands of a man, and I want him to put his fingers in my mouth.

Are you serious? Stop.

He checks my name and the license plate. "Cassandra."

"That's my name."

"Do you know the Cassandra complex?"

"You're getting wet."

He hands me the registration. He must have memorized everything already. "Cassandra was an ancient Greek woman with the power to see how the world was going to end, but no power to stop it."

"Let me guess. No one would listen to her."

He smirks and crosses in front of the car, touching the hood with the graceful tips of his fingers as he cuts the turn around it. I hit the unlock button. When the passenger door slaps shut, he and I are in a tight space. Was the car always this small? Was the roof this low? The seats this cramped?

He slides the seat all the way back, but the length of his legs isn't the issue. He's fine. The car is suddenly too small for *me*. His presence fills the space between the dashboard and the back window, floor to ceiling with a sense of thick menace. He's as stationary and lethal as a bullet in the chamber. As perfect as a polished barrel shining in the moonlight.

Without the protection of my badge, the two-way mirror, or the buffer of a threat, I am small and vulnerable. I am made of alarms and denials. I'm water being poured into a container shaped like him.

"So," he says. "How is it you can be in the field office parking lot with me?"

I close the windows and turn on the heat. Everything turns to steam. The air gets heavy, weighing down my eyelids in a way I know will be construed as seductive. I'm conflicted about giving that impression. I'm pretty sure there's no way I can hide how beautiful I find him.

"We have nothing on you. That doesn't mean we aren't close."

"I don't know you, Agent Grinstead, but if I were a betting man, I'd bet entrapment was beneath you."

I look him in the eye, and the force of his gaze silences me. I feel powerless. Like cornered prey. The thickness of the air delivers his smell directly between my legs, which reacts with a sudden throb that's almost painful, as if an unused delivery system is asked to do too much, too fast.

I point out the half-fogged window, up at the light posts. "Those cameras?"

He's looking at me, not in the direction I'm pointing. I'm about to trust him with a piece of information. It's easy negotiation calculus. I have to expose myself if he's going to expose himself.

I continue. "Out here in Doverton, they put them up, but they don't have the resources to monitor them. Some work. Some don't. That one in particular hasn't worked in three months. That one over there." I point behind him, but he doesn't turn. "Couple of high school kids hit it with a rock and it points at the sky. It works if you want to know the weather."

"It's raining."

"Yeah."

"It bothers you that they don't work."

For a guy who makes a living hiding behind a computer screen, he sure can read people. Now, in addition to feeling turned on to the point of being liquid, I feel naked.

"It bothers me. If you're going to do something, you should do it. If they don't want a field office in Doverton, they should close us. Don't do this half-assed shit."

"Are you from here?"

"I'm from Flint. Just outside Detroit."

"I know where Flint is."

Of course he does.

After clearing my throat, I say, "So you're wondering why I asked you to come into my car."

He smiles. He has great teeth. Not fake. Ever so slightly uneven. I notice the canines aren't any longer or sharper than a normal person's, then I wonder if that's a trick to make his prey relax.

"Not really," he says. "I can work it out."

"Oh?" My apprehension gives way to curiosity. I turn off the heat, cutting the ambient noise so we can hear the *pit pat* of rain on the windshield.

He taps his finger on his knee. His trousers are a nice tweed. He was on his way to the Barrington bottling plant for a celebration. He's missed it, and I don't feel bad about that at all.

"You're an open book, Ms. Grinstead." He adjusts himself in his seat, looks away from a beat. He turns the heat back up, drowning out the sound of the rain.

He waits.

"You're testing me," I say. "I turned the heat off. You think it might be to unmask our voices because the car is wired? You don't know."

"Now I do. You didn't react when I turned it back on."

"The car isn't bugged."

"It's not." He turns to face me with more of his body. "You're taking a risk. You knew you had nothing on me. This meeting we're having here isn't planned. Maybe it's personal. Looking to get information on an ex-boyfriend perhaps?"

I huff out a laugh. My most recent ex-boyfriend, Doug, is harmless to the point of invisibility. If I want information from him, all I ever have to do is ask, except there's nothing in his brain I want to know.

But Keaton Bridge? Sitting so close to him, pressed against his presence like a raisin kneaded into cookie dough, I realize I want to know everything in his mind.

"It's not personal." I pull my laptop out of my jacket. "But the bureau won't let me be direct about it until you're an asset."

"Ah. I have no intention of getting entered in your little database of informants."

I start to tell him that I know, but stop. I shouldn't agree. I should ask him how he's so sure, but I trip on the response. I wonder if I'm having the same effect on him as he is on me. Is he turned on to the point of distraction? Does he have an ache between his legs? Everything about him is distance and control.

Imagine cracking through that.

Imagine him losing control.

Stop.

I lay the laptop on my knee, and as I'm about to open it, he holds the top down. "Don't open that." He spreads his beautiful hand over the top. I look into his twilight eyes. "Tell me first."

"There's an onion site."

"There are many."

The dark web is larger than the web we can see. No one knows how much larger, except maybe 4lph4_W0lF a.k.a. Alpha Wolf, the king of the underworld who is rumored to be Keaton Bridge.

"I know, and I know Alpha Wolf—"

"I didn't say that was me."

"He was one of the ones who took down New Peanut Butter."

New Peanut Butter was a site for the utter destruction of innocence, like putting a knife into a new jar of peanut butter. They were taken down and unmasked to law enforcement by an anonymous group of hackers.

"Good for him," he says.

"So you're a moral person. On some level, you're not evil."

"Thank you for your vote of confidence."

His answer doesn't have a denial inside it. Is that calculated? Or did it slip?

"I do know some friends of his"—I use the third person as a buffer for his non-denial—"were in a white supremacist forum that moved a few months ago. I need the link."

That isn't uncommon. There's no Google of the dark web. You have a link or you don't, and the links are randomly generated alphabet soup. Once a moderator gets a whiff of infiltration, he'll send a new link to people he trusts and the forum will be left with a bunch of outsiders banging around in an otherwise empty room.

"There are no friends on the dark web," Keaton says.

"Fine. Associates. The forum went dead, and I have no idea where it moved. It's called Third Psyche."

"If you think I keep company with Nazis, you have something coming."

The rain gets heavier. *Pat-patter* on the windshield turns into the whoosh of rapid fire *pah-pah-pah-pah*.

"So you've heard of it?"

"I never claimed to know nothing."

"Are you going to help me?"

"*Me?* Not *us?*"

"Are you going to help or not?" I repeat without the pronoun.

He hesitates. It's not a pause. It's indecision. Maybe the forwardness of the question has shocked him. "No."

"We may have nothing on you to arrest you today, Mr. Bridge, but we're working on it."

"Call me Keaton. We're old friends now."

"Your identity is out. We're going to prove it."

"Back to *we* I see."

"*We* know the money you invested in QI4 was laundered, which makes the entire company subject to asset seizure."

He leans forward and puts his hand over mine. It's dry and warm. I never knew I had nerves that went directly from the skin on my hand to the glands inside my thighs, but now I do.

"You have nothing. The money is untraceable, and it was made honestly, taxed honestly, and used in an honest venture."

I hear a car pull up behind us. We both look. His cab.

When he takes his hand from mine, the skin goes cold. He opens the passenger door. The muffled clop of raindrop sounds get sharper and more urgent.

With one foot out the door, he stops and looks me in the eye. "If you want out of Doverton, you should try catching a criminal, Agent Grinstead."

"Call me Cassandra."

He smirks and slaps the door closed. The cracking rain goes back to muffled tapping. I am alone with plenty of room in my car, the air thin enough to breathe.

In the rearview, I see him canter across the street and get into the taxi.

It's not until he's gone that I wonder what just happened.

CHAPTER 6.

KEATON - FOUR MONTHS LATER

I couldn't forget the FBI agent with the raven hair and the fog-grey eyes. I'd promised myself I wouldn't look into her background, but I'd lied. I distracted myself with work for the first week, then in a moment of weakness, I uncovered whatever I could, devouring information so I could build a woman out of meaningless details.

I stayed in San Jose until I couldn't anymore. As soon as I crossed into Barrington, I knew I would see her again.

I'm worried about how intrigued I still am by her. She's as harmless as wolfsbane, with its innocuous-looking purple flowers. Touching it with a paper cut can kill a man. Or not. It's a risk I'm not willing to consider. She can derail everything.

I'm not worried about the feds. I thought about moving out of the dark long before the FBI connected Keaton Bridge to Alpha Wolf. I'm prepared for the switch. Nor am I worried about her threats. They have the hollow ring of a prop sword on fake armor.

I won't mistake Cassie's vulnerability for weakness or her silence for lack of interest. She hasn't gotten what she asked for. She'll make sure she comes for me to get the link. I'll find a way to give her what she needs without giving her what she wants.

The taxi speeds over the empty road, rain splashing everywhere. The layer of water on the windows marbles everything into a moving grey mass, but the driver speeds along as if he can find Barrington by smell.

I've dissected my last contact with Cassandra dozens of times since leaving. She'd turned skittish in her car, like a tamed horse who only remembered her wild past when cornered. Her domestication cracked, and something unruly seeped through. Something sexy and musky. Her sweet steel smell and the soft sound of her voice is stuck to my senses, latching on like a puzzle piece.

I'm sure I'd fancy getting the girl with the long sable hair to scream my name. I'm sure her sexual obedience would be more satisfying than any other woman's.

By the time the cab pulls off onto a long road, the beating rain has slowed to a thick drizzle. The factory's details are shrouded by the mist and the setting sun. Three cranes surround it, ready to remove the roof so the equipment can be dropped in.

The guard at the factory entrance sees me in the backseat and knows the driver because everyone knows everyone here. We're waved past the gate and navigate the delivery trucks, then a flatbed with a ten-meter-high wooden box with QI4 stenciled on the side.

I pay the driver and hop up on the loading bay. I know the man with the clipboard and the woman operating the forklift. I know the name of the architect who points at the doorframe. They wave or nod, but they're afraid of me. They don't ask questions and I offer nothing. I'm a ghost, and I like it that way.

The room is cavernous. It's a fucking circus. Forklifts and boxes. Drones stringing cables across the ceiling. Robots being assembled by robots. Sparking arc welding behind screens and the shouts of men and women with clipboards as they check their punch lists.

A male voice breaches the din. "It's done!"

"Yes!"

That's a woman's voice I recognize, and I hitch my attention to it. Harper Barrington sits on a wheeled dolly, staring into a screen. Headphones arc over her blond hair, and six of her phalange knuckles are wrapped in white hacker tape.

I hop on the dolly as she pushes headphones off her ears.

"Hey, K," she says as Taylor Harden hops onto the dolly in trousers and a jacket. They high-five and kiss longer than I find appropriate.

"Hello, Alpha," he says when he's done.

"Hello, Beeze."

Harper shuts her console. "We can do the second half tomorrow."

"Does she even work here?" I ask. "Shouldn't she be in school?"

"Get someone else," she says. "See if I care."

"Winter break." Taylor hops off the platform and calls to me, "You have to see this."

I join him as he takes me across the concrete floor. It's been sanded down and shined. Masking tape outlines the equipment and wall placement.

"We're doing it," Taylor says. "When I saw this, I said damn. We're really doing it."

He bursts out onto the loading dock, where a forklift picks up a pallet of nondescript boxes. It's already cold, but colder air comes from the open back of the truck. SysCo is printed on the side.

"This is it!" Taylor's breath is smoke and his jacket flutters open in the wind. "This is when I said *holy shit*."

"It's a refrigerator car? A food delivery?"

"When I dreamed about making it, I thought about this. Being so big we needed a cafeteria."

"We need a cafeteria because you wanted to buy a factory in the middle of nowhere."

He doesn't even hear me. He's lit up like London Bridge.

A crane lowers a pizza oven onto the dock. We jump to ground level. He knows me well enough to walk toward the river, where there's less noise and confusion. We stop under the shelter built to protect equipment from the elements.

I make him nervous. His life is built on quantum circuits and the software that makes it feasible. If the law finds something on his partner, his life's work is in jeopardy.

"The FBI," he says in a more somber tone. "Have you heard from them since they brought you in?"

I'd told him about the interview, and he hasn't brought it up since. Now he has to. This is why we're by the river.

"I would have mentioned it."

"Not comforting."

He doesn't believe me. Or more accurately, he believes I'm telling the truth, but doesn't believe the truth is mine to tell.

"They were fishing," I say. "I don't have what they want. I told you this."

He looks away, then back at me. "Okay, listen. Here's the thing. I can't…" He takes a deep breath. "I can't take risks right now."

I cross my arms, trying not to laugh at him. He was never half the risk taker he fancied himself.

"Is Harper all right?"

"She's fine. Thanks for pretending you care."

"I do care." I have to jump in front of this, because this idea that I don't care about him, and the love of his life by extension? It bothers me. "Tell me what you're off about, would you? I don't have all day."

"We have a cash flow problem."

"How much?"

"Hundred."

He means a hundred thousand. It's not much in the grand scheme of our investments and liabilities, but moving that amount around to cover it won't be easy.

"Don't we have accountants?" I ask.

"They can't pull it off a money tree. All our shit's tied up."

"I'll take care of it."

"With what? Bitcoin? No." He can't look at me, or he won't. He's doing it on purpose.

"Why not?"

Finally, he looks me in the eye. "Dude."

"Wanker. I set you up clean." The end of each word is clipped, but I keep my voice low. I don't want to alarm him, but he needs to trust me on this.

He closes his eyes for a second as if gathering his own patience. "I know, but… Harper says there's hacker chatter about you. Kaos's people aren't happy you've gone legit. And on the one hand, fuck them. On the other hand, it creates a vulnerability we have to shut down."

"They have no idea who I am."

"Dude, *I* don't even know who you are."

Taylor used to be an impenetrable wall of ambition. Once he met Harper, he started saying what was on his mind whether it serves his goals or not.

"We've been friends since you got your first boil," I say.

"You dropped into New Jersey from nowhere."

"London's hardly nowhere."

"Do you remember the time Mrs. Denver was calling your name in the cafeteria? She kept calling and calling and you just ignored her? Everyone turned around but you and the girl you were talking to. Denver was just, 'Keaton! Mr. Bridge! Keaton! Keaton Bridge!' I had to kick you."

"I was obviously distracted by the bird."

"No, I thought about this a lot. There were other times. The time you had to sign out of class early and you wrote a D instead of a K."

My throat closes. There are some things I don't talk about. Not with my best friend. Not even with those in my family with the same secrets. There are things that are off-limits, but if I tell him that, he'll know by deduction. Taylor's no dolt. In fact, he's brilliant enough to get me killed.

I step out of the shelter. The rain's slowed. "Reliving the glory days has been fun."

"You didn't know yourself by that name," Taylor continues. "Keaton Bridge isn't your name. It's what it is, bro." Taylor's words come from far away, and I hang on every syllable. "It's cool. You're a mystery man. Cool. But maybe the FBI showed up here for a reason."

"You have nothing to worry about. The fed will never be a problem. Ever."

"And Kaos?"

"He's not your concern."

"That's not comforting."

"I'm not here to comfort you."

"Why are you here?"

I answer by putting a hand on each of his shoulders and looking him in the eye. I'm here for him, but I can't say that. He'd never believe it.

"I have this," I say.

He looks at me in a way meant to threaten. I love him, but he's a knob if he thinks he can scare me away from disappearing.

CHAPTER 7.

CASSIE

The club restaurant is crowded with Doverton's élite. Heavy silver-ware clinks, and voices are dampened by the damask curtains with a rose pattern.

The busboy takes our dinner plates.

Frieda has one eyebrow that fades in the center of her nose but doesn't disappear. Where most women would remove the connection, my friend owns it. She tweaks the shape of her brow to beautiful, subtle arches, and can raise one or the other to express a question or doubt, but with the dark line connecting both sides, every expression comes with an undercurrent of strength.

Her dark brown hair is pulled back and parted in the middle. Her gold hoops swing back and forth when she shakes her head. She's a year behind me at the bureau, and the only other woman agent in the office.

"You see that factory? They're building so fast." She slides her thick black glasses to the top of her head and picks up the check.

"Barrington loves it."

"I don't trust these California guys." She puts down the check and picks her bag off the back of the chair. It's basically a leather sack Santa would find quite roomy. "Of course, you knew. You're always so on top of it."

It's my turn to pick up the check while her hand is frozen in her bag as if she's found a prize at the bottom of a cereal box.

"Yeah. Besides being one of the absolute worst, I mean *best*, hackers in the world, he's so cocky about it, I want to slap him with an indictment just for smirking."

My wallet's out before hers. We drop our credit cards on the tray and the waitress whisks it away.

Frieda puts her elbows on the table and circles the air with a finger. "What was this that happened to your face just now?"

"What?" I have no idea what my face did before she asked the question, but it's turning red once she does the circle-thing.

"This glint when you say 'smirk' like you have a picture in your head."

"Of course I have a picture in my head."

"And you like this picture?"

I shrug, but she knows me. She raises that one gorgeous eyebrow, one side higher than the other, and tilts her head.

"Whatever," I say. "Where are they with that check?"

"Tell me something about him."

"There's nothing to tell."

"Anything. Just to pass the time."

I'm not going anywhere until the check comes, so I might as well just spill it. "British."

"Oh, and an accent?"

"Yeah. But he's been living here since he was sixteen."

"Some people don't shake it so easy. Tall? Short?" She slams the last drop of cola and places her glass in the condensation circle on the tablecloth. "Tell me."

"Tall, I guess? Six four?" I slide my own wine glass onto my own grey circle, matching hers. I don't know why I'm equivocating. "Really, really beautiful, to be honest. Like a jaguar. Not the car."

"I like this picture you're painting."

We get the check back and sign on the dotted lines. I'm uncomfortable talking about how I felt around Keaton.

I stand and grab my bag and coat. "I like the picture of him having information I can use to get one up on Ken."

Frieda snorts and throws her twenty-pound bag over her shoulder. "I like that picture too. Ken is one hundred percent *bro*." She drops *bro* like most people drop *shit*. "And he has a sneaky face I don't like."

"His face suits him. And he's going to be the one moved to CID unless I can find something to leverage to my advantage."

CID is the FBI's Criminal Investigative Division. My dream job. I've been passed over four times.

"Can you leverage Mister-Not-The-Car?"

"I can't," I say right away then stop, because I'm flooded with distracting pictures of ripped sheets and knotted bodies. "He's an asset. Off-limits."

"Ah. Well, then. The cat must disappear back into the jungle without you."

She yanks one handle of her hobo bag over her shoulder and opens it, digging for her keys as we walk through the bar. She spends half her waking hours with her arm buried to the elbow. She stops in front of me in the middle of the half-empty, post-dinner-seating bar area to rummage for her keys. There's a football game on the TV, cheers and groans in the air, laughter and clinked bottles. Our team must be winning.

I know exactly where my keys are, but I wait with her, watching the TV as the next play is set up.

In the tense silence, a voice breaks through, and I'd know it even without the British accent. I scan for Keaton and find him when the guy in front of me leans over to talk to the woman next to him. The British businessman/tech giant/hacker sits at the corner of the bar, ordering a drink.

Keaton looks calm, almost serene, more the threatening villain than I ever thought possible.

"Got them!" Frieda exclaims to a jingle of keys.

The play completes. The crowd cheers. Keaton's drink arrives.

She pulls me forward. "Let's go."

The man next to Keaton gets up, and our eyes meet. Keaton looks right at me, picking up his glass and tipping it in my direction. I'm frozen still, shot through with hot steel.

I can't turn away. He's half in shadow, one foot on the floor and the other tensed against the rail of the stool, holding me still with his gaze where most men would have bored me already.

Frieda snaps her fingers in front of my face. "What are you looking at?"

She follows my stare to him just as he puts his drink on the bar as if he's not relieving his hand of weight but making a statement about who he is and what he intends. Everything about him is calculated and deliberate.

"Let's go," I say.

I don't want Frieda to see him. She won't approve, and I'm just not in the mood for it. She'll ask me to make sense of the way I feel around him, and I know I don't have an answer for it.

What do I want out of Keaton? He'd refused to get me into Third Psyche four months ago, and he won't do it now. He's not going to do anything but make me feel unsure and vulnerable. He's going to set off alarm bells and a war between heart and head.

Nobody. No one needs to be all liquid under their skirt. No one needs to feel their heart pound or feel the air press up against them.

A guy in full team regalia tries to sit in the empty stool but makes the mistake of looking at Keaton first. I can't see what passes between them, but the guy, who has tattoos up his arms and a goatee, holds up his hands as if he's sorry for causing offense.

Keaton puts his fingers together and points all four at the seat as if to say, *Are you sitting or not?*

"Are you coming on or not?" Frieda shouts over the growing din before the next play.

Who needs to feel as though they're being devoured by a man's seven o'clock eyes, a four-course meal for a hungry jaguar. Who needs to be touched by a man shrouded in mystery? To fall into the music of his voice?

I am a federal agent. I have a law degree. I worked my ass off to get this far and I'm not jeopardizing it with an untrustworthy businessman.

Do you want to go to CID or not?

If I want to get this done, I'm going to have to stretch my values thin.

Frieda's looking at me as if I have lipstick on my teeth. "Is this Mister Smirkypants?" She jerks her head in Keaton's direction. Her voice is flirtatious, as if she's trying to pack a hundred syllables worth of *yowza* into one word.

"How did you guess?"

She draws the same circle in the air as she did over the dinner table. My face gives me away apparently. Somehow, that's enough for me to know I've already made a decision.

"I'll see you later," I say.

"You going to be all right?" *Yowza* off. Concerned friend on.

"Yeah."

"Call me." She holds up her fist, and we bump.

"I will, my sister-in-the-law."

She hugs me and heads for the exit.

Taking a long, deep breath, I stride over to Keaton. That happened so fast, I have to take my steps slowly before standing by the barstool he's saved for me.

His eyes take a quick, almost imperceptible tour of my body. I'm in sensible work clothes and naked at the same time.

I'm wary. He senses it.

I'm turned on. I'm sure he senses that too.

"Fancy meeting you here," I say.

"I stay in the club when I'm in town. The suites are quite nice."

Is that an invitation? Am I supposed to answer that with a yes or no?

He doesn't wait for my response. "You'd better sit before I have to kill a man to save it for you."

"I want to be clear," I say. "And honest."

"I expect no less."

"I'm not sleeping with you."

"Indeed."

He indicates the stool again, and this time I slide onto it. For the first time, I wonder how this will look. The patrons seem like regular folk from Barrington and Doverton. The Doverton customers have the smack of wealth. I could separate them out if I had to, but I don't. I'm not interested in who's from where. I'm concerned with being seen. I don't see anyone from the bureau in the bar, but you never can tell.

"Are you looking for a boyfriend who might see you with me?" Keaton asks.

"No."

"Then who?"

I don't answer. He knows damn well.

"What are you drinking?" he asks.

"What are *you* drinking?" I touch his half-empty glass with its pale fizzy liquid and mint leaf.

"Bitters and ginger beer."

I think that's non-alcoholic. I don't want to drink around him. I already had a glass of wine, and that's my limit if I want to keep my wits about me.

"I'll have one of those," I say, hoping I'm right.

He orders it with a tilt of his chin and a flick of his fingers. The bar is packed but the bartender gets right on it.

"Wow," I say. "I would've had to wave a twenty at her for half an hour."

He shrugs as if he doesn't know the reason for his superpowers. I've noticed no one with them knows where they come from.

"How have you been?" he asks.

"Fine."

"Did you ever get where you wanted to go?"

"No," I say with regret and a little shame. I tried and failed the forums while Ken and I followed other leads.

"Do you like puzzles?" he asks.

"Actually, yes."

He leans forward, elbows on the bar, closer to me than I expect but not as close as my body wants.

"To your left," he says, pointing at the couple next to us. His limbs are so long he could wrap himself around me. If I turn, my nose will brush his neck, and that's exactly what I want/don't want.

I look at the couple. He's young, with a short haircut and a clean-shaven face. She's got long curly brown hair, a skinny-strapped, over-the-shoulder bag, and a giggle. She likes him, and he's trying to impress her with a bar game. He's set up drinking straws in a tic-tac-toe pattern, and he shakes a little stack of coins in his closed fist.

The crowd groans at something on the screen, but these two don't care. He hands her the coins.

"Six coins," Keaton says. "Place them so that they don't make a line of three."

She places the first one in the middle.

"She's already lost," I say.

"Really? You know this one?"

"Four sides and two corners. You don't have to know the game to win."

"But you do."

"I know them all."

He leans back. The bar has settled into a murmur. It's the half-time show, and no one cares about dancing girls.

My drink arrives. He gets a refill without asking.

"Let's make a bet," he says.

"I don't make bets I can't win."

"If you show me a pub game I don't know, I'll answer any question truthfully. If I show you one, you'll do the same."

"I can't give you any classified information. Anything I know from the bureau."

"Personal information only."

Is his connection to Alpha Wolf personal? Can I ask, and will he answer?

Is that the question I want answered?

I want more, somehow. I know he's Alpha Wolf, but I can't prove it. A verbal confirmation is meaningless. I want to know about *him*, who he is, what he does, what he likes. I want to know things about his past that I can't find in a dossier, and things about his future outside the newspapers.

"Deal," I say.

"Let's make it even more interesting."

Spoken like a true gambler. Interesting means riskier.

"How?"

"We'll each mention a pub game and answer a short question if the other knows it."

"Fine. But that's as interesting as I'm getting tonight."

He nods. Reaches for bar straws. "Front-facing dog."

I stay his hand, then pull it away. "No need to demonstrate. Pivot the nose so he's looking back."

"Yes. Your question?"

"Are you single?" It shoots out of my mouth before I even filter it. "Still not sleeping with you," I add when he looks at me. His eyes don't wander away from mine, but I feel naked again. "Just asking."

"I am single. And I promise, you won't do much sleeping."

My cheeks tingle. I'm glad it's dark because my face must be beet red. I rush to the next game. "Dime in a shot glass. Remove it without touching it."

"Blow on it. Hard." When he takes a drink, he moves the straw to the side and sips from the edge of the glass. He puts it down before his question. "Are you single?"

"Yes." My face tingles. I don't know if he can see it in the dim light of the bar.

He reaches behind the bar for two brandy snifters. The bartender shoots him a look but lets him get away with it. Being seen, caught, and walking away is its own superpower.

He drops an olive on the bar and covers it with one of the snifters, leaving the other face up. "Move the olive—"

"Please." I hold up my hand. "Allow me."

I rotate the down-facing snifter against the bar until centrifugal force pulls the olive into the deep part of the glass. I pick it up and drop the olive into the upturned one.

"Very nice," he says.

Without the football game on, my trick has gotten us some attention. The couple with the tic-tac-toe quarters is leaning forward with the guy explaining the trick to the shoulder-bag girl.

I hold out the snifter with the olive in it. "Want it?"

"No, thank you."

"Are you Alpha Wolf?"

"*Want it?* is a question." He smirks. "But I'll change the answer." He plucks the olive out of the glass and pops it in his mouth.

"Fine." I put down the glass. "Let's make this more interesting." The tilt of his head is a show of respect, and I let it warm me. "Let's play a lying game."

"As opposed to this dance we're doing now?"

"If you don't know the next trick, you lie to me for as long as it takes the trick to complete. If you know it, I'll lie to you."

"You're on."

I get the bartender's attention. "Can I have a shot of whiskey and a shot of water? Fill both to the rim. And if you have a playing card?"

"Yep." She pours out the whiskey.

"Do you know this one?" I ask him. I haven't done this trick in years. I almost hope he knows it.

"Nope. Spent a lot of time at the pub, have you?" Keaton asks.

"My mother taught me."

I swallow the rest of the story. How she practiced on me. How she told me her cons, testing the tricks to see if they were easy enough for a child to figure out.

The bartender places the two shot glasses and a joker card on the bar.

"I'm going to move…" In the middle of the sentence, I stop, because I'm not invisible. A dozen sets of eyes are on me, not the least of which are as blue as the deep side of twilight. "I can switch the whiskey and the water without dumping either glass out."

He stares at the glasses and the playing card. Glances at me as if the instructions might be written on my face, then turns back to the tools of the trick. "You'd better start the trick."

"And you'd better start lying."

Placing the card over the water-filled shot glass, I turn it upside down and place it over the whiskey so that the rims would touch if the card wasn't there. It stays. Everyone in the bar gasps, and Keaton leans forward so only I can hear him.

"My lies are facts." His shoulder is an inch from my lips. I smell the tweed and the remnants of the morning's aftershave. "I'm a black hat hacker trying to establish an honest career."

Turning away just enough to finish the trick, I tap the card. Nothing. Tap harder. It shifts.

What does he mean by his lies being facts? I keep tapping while Keaton keeps talking.

"I have a long list of criminal activity I've covered up. I have no morals. No ruler except money."

The tapping moves the card enough to open a space between the glasses. The bartender gasps, but there's no need. Because both glasses are full, they create a vacuum and there's no spill.

Keaton continues. "I'm a cold, empty person and I don't want you." I hold my breath, watching the whiskey swirl upward like a marble cake. "I don't wonder what you taste like behind your knees, inside your thighs, or where your cunt is soft and wet."

"Keaton."

"That's my name."

I turn my head slightly, and he's turned his. Our noses are so close, I feel his breath on my lip.

"This isn't what I had in mind," I say.

"I haven't thought about holding your arms behind your back while I fuck you from behind. Taking you by the hair and pulling your head back until I see you breathless when you come."

I sit back with my hands clutching the seat. My face is frozen in a rictus of shock, but my body's melted into a puddle of desire.

He smirks. Without taking his gaze off me or moving away, he says, "I think your trick is complete."

"You knew it," I say without even looking at the glasses. The lying is over. The football game has started again. I can see the green mass around the line of scrimmage in the mirror behind Keaton.

He shrugs. "There are some lies that need telling."

The spell is broken, but the damage is done. I cross my legs, but I'm engorged and it sends a shot of pleasure through me.

Snap out of it.

Holding the card in place, I flip the whiskey, losing only a few drops.

"Now you know." I push the whiskey toward him. "I'm driving."

He picks it up and drops the liquid in one of the brandy snifters he took for the olive game, swishing it around. "What do you want, Cassandra? No games. What do you *want*?"

I want a reason to touch you.

"I want a lot of things."

"What do you want badly enough to invite me into your car?"

One glass of wine isn't enough to affect my judgment. I sip my drink, thinking of what I want and how much of it I can tell him. "I want to get reassigned out of Doverton. I want to say I'm Special Agent Grinstead with CID. But I'm not part of the old-boy network. I don't get invited out. I don't get mentored. I'm not good at cozying up to my boss. So I need to do something big enough that someone notices. Something they can't ignore."

"And getting into Third Psyche will do that?"

"Yes." I'm so sure of it that there's not an ounce of doubt in my voice.

He drinks the whiskey in a gulp. "I think you're beautiful and sexy. But mostly, you are fascinating."

"That was a cute trick you just did." I put a ten on the bar for the whiskey. "But I'm not available for you, and I'm not fishing for compliments."

He pushes the ten back toward me. "I have a tab."

"Leave it for a tip then." I slide off the stool and shoulder my bag. "It's been nice hearing your lies. Bring your A-game next time."

He helps me get my jacket on. It's silly to think so hard about how he does it, but I have time, because his motions are efficient and languid. The sleeves are placed perfectly. The satin lining is cool against my skin, and when the coat drops on my shoulders, I feel the weight folding around me as a comfort.

Which is a completely pointless thought process, but I can't help it. Being around him is like stepping into a world where every part of my body is sending data to my brain.

As I tie the belt around me, he grips my shoulders from behind. My hair flicks against my ear when he speaks. "Come upstairs with me. Like I said, we won't be sleeping together. You don't have enough fingers to count all the times you'd come."

I'm red. For the record, my cheeks don't tingle. I don't get flushed. I started perfecting my poker face in third grade. Sure, the unexpected sex talk is enough to make any girl tingle, and he delivers it with a matter-of-factness in his English accent that only accentuates how damn sexy it is.

"I can't."

I finish tying my belt, and his hands slide down my arms. When he's no longer touching me, I feel my attention turn back to the room, the sound of the game, the placement of my body as it relates to the world, not to him.

"I'll walk you out," he says when my silence is long enough to tell him how far off course he's thrown me.

"No." I'm too curt. I blink hard. Soften. Impulsively, I take his hand and squeeze it. "Just let me go. I had a really nice time."

He brushes his thumb along the top of my hand, and it feels so good, he might as well be drawing his tongue along the seam between my thighs. My cheeks tingle all over again.

"Me too," he says, bowing slightly. He lowers his head further and brings his lips to my hand, kissing it.

He's chaste and respectful, but those lips on my skin will be the end of me. Every nerve in my body goes dead so my brain can process the softness of their touch and the firmness of their intent.

I pull my hand away.

"I hope I see you again," he says.

"I hope it's not at the field office," I reply, leaving open a door I shouldn't. I should cut this off right now. Tell him not at the field office or anywhere. I have to get my shit together. He's a potential informant. A person of interest. Maybe a target.

Backing away, I wave at the statuesque man against the backdrop of a busy bar, then I use every ounce of my willpower to spin on my heel and walk out.

I can barely breathe.

CHAPTER 8.

KEATON

The strands of my plans are like strands of yarn waiting to be woven into a fabric. In the dark, I ask myself how much I'm willing to unravel for her. For one night. Two. A fling. A relationship that takes its course.

When Cassie turns, she takes a bit of my willpower with her. When I first arrived in New Jersey, tired and dirty, blood boiling with adolescent desires, America seemed like a dangerous jungle. Once I had the lay of the land and the jungle lost its danger, it was boring. The newness of everything wasn't posh. It was flat. Dull.

Until her.

I have a plan to fold myself back into a world built on facts and realities, leaving this name behind. I will disappear. I will turn my back on her because I don't know her. I don't love her. I owe her nothing and she owes me the same. By the time the FBI has enough to get me back into an interrogation room, I'll be—

I need to make a mark on her life. Now.

How long are my feet nailed to the floor before I run outside? Too long. She's in her car. She's pulling along the drive.

I can hack her. I can get her phone. Email. Address. I can have her social security number on the tip of my tongue, but that's not the kind of intimacy I crave.

The cold air is dry tonight, cutting through the thin fabric of my shirt and snaking along my open collar as I run across the club's drive. She's stopped at the sign, but not for long. The car starts forward. I bang on the boot. The car jumps when she hits the brake.

Her window is half open when I get around the car.

"What is—"

But I cut her off. Rude. My mother would have my head. "Special Agent?"

Once the window is all the way down, I put my hands on the top of the door. She's incredulous, beautiful, her nose red at the tip from the cold.

"What?"

"You want to be a special agent with criminal investigations. Yes?"

"Yeah? I mean, everyone wants that."

I put my elbows on the bottom of the window and fold my arms together. "If you get into this forum you asked me for?"

"Third Psyche?"

"Will you get the promotion?"

"Maybe? I mean, I want to get in to stop what's happening in there. Or what we *hear* is happening. That's first."

"And second?"

"They won't be able to ignore me."

Her sentence is loaded with disappointment and isolation. "They" have ignored her for the last time, the blind buggers.

"Go home and sleep," I say, standing. "I'll do what I can."

She doesn't move, looking up at me from the open window. Her breath clouds and dissipates, as does mine. Our streams do not meet. There's a discontent in the early disintegration.

She jumps when a horn blasts. I find the source. The car behind her. I want to punch the driver for giving her a fright.

"Thank you," she says. "Do you know how to get me? If you find it?"

"I do." I step back, giving the twat behind her a dirty look, as though I can shove that horn right up his arse.

When I look back at her, she's pulled onto the road, left indicator on. She makes a turn into the darkness and is gone.

CHAPTER 9.

CASSIE

Nana's up watching QVC. The sound is off, and the diamond solitaire that fills the screen gets rotated by disembodied female fingers so it reflects the spotlights over and over. When I got stationed in the Doverton field office, she came with me from Flint "to take care of Cassie." It was the only way to get her to join me here, but it's pretty clear to me who's taking care of who in the Doverton suburbs.

"Hi, Nana," I say, hanging up my coat. "Were Fredo and Carol over?"

"Just left." She points at the screen. "I bought you that ring. It's perfect until you find a man to marry you."

I'm not insulted by her anymore. She's my nana. She can say whatever she wants about me. The purchase of a four-thousand-dollar ring would be a concern if her payment method was more than a Fisher-Price version of a credit card with a twenty-dollar spending limit. I set it up specifically for daily QVC emergencies. They take her orders over the phone and it declines the next day when she either regrets the purchase or forgets about it. I have the sneaking suspicion she knows the card won't go through but plays along to please me.

"Thanks. I'm not looking for a man, but I like diamonds."

I sit next to Nana. She's four-foot ten. Seventy-three and counting. My mother's mother. In front of us is a one-third-complete thousand-piece puzzle of the White House in spring. The outside edge is placed just fine, but the "completed" parts of the inside look like a shingled roof after a storm. Pieces are jammed in sideways or forced together. Some pieces have their blanks choked by ill-fitting tabs, or little slivers of open space between pieces when the tab is too small.

"I don't think these two go together," I say as if the problem is with two pieces and not with eighty percent of her decisions.

"The perfect's the enemy of the good." She says it as if it's the first time she's dropped this nugget of wisdom on me. It isn't. "You smell like a man."

I'm about to smell under my arm to see what she's talking about but stop myself when her meaning clicks into place. "I do not."

"English Leather. Had a boy like that once. We drove to Woodstock together in his Buick Skylark. Ran all 350 horses into the ground. Big backseat too."

Nana's from Detroit. She knows her cars and she knows her backseats. She knows what a man smells like, and she'll call me Agent-Pants-On-Fire for a week unless I come clean immediately.

"If I smell like English Leather, then you smell the guy I was talking to at the bar."

"Knew it."

I gently take more of the puzzle apart. Nana puts on her glasses. She doesn't like wearing them even though she's so farsighted she can't see an inch or three feet in front of her face.

She leans into the puzzle. "You're making a mess out of this, Cassandra." She joins me in taking apart the jammed-together pieces.

"Sorry. I'm not good at puzzles." I say it with the same tone I used to convince her I needed her to come to Doverton with me.

"I'll say. Tell me about English Leather. Should I return the ring?"

She never wore a ring on her left hand that she didn't buy herself, and no man ever wore a match to hers. I'm from a long line of single women. I figure I'll be single my whole life too. I've stopped calling it the Grinstead curse. Now I call it the Grinstead blessing.

"I'll cancel the ring," I say.

"So it's serious?" She looks at me above the frames as if that helps her see. I'm not sure that it does.

"No. No, it's not. It was just a conversation. I'm not interested in getting involved right now."

"Not gonna get easier when you move us to Quantico, you know." She snaps a piece into place. It lays flat. "Got the ring in a size six. That okay for you?"

"I don't like square cut."

"Carol noticed all the rich bitches at the club have square cut."

"I'm neither rich, nor a member of the club."

"Ha!" She slaps my knee with her paper-skinned hand when she realizes I didn't deny being a bitch. "You're too good for them, my girl." She pats my cheek. "Every last one of them. Get their smell on you but don't let them own you. Never trust them."

"Darn right, Nana." I put down the pieces I've pried apart. "Are you going to bed?"

"In a bit. I'm going to watch that guy." She waves at the TV. "The one with the moustache who doesn't wear a shirt."

I stand. "I'm going then." I kiss her cheek.

"I love you, Cassandra," she says absently, looking over her puzzle.

"I love you too, Nana."

• • •

I get through brushing my teeth and putting on pajamas. I even make it to bed, more or less. My butt is on the mattress but feet are still on the floor when I can smell him as clearly as my grandmother did. I feel him where his hands and lips touched me. I put my hand under my clothes and slip them inside my seam. I'm throbbing like a teenager. His words. His touch. The lies that revealed truths just as the game intended.

He could be a dark web madman, but maybe not. Maybe I'm wrong. Maybe we're all wrong and he's just a legitimate businessman.

That was one of his lies.

Four fingers deep, with the heel of my hand jerking the surface of my nub, I consider the possibility that he is a decent man. His integrity must be battered raw with insinuation. He's beautiful, prideful, and falsely accused. He's a good man doing good things.

He has a magnetism. It's almost frightening, but I never—not for one second—felt fear. The danger of him sends me to new heights. The idea that I was walking some kind of edge at the bar sends shivers to the base of my spine.

I haven't even drawn the duvet down and I'm on my hands and knees, rubbing myself in the dark, remembering the look he gave the driver behind me.

I come so hard I have to bite back a scream that might scare my grandmother.

CHAPTER 10.

CASSIE

In the first days of my training, my hands weren't strong enough to discharge a weapon with speed. After three rounds, pain shot through my palm. I worked at it until I could empty a magazine, but the recoil and vibration were so intense, my hand wasn't agile enough to change the magazine afterward. I dropped it and everyone laughed. I went to bed with a hand stiffly curled into a claw.

Now, the shooting range clears away the fog of my emotions. After the emergency meeting today, I need a lot of head-clearing. The gun *pop-pop-pops*.

Ken has uncovered a lead into Third Psyche's plans, and they're a doozy.

Orlando called him out for great work in front of everyone. I'm jealous and pleased at the same time. But more than that, I'm not getting promoted unless I do what he's done.

Pop-pop-pop

I need to make rain.

I review Orlando's speech in my head.

Ken's lead is flesh and blood. This was good, solid investigative work. Old-school. We cannot do this all online.

Of course that was the issue. Online leads meant looping in the cybercrime division. I'd been too stupid to see that Orlando wanted all the credit. Once another division is on the case, we go back to being a sleepy field office in the middle of nowhere.

We're getting together a team to head up to Springfield. The subjects are operating out of a strip club, so ladies, you'll be giving us backup from here while we talk to the asset.

Pop-pop-pop. I shoot until my hand hurts.

You mean stuffing dollar bills in g-strings.

Tito believed they were going for better-looking strippers. As if. Ken has a smooth fucking lump where his dick should be, but he plays such a man to the crowd.

It's a sacrifice I'm willing to make to serve my country.

Lolz. Fucking rolling on the fucking floor, you assholes.

This FBI thing is going nowhere. I have to find another path, but where? To do what?

I don't know how to quit. Ken or no Ken, I don't know how to just give up, even when I should.

I squeeze the fourteenth round into the target's chest. Chamber the last one. Pop a new magazine and empty my anger into the target.

Pop-pop-pop.

"Grinstead!"

It's Shadow Horse Brady, the guy who runs the field office's tiny firing range. He's in his thirties, built like a football player, with a long black braid over each shoulder. FBI agents don't usually have long hair, but they're not usually Sequoia tribesmen either.

"Yeah?" I take off my earmuffs.

"Someone left you a note." He holds out his hand. A yellow Post-It is stuck to his middle finger. It's blank on top.

"Thank you." I take it off, flip it. There's a phone number on the back. "Did he just walk in and leave this?" The range is pretty secure, but maybe not as secure as I thought.

"It was here when I got in. Is it civilian?"

"I don't think so. Just asking."

"Nice shooting." He points at the poor black silhouette I've left with a nearly hollow chest.

"Missed three." I point at the three holes in the white area around the target.

"Perfect's the enemy of the good, Agent."

"So I hear."

• • •

I pull the car to the side of the road and call the number on the back of the Post-It. The two-lane road is thinly lined with trees, newly paved, with a sharp double yellow in the middle that goes straight a long way before disappearing into a single point.

"Keaton," I say when a ring cuts off and I can hear someone breathing. "You left this number."

"I have something for you." He's clipped and businesslike. I thought I'd never hear his demanding British voice again, and when I do, I catch myself smiling. With Ken outrunning me, I needed the help, and the package it came in made my nerves vibrate.

He continues. "It might be of use."

"Might?"

"I believe—"

"You believe?" I tap the steering wheel as I decide how much more to tell him, and how, because it will determine how much I want from him. I open my mouth to carefully ask what "might" might mean. That's not what comes out. "I don't have time for 'might,' okay? Or 'I believe.' I'm getting steamrolled over here. Actually, if I come in with something 'you believe might' not be exactly perfect, I'm going to get laughed at, and I have to tell you, getting laughed at is going to put me over the fucking edge."

I should be ashamed of my behavior in front of a man I barely know, but here's the rub. I'm not ashamed at all. As a matter of fact, I feel a little relieved to have it off my chest.

"I like the fight in you," he says.

"I don't like having to show it."

There's a silence that's kind of comfortable, kind of tense. I can't discern where he is from the background buzz.

"Cassie?"

"Yeah?"

"I want to see you again."

He doesn't mean he wants to wave from the window. That's for sure.

"Is that a good idea?"

It isn't. He knows it. For better or worse, once he passes me information on an active case, he's an asset. I don't know what kind of trouble this can land him in with the players in his world, but for me it's a no-no.

"It's a terrible idea," he says flatly.

I smile and look at my lap. He said it as a fact, and in stating it as a fact, he made it somewhat less terrible and completely unavoidable.

When I ask the next question, my voice sounds softer and lower than I intend. "When?"

CHAPTER 11.

CASSIE

While Ken, Orlando, and a couple of the guys are in Springfield questioning an asset at a strip club, I'm standing over my bed in my underwear. My phone lies next to the dress I've laid out. Frieda's voice comes through the speakerphone.

"Is it business or pleasure?" she asks as I rummage through my closet.

I haven't told her what Keaton and I are meeting about, and as friends who work with sensitive material, we're used to giving each other half-stories.

"Business," I say. "But I can't ignore the overtones."

"Well, do you like the overtones? If you like them, you wear something sexy. If you don't, then you wear work clothes."

I throw a blue pantsuit on the bed. It looks like a cloak of invisibility. "What if I just wore sneakers and jeans?"

"Then you are neither business, nor overtone, but you'll be able to run fast."

I laugh. "I don't think I'll have to run. At least not fast."

• • •

As soon as I see Keaton in the supermarket parking lot, I wish I'd chosen the invisible pantsuit. What was I thinking? I'm leaning against my car with the dress safely under my coat, but when he pulls his car next to mine, he rolls down the passenger side window and leans over, looking at my stocking-covered calves. It's as if he knows I have on a sexy dress.

"Hi," I say.

He gets out but doesn't shut the engine. "You found the one dark parking lot in the state."

He's right. We're in a dark corner that smells of piss and Dumpsters. The only light is from his headlamps. The rest of the lot is bathed in floodlights, as is the one for the Home Depot across the street.

"I don't like being seen," I say. "I assumed you felt the same way."

In the dark, he's no more than an outline of a man. What's inside the framework? Does it show in the light? Or am I only seeing a scaffolding?

"You deserve to be seen."

Is he made of kind words and compliments? Does the rhythmic accent hide truths or lies? Is he empty inside the outline? Or is he made of skin and muscle?

"Maybe," I say. "Do you have it?"

"Not with me."

What is the silhouette filled with? Kindness or cruelty? Life or death? Keaton Bridge or Alpha Wolf? Both? Neither?

"Not with you?" I say. "That's such a cliché."

"Too much American television as a kid."

He opens the passenger door. When the dome light comes on, he is rendered in three dimensions again.

I don't have to get in. I can just go home and wait for my team to get back from Springfield and tell me what happened.

I step forward. One step closer to the car and one step closer to him. "Where are we going?"

"Little place I know."

There's no "little place" in Doverton or Barrington. There are box stores and mom-and-pop shops that are already closed. There's a bar off the highway and a twenty-four-hour sandwich place. There are plenty of nice places to go and good places to sit, but none match his cozy implications.

I get in the car, wondering if I should have worn my sneakers.

CHAPTER 12.

KEATON

It's twenty-two miles to Barrington. The highway is dry, and the air is cold and crisp. I go the speed limit and no more, as is my habit. I don't risk exposing myself by getting tickets.

"It is too cold?" I ask as she rubs her hands together.

"No, I'm fine."

"Do you like Doverton?" I ask.

She laughs a little. A short, sharp thing meant to say more than words can. "It's fine."

"Fine?"

"It's small." She shrugs. "Catty."

"Bigger than Barrington. Some people in Doverton say they inbreed."

"Like I said." She looks at me just as I'm looking at her. She is just stunning. "Catty."

I have to look back at the road. "How long have you been here? From Flint?"

"Can we stop this?"

"Stop what?"

"You know everything about me."

I know what she means, and I'm not going to waste time denying it.

"And have you not looked for me in your records?" I shoot back.

She looks straight ahead, lips pressed together. Up ahead, lights dot the sky at the factory roof and on the very tops of the cranes. I pull off the highway.

"What did you find?" I ask.

"Nothing."

"That's disappointing."

"Not a stub. People whose families immigrate usually get a stub. But you? Nada."

There had been an FBI stub as recently as six months ago. In a way, knowing it's gone is comforting. It means they've started.

In another way, it's chilling.

"Where are we going?" she asks.

"You know the factory?"

"That's a great place to murder someone."

"Not if you want to get away with it. Half the town descends on it at seven a.m."

"Are you on schedule to open?"

"Yes." I don't offer more because I don't want to talk about the fucking factory.

The service road is rutted and bumpy. We'll clean it up after we bring in the heavy stuff. For now, the car rocks like a boat on a stormy sea.

"How much do you know about me?" she asks.

"Not much."

"Please. If you don't know my social security number and the name of my first pet, I'll eat my shoe."

She thinks I'm lying. She doesn't trust me, and she shouldn't. My anger is in inverse proportion to how much of her trust I've earned.

"If you need salt, I'll allow it."

I stop at the factory gate. A guard sits in the little house. He's not an ounce under three hundred pounds. His name is Bernard, but everyone calls him Butthead.

I roll down the window. "Bernard."

"Mr. Bridge."

"Keaton. Please."

"Sure." He peers into the window to see Cassie. "Ma'am. Can I see your driver's license?"

"She's all right," I snap. Worse than Cassie's distrust is her seeing someone else not trust me.

"Mr. Harden says."

"I practically invented corporate espionage," I say, losing patience. "I daresay this lady won't pull a trick I can't see coming."

Cassie reaches one hand over me with her wallet stretched open with her fingertips. She's closer. I can smell her. Vanilla and gunpowder. My God. She's made of candy-coated bullets.

Bernard takes one look at the FBI ID and opens the gate. Cassie leans back, but I caught a whiff of her already, and it's enough.

"You invented corporate espionage?" she says. "That was exculpatory."

"Not really. It's a quote from *Gizmodo*."

I drive through the gate. The hulk of the factory grows larger as I approach. The windows on the first and third floors are lit with low-wattage LEDs. I pull into my spot and put the car in park.

"Want to make a wager?" I say.

"Again?"

I look at her. She's leaning forward, genuinely interested. I like her curiosity mirroring mine.

"I bet you can surprise me."

"I'm really boring."

"That would surprise me indeed."

I get out of the car.

CHAPTER 13.

CASSIE

Keaton opens the door for me. The parking lot is in crappy condition, and even though my shoes aren't too high, my heel lands on half a rock and I lose my balance. He has me by the elbow before I even realize I'm falling. His hand is strong and gentle. He lets me go as soon as I'm on my feet.

"Thank you."

We walk along the side of the building. Dim lights on the ground floor glow through the web of scaffolding, cross-hatching the ground in front of us.

"We can take the lift," he says.

"I'm not afraid of a few stairs."

"Really?"

"I can make four flights in under a minute and a half, carrying a firearm and spare cartridges."

He reaches into the darkness and clicks something. A light goes on to reveal an elevator car built inside the scaffolding. It's for construction, with a wood plank floor and a big orange lever. We get in, and he slides the gate closed. With a tap of the lever, we move up.

"Don't be afraid," he says.

"I'm not."

He flicks a switch and the car goes dark.

"Oh," I gasp.

The lights over Barrington are visible, and behind it, Doverton glows just in front of the curve of the earth against the navy sky. The stars are a pin-poked wrap over the earth. We stand in silence, our perspective changing as we rise ninety feet and stop with a jerk.

Keaton slides open the gate on the factory side with a clatter and slap. He holds out his hand and I take it. Pause. His face is in shadow. His expression as we touch is hidden from me, but as his thumb brushes the tops of my fingers, I don't need to see it to know the contact is intentional and sexual.

I step onto the roof. He follows, laying his hand on my shoulder. Touching. Again. I'm conscious of how disproportionately carnal the pressure and placement feel against how tame they really are.

"Here," he says, leading me to a little café table with two folding chairs surrounded by outdoor heat lamps.

The floodlights clack on when the motions sensors detect our bodies, making the roof both bright and black. The table is in a trapezoid of shadow. There's a pitcher of water and glasses. I glance quickly into the glasses. Dry from what I can tell. Good.

Keaton pulls out a chair and I sit, noticing a square yellow Post-It stuck to the center of the table. He sits across from me and pours water in my glass first.

"Not trying to get me drunk, I see."

"If I had wine, would you drink it?"

"No."

"Why not?" He pulls his glass closer to him.

I touch mine. I'm thirsty, but don't pick it up. "It's hard to hide drugs in water. Easier in alcohol."

"You think I'm the kind of man who needs to drug women?"

"To get laid?" I go right for the point. "No."

"What then?"

"You might drug an FBI agent."

He leans forward, into a patch of light. His brown hair's brushed back, but a curve of it escapes and falls against his forehead. His left ear has a thin gold hoop tight around the lobe, hinting at a history I can only guess. Gorgeous, yes, but the promises of secrets, knowledge, depth are what make me throb between my crossed legs.

He's breathtaking.

"There's no need to drug you or any agent. If I want something from the part of you that carries a badge and a gun, I can take it without you even knowing it. I can own you. I can own your job. Your family and friends are safe because I choose it."

I'm tricked by his looks. His promise. The timbre of his voice. I've been lulled. He is what he is and has always been. And here I am—alone on a rooftop with him.

"So are you Alpha Wolf?"

"I can neither confirm nor deny any digital persona is linked to me."

"You don't scare me."

His smirk is devilish and comforting, as if mischief has a charm all its own. Then he leans back and drinks his water as if he knew I was waiting for him to go first. He puts down the empty glass. "Good."

I sip my water.

"So," he says. "You heard there are plans being made on an onion site."

"Third Psyche."

"The link's written on the back of that Post-It." He flicks his fingers at the yellow square stuck to the center of the table. I reach for it. With an efficient but languid gesture, he covers my hand as it's over the paper. "Not so fast, Ms. Grinstead."

"Cassie's fine." There's a snap in my voice. I don't care if he knows I'm annoyed.

"Cassie. First you tell me why you want the link."

"I told you."

"I believe you. But there's more. No one wants a promotion for the sake of one."

He's touching me. Skin on skin. He doesn't move his fingers across mine, but if he does, I'm going to melt into the chair. I can stay like this all night, until he tightens his palm and puts downward pressure on his fingers. It's encouraging. A barely perceptible invitation to speak what's in my heart.

It's all I need at a time when I would have denied needing anything.

"Because I want to catch criminals. I can catch bigger and better from CID."

I don't take my eyes off the way his hand covers mine. Not as I speak, nor during the long silence after I'm done.

"Small-time crooks don't cause enough trouble?"

"Maybe."

"Or do you have too much empathy for them?"

I snap my hand away. "What's that supposed to mean?"

"Oh, the lady doth protest too much. You have to know law enforcement attracts a criminal element."

I will my lips shut, but my mind simmers, then boils. "You can go to hell then." I wish I could get up and walk away, but that yellow Post-It is calling.

"I will. I'm sure of it."

"Said the black hat who's going straight."

"We have more in common than I thought."

"My record's clean." I lean back. "I don't know what you think you saw or where you saw it, but it's fake."

"I didn't say you were guilty of anything. Your mother was obviously a petty reprobate by choice. You were dragged along for the ride. Yet I saw a little flicker in your eyes when you said your record was clean." He points at each eye as if trying to recall the little glints. "You're proud of not getting caught."

I have to divert this conversation before I get sucked into it. "You were the king of the dark web. You were making millions in hacked accounts."

"I was."

"Guns."

"Yes."

"Drugs."

"No. Never. No drugs, no people."

"Every thief has a code." I know that all too well. "Why leave it?"

"Taylor needed the money."

"Are we done here?" I ask.

"As you wish."

I reach for the Post-It again, and again he puts his hand over mine. I let it stay. With everything that was said and revealed in the last five minutes, that pause before I shake him off is the moment I let myself like his touch.

He slides his hand away, and I curl my fist around the paper, snapping the glue off the tabletop.

"The link comes with a warning," he says.

I turn over the paper. The link is written in pencil. "A warning?" I fold the Post-It and put it in my pocket. "Are we enemies now?"

"No, but I don't want you to make any." He looks at the sky, apparently thinking. "You're not callous. If you have to believe you are, I understand. And working in law enforcement, you'll get callous or die. But not you. Not yet. But…" He laces his fingers together across his belt. "When I went looking for something to put on this piece of paper, I might have been noticed."

"You?"

He knows what I'm asking. Was Keaton Bridge noticed or was Alpha Wolf? I don't go further because I know he's not going to answer.

"It's not my intention to expose you to danger. If I had my way, you'd toss that paper in the rubbish and forget the whole thing. But you're too far gone. So take it. Catch the bastards." He leans forward now, putting his elbows on his knees. His head is only slightly lower than mine and he's dead serious. "Do not speak to Keyser Kaos. Do not speak to anyone who knows him. If you're wise, don't speak to anyone whose identity isn't known."

His voice is so even that I shutter any thoughts of disobeying him.

"Are you going to be all right? Are they going to come after you?"

He starts to say something. Stops himself. Leans back.

What have I done? I tuck my hands into my sleeves. The heat lamps only do so much to chase a chill.

"I wouldn't worry about it," is his final answer. "I want you to have this. I want to do something for you."

The link could be a setup. He could be a beautiful trap. But he's not. I can't know the results of his gift, but when he says he wants to do something for me, I believe he's telling me the entirety of his intentions.

"Why did you decide to go straight?"

His look is quizzical, as if he's revving up to deflect.

"Surprise me. I know you want me to surprise you, but you gotta meet me halfway here."

"How do I know you won't use it against me?"

"You don't."

I figure it's over after that. We're at some kind of stalemate. This isn't a guy who gives up a piece of information without a fight. He knows its worth too well. His eyes flick across my face as if he's reading me, but that's not what he's doing. I know it as well as I know when a mark is just distracted enough to think she's not. He's calculating the value of his story.

"I went straight, as you call it, because there are some things I can only do with a name, and a face, and a history in this world. I needed to do those things."

"You needed to invest in QI4? Why?"

"Some things can't be written and explained in a tight little fable. The short version is—I did it for friendship."

The alarm bells that bark when I'm around him shut down for a second. That wasn't the answer I expected. The fact that he'd make a sacrifice for a friend clues me in to the existence of a complex, layered person, not just a sexy, secretive criminal.

"I'd like to hear the long version some time."

"There won't be a long version."

Won't be?

He says it as if the story is still being written and it's about to be cut off.

CHAPTER 14.

KEATON

The yellow Post-It is folded between two fingers. She's rubbing the paper against itself as she looks outward, at me, and inward, dissecting every word I've said.

"You're planning something," she says.

"Nothing that should concern you." I lean forward. I want to smell her. Feel her warmth. "How do you feel, now that you have what you want?"

She casts her eyes down. The lashes cast shadows on her cheeks. "Honestly?"

"Of course."

"A little scared of what I'll find."

She's so proud and so honest. I admire the way she couples strength to vulnerability, beauty to humility.

"You're smart to be scared. But you know how to do it."

I mean, how to stay invisible in the forums. Set up a fake profile behind a data wall. They'll find the FBI eventually, but they won't tie the discovery to a particular agent.

"I do know how to do it."

Her smile is confident, cocky even. I like that too.

She stands and puts out her hand. She wants me to shake it. And what am I supposed to do? Shake it and let her go? I don't know a thing about her. Sure, I've dug up plenty, but I want to hear her story from her mouth.

Her hand hangs in the cold air while I decide how I'm going to keep her.

"Thank you," she says.

I stand and take her hand. "My pleasure."

The word "pleasure" rolls out of my mouth on eighteen wheels with a payload of meaning behind it. Even if I want to keep the word clean, I don't have a choice with her.

She looks down at our clasped hands.

"Let me walk you out," I say.

"You're a real chivalrous guy."

"I'm British. It's a default setting."

She lets go of my hand and turns away. "I like your default setting."

I turn off the heat lamp and catch up to her. She takes my arm when I offer it, letting me guide her into the lift.

I get in and press the red button.

The car jerks downward. I want to kiss her in this tight little space, but her hands are in her pockets. She won't look at me. She's not ready or she doesn't want me to.

The lift bounces at the ground floor. I slide open the gate with a clatter that shakes the silence. I step aside so she can go first.

What do I want out of her? I want to fuck her, but that shouldn't be surprising. She's an attractive and intelligent woman. She's also dangerous at this point. Not because of her job, but because of the way I react to her. I lock up the lift, letting her walk ahead.

She's a siren, pulling me toward this burdensome identity when all I want to do is get away. She's halfway to the car, hands jammed in her coat pockets. I trot to her. I bridge the distance in six and a half steps. The last half-step to seven puts me between her and the car. I can't read her expression, but I caption the picture anyway, telling the story of a woman who wants to go home and blow dry her hair or rearrange the jumpers in her wardrobe.

Just as I catch up, her ankle bends when she steps on a rock. She tips. I catch her because I don't want her to fall, and I feel in my gut that she's my responsibility.

I don't know why I care, but I do. If I don't connect now, there's no future and I don't know why it matters but it bloody fucking does and if I could just—

So I kiss her.

CHAPTER 15.

CASSIE

The deal is done. I can have the guard call me a cab and wait for an hour, or I can let Keaton drive me back to my car. Either way it should be fine, but his little café table setup on the roof was romantic. His trade gives him no weapon against me. He wanted to know why I needed the link, but the knowledge is useless. There are no rules against trying to get a promotion.

He wants me as much as I want him, and that scares me. It means I have to make a decision, and either choice could have a terrible outcome.

He's just about admitted he's Alpha Wolf.

A criminal.

What has he done? What evil has he fomented? What goes on in the dark web?

Drug-trade-human-trafficking-hacking-whistleblowing-cheese-pizza-slavery-war-guns-murder-for-hire-revolution.

I'm a few feet from the car when my heel catches a rock. I slide my hands from my pockets to reweight my balance, but he's got his hands under my arms, holding me up.

Holding me still.

The list of crimes that happen on the dark net bounces through my brain as he holds me. Is he going to kill me? Strangle me right here in the parking lot of his own factory? Maybe he wants to try. He's well-built, but I'm pretty sure I can take a computer nerd in hand-to-hand combat. I just can't let him get the jump.

He goes for me.

I'm surprised and prepared for it at the same time. I didn't actually believe he'd try, but I'm reaching to block an attack while he's leading with his head, which is weird, but I got this.

When his lips smash against mine, my body is a split second ahead of my brain. It's processed the list of dark net violence and thus completes a series of moves to bring down a frontal attack.

Even as I'm using his weight against him by holding his arm still while I swing him, letting his high center of gravity do all the work of stripping him of his balance, my mind processes the kiss. Because it was a kiss. A real soft-lipped-slightly-open-mouthed-I want-her-to-like-it kind of kiss.

By the time those nice thoughts register, I'm slamming him up against the car. I'm a little disappointed that I can't take back my counterattack. I would have let him kiss me a few more seconds before taking him down.

His eyes are open wide and the breath's knocked out of him. The thump of his body against the car door fades into the night.

"Why did you do that?" I ask.

He looks at me as if I asked him why he pees standing up. Brows knotted. Arms out. Mouth half open as if he can't contain the sheer number of answers he could give me right now.

"What?" He says it like *whot* and it's endearing and haughty at the same time. Damnit. I should have taken that kiss and not gotten all black belt on him.

"Don't sneak up on a girl like that." I sound like a brat.

He straightens himself out, pulling his cuffs down and realigning his jacket. "I'm going to pretend you didn't just do a very impressive judo throw and tell you, out front, that I'm going to kiss you. First, I'm going to put my hands on your face, because I would like to feel your mouth move when I do it. Then I'm going to tilt my head to the right, so please, you should also tilt your head to the right." He waits for me to nod, and when I do, he comes close to me and lowers his voice. "I'm going to wait a second once our lips touch, just to make sure we're both appreciating this first contact. When I open my mouth a little, I want you to do the same. You need to accept my tongue in your mouth." He puts his hands on my shoulders. "Is that enough of a warning?"

"What happens after that?"

"It's unwritten."

He moves his hands up to my jaw, laying his thumbs against my cheeks. He strokes them and I lean forward.

He kisses me just as he said he would. His tongue tastes like ice water, and his lips curve into the shape of mine. The adrenaline in my veins blends with something newer and warmer. He slides one hand back and tugs my hair, which sends fluids and sensation and pleasure and all my attention between my legs. I push against him just so I can feel him resist. I need to fight him as hard as I want him.

He's rigid and yielding all at once, turning us around until I'm the one with my back against the car. I shove him away, and he separates from me with a sharp intake of breath.

He doesn't say a word, still holding me by a fistful of hair. The cold clouds of our breath mingle between us. He's a predator, a criminal, and a mistake. But his jaw is tight and his nostrils flare when he breathes. He's all those things and a bull charging for the red cape.

"Push me away again," he says finally, "and we're done here. And I know for a fact that's not what you want."

I am the red cape, and I need to be yanked away as much as I need him to charge at me again and again. "When I want you to stop, I'll say so."

I shove him again, and he smiles before laying a kiss on me. It's not a kiss I fight. It's a kiss I want. He pulls his mouth away as if giving me a second to tell him to stop, but I don't. I don't push against him until our mouths are locked again. His hips grind into me. I feel his erection through our clothes.

I'm clutching his coat without any sense. I want to tear away every stitch of fabric. I push and pull with equal ferocity. I want to spread my legs, but my coat's too long. I want to punch him. I want that hard dick stretching me and I want it to hurt. My mind is wiped clean of everything but need. I don't have a job or a career. I don't have dreams built from childhood. I don't have a name. I'm just a pillar of desire. I'm reduced to movement and hunger. I want his body inside mine. Nothing else.

"Hey, uh…"

Keaton snaps away from me at the sound of the security guard's voice. My body wants him back, but my mind fills up again.

"Yes, Bernard?" Keaton has on a full British jacket of *what-could-you-possibly-want-now?*

Bernard looks as embarrassed as I should be. I pull on my coat ties as if they could be any tighter.

"Just wanted to let you know my shift's over in ten minutes and I'll let Trey know—"

"Thank you," Keaton snaps.

Bernard nods and backs away. Keaton turns back to me as the guard's boots crunch against the loose gravel. We don't say anything until the footsteps disappear.

"Well," Keaton says, inviting me to begin the mindful part of this thing we started—whatever it is.

"Well. That was…" I swallow. Was it great? An eye-opener? An earth-shattering beginning to something that will stop my ambitions dead in their tracks? "Complicated."

"It doesn't need to be. I don't live here. There's no threat of permanence."

I know what he's suggesting. This can be very short, very simple, and very pleasurable. It's tempting. He moves a swatch of hair from my cheek, letting his fingers brush my skin.

"You'll be back a lot to manage this." I wave at the factory.

"They need me in California. This"—he waves at the factory, mirroring my gesture—"is not my area of expertise."

"But you will be back. And I can't… getting caught having an affair with someone like you? It's not—"

"It's now or never." He brushes his finger along the length of my throat. I'm collapsing like a house of cards. "By the time I come back, you'll be in Quantico making the world safe from people like me."

He's close again. I can smell his aftershave cutting the cool air. His lips are on my throat, flipping me like a switch.

"What if I'm not?"

"We'll ignore each other."

I know that's not possible. His hands are on my jaw and his mouth is on mine. My body has never responded to a man this strongly. I've never felt so little control over it. I won't be able to ignore him when he comes back or when he's away.

But the logic is manageable. I use it to shut up the klaxons enough to hear my screaming inner child.

She's telling me I could lose everything. She says I need to be safe. For once, I need to feel safe and Keaton Bridge is anything but safe.

I soothe her. I promise her the adults are in charge. She doesn't believe me, but she trusts me. She was always foolish. She trusted the men she brought home. Trusted Mom's word that the piles of wrapped dollar bills on the coffee table were from a greeter's gig at Wal-Mart, not the results of a long con.

I'm thinking about those bills when Keaton reaches behind me and opens the car door. The pulsing beep of the open door alarm matches the thrum of my heart. I'm thinking about how I believed her because I wanted to. The bills meant food and maybe a month of cable TV. They meant comfort, and I wanted comfort more than the truth. They never meant a different life.

I'm grown up now and my comforts may have changed, but my inner child's excuse-making hasn't. I'm better than that. The adults are in charge.

"Thanks," I say. "But no thanks."

With a little push, he steps away from me. I don't know what's going on in his love life, if getting sex is easy or hard for him, but the look on his face is layered with so much confidence with its contrasting disappointment that I can only assume he usually gets "yes" for an answer.

"I'm sorry," I say. "For leading you on."

"It's nothing." He brushes my hair away from my face, and I'm suddenly aware of the cold air creeping up my sleeves. "Can I return you to the only dark parking lot in the state?"

I look over the desolate nightscape. I hear the trickle of the nearby river and the buzz of the overhead lights. I don't want to wait at the guardhouse for a cab. I want to go home. "Sure."

He steps out of the way and I get in the car, relieved, disappointed, and regretful all at the same time.

CHAPTER 16.

KEATON

We cross a narrow bridge in the center of Doverton, wheels clacking on the wooden boards bolted into the steel frame. The bridge has low guardrails and a thin walk on each side that's used more for fishing in the Winnepak River upstream from the factory than for crossing it. The steel-colored water runs narrow and shallow in the summer, but in the winter or during rains, it thrashes between the banks.

There is no small talk between Cassie and me. Every word is loaded. Every pause has meaning. So when we drive for five minutes in silence, I know something's on her mind.

I appreciate this, because I have plenty on mine.

"This link?" she says, breaking the silence.

"Yes?"

"The fact that you gave it to me means I have to register you as an asset. It's a totally confidential process."

I laugh. How could I not?

"What's so funny?"

"Darling, if you want to find criminals, the first thing you have to know is that there's no such thing as confidential."

She looks out the window. Was I too hard on her?

No. When it comes to this, she needs a little tough love.

I pull into the supermarket lot and make my way to the dark corner where her car is parked.

"You do what you have to," I say.

She nods. I get out and open her door for her.

She's a few steps toward her car when she turns, keys in her hand. "I have a question."

"Go on then."

"You don't believe you're protected, and getting me this link has made people mad at you. Why expose yourself like this?"

Because in the little time I have left, I want to leave a mark. An anonymous mark, yes, but a trail of good things astride the bad. I want to know people I care about are settled, and in the little time I've known Cassie, I care about her. I want her to have her promotion. I want her to get what she wants out of life.

I don't know why she's important to me or how she's weaseled her way into my heart, but the fact of it is indisputable.

However, I can't tell her that.

"I don't care for Nazis," I say.

"Yeah." She presses a button on her keys and her car unlocks. "Ain't that the truth."

I open her door for her. She gets in. She keeps her head turned away from me, signaling that there will be no goodbye kiss unless it's taken.

Getting slammed into the side of my car was pleasant in a way, but I won't take what's not offered again. I slap her door closed and watch her rear lights get smaller in the distance.

When I reach for my phone, I realize my wallet is gone.

CHAPTER 17.

CASSIE

I am seven and a half the first time I slip my hands into a stranger's bag. I am too young to know better and old enough to be good at it. I've practiced on my mother for weeks. I've dug her leather wallet from her bag as she leans over the kitchen counter a hundred times. If she feels it, I get a death glare that reminds me that my competence is important. I could be the difference between ramen and pizza for dinner. If she doesn't feel my hand, I get three M&Ms.

I really like M&Ms. They taste like safety. They taste like approval. The hard crunch is the glassy crackle of her disapproval. The sweet chocolate melting on my tongue is the warmth of her love.

She's a tough critic. She does not lie. She knows I'm coming, so she is ready to feel any jerk or pressure on her back. Both the bag and the wallet are leather. She paired them to make it harder for me to feel the difference between bag and wallet. The actual leather parts of the bag have faded in the sun. The man-made pleather is bright, deep blue-green. She holds it more tightly than our mark will. She makes it hard. It frustrates me, but I'm not supposed to pout over it.

The first time I do it correctly, she's leaning over the kitchen counter with a cigarette and the phone pressed to her ear. She's talking about a TV show to a friend, or a lover, or a mark she's working on. Behind her, the cast iron pan sits on the stove with the little chunks of scrambled egg drying on the edge. Just in front of her, on the counter, sits a salt shaker like the ones you find in a diner. A chrome crown over a white gown. Little pieces of beige rice swim inside the sparkling salt.

The teal bag is unzipped, but not wide open. She never makes it too easy, but she doesn't want me choosing marks that are too diffi-cult. I don't sneak behind her, because other people will be watching. I come from behind her and reach for the salt shaker with my left hand while my tiny right hand slides into her bag.

Of course, the wallet is wedged under a pamphlet and a pair of sunglasses. I don't hesitate. I've done this before and even though I failed, I know she's added the obstacles for my own good.

I say "excuse me," in the little girl voice we've worked on, just as I pick up the salt and slip the wallet away.

She keeps talking into the phone. She knows that when I pick up the salt, I'm supposed to take her wallet. But she's also honest, and as she's listening to whomever is on the other side of the phone, she turns around, clasps her hand into a fist, and pumps it downward, raising her knee in victory.

I did it.

Those M&Ms—one red, one blue, one yellow—taste like victory. They taste like worthiness. The sweetness of personal contribution to my own well-being.

We do it a few more times, and each time I get better. Each time she offers me little tips and tricks. Her knowledge is endless. She's a wonderful mother who knows everything that is important. I'm the luckiest kid in the world.

On Friday, we go to the zoo. Every year, if there're fewer than two snow days, schools in the Detroit area are closed on the first Friday in May. The zoo lets in all school-age children for free, but adults pay full price. The result in this poor community is that one adult in a group of friends will take the day off so the rest can go to work. The adult-to-child ratio is huge on this day. There's a sense of unending chaos, and that works in our favor.

Mom says to try to find wealthy people. There aren't many truly rich people at the Detroit Zoo on the first Friday in May. But I know what she means, and she knows what she means. Find someone who can afford to lose their wallet today.

The zoo is a two hour drive from home, so I'm motivated to get this right. This is going to be worthwhile trip.

I find a woman who takes out a few twenties to pay for three bags of Cracker Jacks. She leaves her bag unzipped. The straps fall low on her hip. Low enough for me to reach. When she takes her three children to the penguins, I follow.

The kids she's with look like her, with rich brown skin. One is my age, and one a little bit older, and the last is around two and totally focused on his sticky popcorn. She leans over the railing to point out how the biggest penguin watches over the small ones.

I lean with the children she's watching. "Which one?"

When she points, I take her wallet.

She looks back at me with a smile. "That one!"

I use the shield of her body to hide the fact that I'm putting her wallet into my bag. Her smile is warm and forgiving, and I imagine that if she knew what I had done she wouldn't mind at all.

"Who here knows where penguins live?"

The question is for the three children she's with, but I'm caught up in the moment and I join them in raising my hand.

"South Pole," I shout.

The prize in this competition is being right. The two other kids shout the same answer, but I was first. For a kid like me, it's Olympic gold.

"That's right," the lady says.

"They have wings, but they can't fly," I add. "They're flightless birds."

I should be gone by now. I should have slipped away seconds ago, and every second counts. Mom says so. Besides that, now the lady is looking at me strangely. The wallet is heavy in my bag, and I can't run away now. Not without her wondering why.

"Emus and ostriches and kiwis too!" I cry.

The kid who's slightly older than me shoots me a look. I don't imagine she knows about the wallet, but I'm encroaching on her birthright. She's supposed to be the one who knows everything in this family. The approval I'm getting from her mother was meant for her.

"Are you with a grown-up?" the lady asks.

This is dangerous. I don't want to hang around this family for another second. If she reaches into her bag for her phone to call the three-digit number grownups use for lost children, she might realize the wallet's gone. I know what to do if I'm caught, but Mom will be disappointed. This is way past M&Ms. Chocolate is nice, but approval is sweeter.

I point at a random adult by the bathroom.

"Bye!" I say before running in that direction.

I don't take a breath of relief until I'm in a stall, snapping the lock shut. My instructions are clear. Go into the bathroom. Go into a stall.

Remove the money and one credit card. Leave the wallet on the back of the tank. My mother has no use for driver's licenses or identification cards. She's not so bitter that she wants to ruin somebody's life, or even their day.

I was very young when I learned about honor among thieves.

The bathroom stinks of accidents and mold. I open the wallet and am greeted with a silver shield. It shines like a diamond. I'm not frightened of it. I only want to please my mother. But that shield is too much temptation for a little girl. I unhook it from its place in the wallet and stick it in my left back pocket. The money and the Visa card are in the right back pocket.

I don't tell my mother about it. It's mine. I don't know what it's for, but it reminds me of the day I earned the approval of someone inside the system. A sheriff's deputy thought I had done a good job. I had said the right thing. Even though I stole from her, I won a nod because I knew about flightless birds.

Sometime around my fourteenth birthday, when my mother is taken away, I realize that the badge is a placeholder. A signpost to my future self that I didn't have to be stuck. I didn't have to be what my mother was. I loved and admired her, now and always. But I didn't have to be what she was. I could choose to change the course of my life.

• • •

When I get home from the factory roof, Nana is still up. I go into the bathroom and start the shower, stripping down. I pull his wallet out of my coat pocket and empty it.

Pressing the leather wallet to my nose, I inhale him. I'm sitting on the toilet naked, shower running hot, fogging up the air, and the contents of his wallet are on the tile floor in front of me. Three credit cards. One driver's license, State of New Jersey. Birth date—not surprising. He's a Scorpio. Then I notice the expiration date.

It's expired.

I check through the credit cards.

All expired.

A supermarket membership card for Alan Smithee. A card for the Library of Alexandria.

Is he fucking with me?

He most certainly is.

The money's real. Hundred fifty-seven in smallish bills and twenties, in denominational order, all facing the same direction.

I plucked the wallet out of his jacket on a whim in the hopes that I would be shocked or surprised, and I am. It was foolish and reckless, but he made me feel both of those things. Foolish for wanting him, reckless for submitting to the want. Every time I saw him and survived, I felt as if risks were not only worth it, but absolutely necessary.

I told myself he would never be fully honest with me unless I forced his hand. Maybe that's true. Maybe it isn't. What I couldn't deny was that the little sleight-of-hand specialist inside me had been sleeping for a long time and was wide awake now that Keaton Bridge was in her life.

And he'd either known I'd steal his wallet or he carried around a lot of useless shit.

Between the last five and the first single is a small yellow Post-It with a note written in pencil.

You will return this to me in two nights.

My blood turns to ice. My fingertips go numb and tingly. He knew. He tested me and I passed, or failed. I have no idea which. I pull it off the five and turn it over.

Artful Dodger.

It sounds as if he approves, at least if he approves of a master pickpocket in *Oliver Twist*. And who doesn't approve of Dickens?

In some twisted way, he wants me to know him, but he wants me to take the information from him.

That kiss. His body. The control and command of him, even when I was throwing him against a car. His hardness against me. His scent is on the collar of my coat. He's a good kisser. A fantastic kisser. In the kissing department, he's king.

I close the wallet and notice a circular worn patch, beige against brown, a size smaller than a dime. I run my finger over it. There's something in there, but I didn't see it when the wallet was open.

I never got caught before, but this time will be different. The time I had the wallet in my hand outside the airport parking lot doesn't count. I cried and claimed I found it. Mom slapped my wrist, and we laughed when the cop let me go. The law's disapproval would never weigh on me with the same force as my mother's approval lifted me.

I turn the wallet around in my hands, looking for the place where the coin sits regularly enough to wear out the leather. I find a place in the billfold where the lining isn't stitched and take out the silver disk. It's heavier than I expected, marked with raised lines that adhere to the shape of the circle. The lines are broken in places that seem random. It's like a fingerprint, a labyrinth, a code pressed into metal. The other side is the same, but with a different random pattern. I click my fingernail along the surface.

I'm going to have to answer for this, and I stop my nail.

My relationship with Keaton is impossible to define, but it's something. It exists. It's a living thing, growing, changing, becoming a part of my life whether I want it or not.

And having stolen his wallet as if this was a game? How's that going to affect it?

I may not trust him, but what have I done to earn his trust?

I question myself, naked, sitting on my toilet, with a stolen wallet in my lap as if I'm seven years old again, when my phone rattles across the vanity.

If it's Keaton, I'm going to apologize right away, even if he calls me Artful Dodger with all the respect and approval in the world.

But it's not Keaton.

<Agent down>
<Shooting>
<All agents report>

I shut the phone, turn the shower to cold, and am out the door in eight minutes.

CHAPTER 18.

CASSIE

We converge on the hospital in Springfield. I'm running like a dog to keep up, collect crime scene evidence, take notes, get the story straight. With no access to a secure channel, the Post-It does no good in my pocket. I can't even tell anyone about it until I know where it leads.

The sun is just about up when we're called into a briefing. No one's tired. Our blood is infused with adrenaline and caffeine. Three agents have been hospitalized. None are in critical condition, but nevertheless, the very idea that someone shot at federal agents is not going down well.

We've taken over a small education room on the first floor of the hospital. The blinds are open onto the parking lot. The chairs are kid-sized and the walls are decorated with the letters of the alphabet. Frieda sits next to me. She's dug her notebook from the bottom of her bag, and she taps her pen on an open page.

"They're going to want to wipe these guys from the face of the earth now," Frieda says softly as I get out my own notebook.

"Any intel on how they were tipped off?"

"Nope."

You're at greatest risk of being attacked when you attack, and greatest risk of being seen when you seek.

Was it me? Everyone knows I've been trying to access Third Psyche for months. Did my single-minded pursuit of Third Psyche cause the ambush?

I turn away, looking out the window. I hear Orlando quite clearly.

I catch every word he's saying, every fact he states, and take notes. But I'm completely distracted by what part I may have had in this.

A black Lexus pulls into the lot, going too fast, screeching into a spot. I'm not the only one looking out, but I'm the only one who knows who's driving before the car's in park.

I shut the blinds. "Focus, people."

Orlando nods his thanks, and I nod back. So I'm sure it looks strange when I slip out of the briefing into the hallway. When the room's door clicks shut behind me, I bolt through the double doors.

"No running!" a nurse calls as I pass.

Fuck her. I burst into the empty ER waiting room just as the doors slide open for Keaton.

He's a wreck. Shirt untucked. Hair uncombed. A wild look in his eye that's not hungry or sexual, but violent; as if he came to settle scores. His gaze lands on me and I freeze in place, watching his hands go from fists to question marks. Feeling the tension crack and break.

"Sir?"

A man's voice. To my right.

Security or police.

If he's waylaid, he might be seen, might be held or questioned.

Nope. Not today.

I reach for my back pocket and take out my wallet, flipping it open so the badge and ID show. "Federal agent." I don't take my eyes off Keaton as he takes heavy breaths, chest rising and falling as if he's run a mile. "I need a secure location."

In my peripheral vision, the security guard looks at my ID. "This way."

I tilt my head to Keaton and follow the security guard without a word. He unlocks a door to a small, utilitarian office.

"Thank you." I point at Keaton, who's two steps behind me. "Sir."

He's in. I'm in. The door is closed. Locked.

"What the—?"

I never finish my sentence. He's kissing me, and I don't have the alarm bells whistling loud enough to use a defensive maneuver. I let him kiss me, run his hands over my back, take me in his arms as if we've just survived something traumatic.

"I caught it on the scanner this morning," he says between kisses.

"What? The shooting?"

"I thought it was you. I thought they shot you."

"I'm fine."

"I thought it was my fault. I thought they saw you on the forum and came for you."

I push him off me so I can speak for more than two words without getting kissed. "I haven't even logged on yet."

"Thank God. Thank God, thank God. I would have committed murder if they hurt a hair on your head. Cassie. Listen. "

"I was looking in your wallet when I got a call. I'm sorry I took it."

"You think I care about the wallet? Jesus, woman. When I thought you were hurt... I thought I'd never see you again."

I open my mouth to ask him what's happened? What's changed? We haven't even slept together, yet his intensity has a traction I cannot resist, and no words come out.

"You don't trust me," he says.

The words come out without a thought. Instinct speaks. "I don't."

His hand goes under my skirt, between my legs, over the fabric of my underwear. He presses against me. I'm swollen and wet already.

"Should I touch you?"

"Yes," I whisper in the shape of a groan, leaning back on the desk.

He presses my legs open. "Say my name."

"Keaton," I gasp as he rubs against me.

He's fierce and demanding. His hand has one goal only. To make me feel him through the fabric. "Wrong. Tell me my name."

I can barely breathe. I don't know what he wants, but I sure as hell want to give it to him. "Alpha Wolf, a.k.a.... whatever. You have a million aliases."

His fingers swirl, gathering up sensation as if he wants to mold it around me, but he does not get under the fabric, where my deepest want lies. "My real name. Cassandra, tell me my real name."

His real name? Is that an option? He has a real name? Of course he does. Of course Keaton Bridge isn't his real name. I knew this, and he knows I know this. Is this a test? A trick? I open my mouth to ask what I'm supposed to know and how it overlays what he thinks I know and what he wants out of me, but he finally slides his hand under my underwear and touches me where I'm tender and wet. My back arches, but he only strokes gently enough to push me against my orgasm without pushing me over into it.

"Do you want me to stop?"

"No, please don't stop." I can only whine and beg at this point.

He leans close to me until I feel his words more clearly than I hear them. "You don't know my real name. And you want me to touch you between your legs?"

I look him in the eye. The twilight blue of them is almost navy in the shadows.

"Yes," I whisper.

"You want me to make you come?"

"Make me come."

His fingers move along my seam, gathering moisture. I'm so close, and so at his command, that I will say anything. I'll even tell him the truth that I haven't told myself. Slowly and deliberately, he slides three fingers inside me. I push against him until they can't go deeper.

"First, I'm going to own your pussy, then I'm taking the rest of you. Every day is precious, Cassie." His thumb brushes against my clit. "I realized today that your trust is too. I want it, and I'm going to have it."

His hand works me, pushing inside, thumb giving friction against my slick nub.

He lets me come, and he stretches my orgasm to obscene heights, watching me squirm and bite back a groan as he touches me only enough to give me more pleasure than I ever thought possible.

When I'm reduced to panting and pain, he cups his hand between my legs as if he's protecting what's under there.

"I'm glad you're all right," he says when he pulls his hand out of my underwear.

"Me too. Next time just call me."

He picks a handkerchief out of his jacket pocket and wipes his hand, smiles a little, then kisses my cheek tenderly. His lips brush the heat away from my skin and replace it with a new warmth that runs hot with passion and warm with comfort. Whatever enflamed him when he arrived had dissipated.

"What would be the fun of that?" He helps me up, smoothing my skirt.

"You have a point."

He presses his lips to my cheek, lingering over my skin. "Be ready to see me tomorrow night."

CHAPTER 19.

CASSIE

I put Keaton's Post-It on my desk and fold it so I can see the hand-written link. It's been shortened. It'll report back to whoever made it. Keaton will know when I log on. I'm not disturbed. I like that he knows. I feel both protected and aggressive in a show-offy way. I want him to see me.

I set up the secure VPN so the Bureau can track my activity, but hackers can't. I'm completely cloaked when I open Tor, the secure browser that manages access to the dark web, and I carefully type in the link. It connects to the log-in page for Third Psyche.

Thank you, Keaton Bridge.

Before I can note a single element of the site, it flickers and goes to deep blue with yellow letters.

—SORRY—
THIS PAGE HAS BEEN SENT BACK TO HELL

Fuck. I'm glad I didn't open it in front of everyone, only to be embarrassed, but *fuck* just the same.

Was it shut down by hackers? Anonymous? Did they get a whiff that I was looking? Or did Keaton move the link to protect me?

I have a feeling it was a version of the latter.

So what do I want out of Keaton now that he's ripped the site from under his link? Walking down the hall to the coffee machine, I consider what he has to offer and whether or not it's the same as what I want.

The hallway is windowless, and the dull, dead institutional shade of green is the same on the floor, ceiling, and walls. The light over the utility closet has always buzzed. When I think of getting promoted, I think of this hallway. One day I'm going to see it for the last time. On the way out of here, I'm going to say goodbye to that buzzing light and that brain-dulling shade of green.

At the end, I turn left toward coffee and find Frieda's beaten me there.

"Hey, I have gossip." She blows on her coffee. "We're getting a pay grade packet next week. I'm due for a GS-12."

The packets are sent quarterly from Quantico, and include all our promotions and pay grade changes. I'd totally forgotten to worry about it.

"You'll get it," I say.

"Keep your nose clean with Smirkypants," she scolds. "At least until this is cleared up."

She knows me. She knows I'm not attracted to a guy that often and she can tell Mr. Smirkypants is different.

"Promise," I say, holding up two fingers.

She pats my shoulder and walks out. She's a good friend. Something about sisterhood flies across my brain and hooks onto my job before it's gone. It demands attention.

There's another sister in town, and she's a hacker.

CHAPTER 20.

CASSIE

It's funny watching a millionaire bag groceries, but Harper Barrington was in the habit of helping the store owners before she met Taylor or went to Stanford.

She has on a masculine plaid car coat with sleeves halfway down her fingers. It doesn't get in the way of her lightningfast cashiering, nor does the length of the line get in the way of her small talk with the customers.

"Hi," I say when I finally get to the front of the line.

"Hey." She does a doubletake on my face as she moves the loaf of bread along. "I've seen you before."

"I think I met you in front of the Barrington mansion?"

She takes a split second to tap her forehead when she remembers. Behind her, a girl in her twenties comes up behind and puts her bag in a cabinet.

"Hey, Trude," Harper says to the girl before she turns her attention back to me and the groceries I've come a long way to get. "The day you came for Keaton. FBI. Agent Grinstead. You want a separate bag for the eggs?"

"No."

"I hope he didn't cause you too much trouble."

"I think I caused him more trouble than he caused me."

"Good. Twenty-seven forty-nine please."

I hand her thirty. "I was wondering—"

"Trudy, honey," Harper calls behind her, "the credit card slips are in the envelope."

Trudy and Harper go on about bags and cash and rolls of quarters as Harper plucks my change out of the drawer. I'm sure she's finished when I continue.

"Thanks," I start. "Do you think—"

"Did Johnny go to the bank?" Trudy asks, unzipping a green canvas case.

"Yesterday," Harper replies, handing me my change.

The pimply boy at the end of the counter bags everything efficiently. I decide this has gone poorly and I'm going to have to try something else after I drop the bags of groceries home.

"You got this?" Harper asks Trudy, pulling the drawer out of the register.

"Yeah," Trudy says as I head out with a heavy bag in each arm.

I'm putting them in my trunk when Harper calls me from the top of the store's steps.

"Hey! Cassie!" She clatters down the wood steps.

"Yes?" I'm pretty amazed that she remembered my name from hearing it once, months ago.

"You sounded like you wanted to talk to me?"

"I've never met anyone so eager to talk to an FBI agent." I close the trunk.

"Here's what I know. If you want to talk to me, you're gonna. I can avoid it or just get on with it. But do I need a lawyer or something?"

Does she need a lawyer? Am I buying groceries in Barrington on official business, or am I here on a personal call?

"Tell you what," I say. "If we get into sketchy territory, I'll let you know."

"You hungry?"

She indicates the hamburger joint next to the store. It had been closed for business until the previous month. Now it's a hub of activity. It's already late. I could use dinner, and I didn't buy anything all too perishable.

"Sure," I say.

Harper trots off toward the restaurant.

• • •

She knows the owners, who are long-time Barrington residents. We're seated in the back where it's quiet. We both order our burgers rare.

"So, you go grocery shopping in Barrington often?" She pokes her Coke with her straw, letting the insinuation that I went very far out of my way for a few boxes of pasta hang in the air.

"Almost never, but you carry Standoff's Bakery. I've been curious about the cupcakes."

"Hm." Poke. Poke. "Where's the guy you came to the door with? Ken, was it?"

"Got shot last night."

She coughs as if she's choking on her own spit.

I wait until she finishes. "It's nothing you can't read in the papers."

"Here? Barrington? Doverton?"

"Springfield. He's going to be fine. Just a flesh wound."

She shakes her head. Springfield is as near to an inner city as we get. The mythology is if bad stuff's going to happen, it's going to be there.

"Gotta tell you, when I got to Stanford, it felt like I could get shot any minute. I didn't know anyone. All new faces. It takes getting used to."

"Did you feel like that at MIT?"

She'd been there a long time ago for less than a year. I mention it because I want her to know I have information, no matter how surface it is. It seems only fair.

"No. My head was up my ass. Anyway, I'm going to be honest now, since you just basically told me stuff I never told you, so you must have a file on me."

"There are a lot of files on a lot of things."

Whatever effect my admission is meant to have—mollifying her, distracting her, lying, because she doesn't have a file—seems irrelevant to her.

"Keaton, the guy you questioned?"

I try to stay relaxed, but my skin tingles at the mention of his name. "Yes."

"He needed heating lamps on the roof and a little round table last night. I needled him about it until he told me why."

"Really?"

"Really. It was fun to watch him squirm."

I can't imagine Keaton Bridge squirming under Harper's interrogation. She looks so young and defenseless as she sucks on her straw until she's getting nothing but air and ice. She's a kid, in a way, but not to be underestimated.

"So." She places the glass to the side. "Here you are this afternoon, over twenty miles out of the way for cupcakes I don't remember seeing on the belt. I figure you're going to ask me a bunch of stuff and get around to Keaton at some point. I don't know what it has to do with who's getting shot or anything, but I don't like people getting shot. Not even in Springfield."

There are rules about what to tell civilians, and I follow them to the letter.

"You hacked into QI4 before it was released." Common knowledge. Even the *NY Times* covered the hack and the revelation that a small-town girl had cracked the world's first quantum system.

"Most fun exploit ever." She smiles as her teeth bite the straw flat.

"So you're a pretty advanced hacker."

"If you say so."

"As is Taylor Harden."

"He's the best."

"And his partner."

"You know I can't say anything about that."

I take the labyrinth coin from my pocket and lay it on the table. Her gaze locks on it as I push it toward her. "Do you have one of these?"

Our food comes. We ignore it.

"Where did you get this?" She doesn't pick it up. She only touches the edge.

"I won't lie. So I won't tell you."

I recognize something brash in her at the moment. Something show-offy and cocky. Something that makes her head sway with defiance as she takes out her phone.

"I can't believe you guys don't know about this." She pokes her phone and points the camera at the coin as if taking a picture. "What do you do all day?"

"Look for crooks," I say as she watches her phone spin. The first thing QI4 did was build cell towers, but the signal out here is still terrible and she probably has seven layers of VPN. "I'm trying to find out if Third Psyche was involved with the shooting."

"Shit, no." She puts her phone face down and regards me seriously. "Those guys are no good. They're the devil."

"I know."

"I'm so glad you're trying to get them, because seriously? That's the kind of thing I can't even look at or I'm going to lose it. Did you hear about the thing last Halloween? When they tried to do a coordinated attack against seven synagogues?"

"Yep. Then they moved servers."

She slides her plate in front of her.

I take the coin back. "Do you mind?"

She picks up her phone instead of answering, holding the glass up to face me. It's a picture of Keaton looking straight at me, and suddenly I'm surrounded by the smell of him and my ears are filled with the danger in his voice.

I glance at the list of names below.

4LPH4_W0LF

X7R3M3_157

D0XX_D3V1L

There were more, but she puts the phone down before I can note them all.

Still chewing, she digs her keys out of her bag. "I should ask where you got this, but obviously you stole it."

I admit nothing. The waitress refills the drinks.

"What is it?"

"You guys." She shakes her head and ribs me. "What do you do all day?"

"Clean our guns."

She isolates a tiny charm on her keyring. The same coin with a different fingerprint. She points her phone at it. This time, the VPN connects immediately and her picture comes up, filling the screen where Keaton's was. She hands me the phone. "Scroll."

She eats her burger as I scroll through a list of avatars, IDs, height and weight stats.

"It's a verification system," I say. "A passport. And the swirls are like a QR code—if you have the software to read it."

"Right." She gently removes the phone from my hand. "Because hackers never really know who we're talking to IRL… in real life."

"I know what IRL means."

"We could meet and you could say you're anyone, unless you have one of these."

"Why did you just show it to me?"

She smirks and takes a pull of her soda. "Keaton said if you came to me with a cert kwon, I should scan it." She wipes her mouth. "You should have told me you were after Third Psyche right away. From now on, you tell me what you need and I'll get it for you. I won't try to romance you on the roof or kiss you in the parking lot..."

I nearly choke on my burger. Harper finds this delightful.

"Come on!" she cries. "Do you think Taylor's not going to look at the security video to see why he needed a heat lamp and a pitcher of water, just so? Please. He's known Keaton since he was fifteen, and he's never seen him try so hard."

I'm flattered. I'm honored.

I'm swooning, which is completely inappropriate and unprofessional.

I clear my throat to get back my bearings and take a bite of my lunch to buy time, because I don't deserve that kind of effort. I'd never say it out loud, but I'm convinced of it. I'm a regular woman in a masculine job. Men don't treat me like a queen. It's disorienting and exciting.

"You all right?" she asks.

I'm all right. Better than all right. I'm high on *never seen him try so hard.*

"I'm concerned." I sip my Coke. Swallow. I pause to feel my feet on the floor and my ass in the chair. Time to get over it. "Keaton alerted them to the fact that we were looking for them so they could ambush our guys."

"Yeah, no." She shakes her head so vigorously, her hair sways under her chin.

"He *is* Alpha Wolf."

"Whatever. I'll tell you something about Keaton that I know and Taylor would totally back me up. Keaton's interested in money. Em-oh-en-ee-why. Long-term dollars. Nazis are losers. Short-term, risky cash that's soaked in blood. I mean, the first thing he did was fuck credit card companies over Luhn's formula."

That's a slip on her part. Not because the crack was a secret. Luhn's formula is the reason you're asked for the expiration date when you buy something with a credit card online or over the phone, and why giving the wrong one leads to a rejection. The formula's used to checksum the credit card account number against the expiration date. If they don't match, the card's rejected, but if they do, the purchase sails through. Anyone who has the formula has the keys to a kingdom of wealth.

"Taylor Harden cracked Luhn's," I say, touching base with known fact before moving on to a new reality.

"*They* did it, and Taylor took the fall with you guys. Keaton didn't even get to look a federal agent in the eye over it." She wags her finger at me. "You're counting in your head. Statute of limitations is up."

Nailed it. I was indeed counting the number of years since Taylor cracked Luhn's.

Harper gathers a skein of French fries in her fingers and bites it in half, runs the raw ends through the last of her ketchup, and finishes them off.

"And then Alpha Wolf was born," I say.

"Wouldn't know anything about that."

Maybe she does. Maybe she doesn't.

"Taylor sent you to talk to me, didn't he?" I ask.

"He said if I saw you, I should say 'hi.' But I'm here because I like the burgers and I like Keaton. I want to check you out. See if you're trouble for him."

"Am I?"

"Probably. Actually, definitely."

"If he hasn't done anything, he has nothing to worry about."

She laughs as if I'm such a card she can't help herself. "Oh, I didn't mean like that. I mean he likes you and you like him. I can see it and I think it's great, but it's trouble. Every time. Especially for that guy. He's allergic to commitment."

"I'm not available for him." My voice snaps as if I'm irritated by the notion that I'd be interested in a man who has to worry about statutes of limitation. Even though I do want him, very much so, and it's that very real threat that he is lawless that piques my interest as much as *never seen him try so hard.*

"Crap," she says, looking at her phone. "I have to go." She slips her coat off the back of the chair. "Keaton's a better guy than Taylor was, that's for sure. And if you have to pretend you don't want him, you go ahead. You do you."

"I'm just doing my job." I reach for my wallet even though we haven't gotten the check yet.

"The bill's taken care of." She swings her coat behind her and gets her arms in the sleeves. "It was nice to meet you again."

She bounces off, hair swinging across her back as she calls everyone in the place by name. I'm left staring at my half-eaten burger and wondering who Keaton Bridge really is, because with the cert kwon, I know more than ever, and less of what makes me truly curious.

Taylor's never seen him try so hard.

• • •

"It's a coin about the size of a dime." I'm in the parking lot of the grocery and the restaurant, watching the edge of the sky go from orange to blue. "Heavy. Steel maybe? Check their personal effects and I'll be there in thirty minutes."

Keaton's cert kwon sits in my fist. I pretend I'm trying to decide whether to show them or not, but I decided before I even called Orlando. I'm going to tell them I know about them, not that I've seen one.

"Where did you get this intel?" Orlando asks.

"A good asset. A different one."

"If we find one on these guys, it's going to break this wide open."

"I know."

"Tell me what you think about the shooting."

"I think my asset either sold us out or revealed himself."

"There's a lot happening between 'either' and 'or,' Agent Grinstead."

"I don't think they sold us out."

He makes a weary sigh. "Who is your asset?"

I don't have to tell him. Not unless I need money to pay him. The fact that I'm under no obligation to tell him does not remove the pressure to do so. I should tell him. He'll keep it under wraps. That's his job.

And if he doesn't?

I've betrayed Keaton, and my guts twist at the idea. My reaction to revealing his name isn't sensible. It's not logical. It is not the result of a thoughtful calculation. My body doesn't want me to say his name. I won't be able to take it back.

"I trust him," I answer by not answering.

"Is this person known to you personally? Or is this an online ID?"

"Personal."

His lips are personal. His touch. The sound of his voice. They're personal, and they're mine.

"You better make sure you know exactly who they are. I don't want you or this office to be distracted by inquiries into this asset. Do you understand?"

"I understand."

"If you need to take some time to vet this person, take it. Come to me if you find out your trust was misplaced."

"It wasn't, sir."

"Prove it to yourself, then prove it to me. I'll get you Level 4 clearance to dig them up."

"Thank you," I say. "One more thing."

"Speak."

"I think the answer is online, in the white supremacist forums. And I think I might have gotten access."

"Really?"

"Yes. But I need to work on it here. I don't want to shirk my duties if you need me in Springfield, but I believe I can do more good here."

"Agreed. Keep me updated."

"Thank you, sir."

"Good work, Agent."

We hang up. On the drive to the field office, I try to remember the last time Orlando told me I'd done good work and how I felt when he did.

The first time he told me I'd done good work was my first two weeks on the job, when I'd found messages inside the comments script of a website no one could prove was behind a money laundering scheme.

Frieda and I had a glass of champagne that night, and I beamed.

But not today. Has the excitement worn off? Or has something else happened? Because I'm happiest about Keaton's trust. Not his approval, but his trust that even if I found out about the coin, I'd protect him.

I'm going to live up to it.

• • •

SUBJECT: KEATON BRIDGE
SEARCH TYPE: LEVEL 4

Everyone is somewhere in the FBI database at Level 4. Having a stub isn't a big deal. Having a file doesn't mean as much as everyone thinks. Most of it is automated anyway.

But Keaton?

He doesn't have shit. For a foreign national with part ownership in a soon-to-be huge company destined for government contracts, he has less than Joe from Petoskey.

I check Interpol.

Nothing.

I check our shared data with MI6.

It was a longshot to begin with, but nothing.

My blood gets cold. My mouth tastes like the inside of my stomach. Something isn't right. I do a quick check for Taylor Harden, just to make sure the system's even working.

—BeezleBoy363636 offers Luhn's formula with bids starting at one million Bitcoin.

—BeezleBoy363636 tracked down to Camden, NJ.

—A bunch of redacted shit.

—Taylor Harden a.k.a. Beezleboy363636, a fifteen-year-old hacker with a nice family who likes to think they raised him better, flips in exchange for expunged records.

—Asset records filed in Delta show Taylor did three years of coding and hacking consultation before heading to MIT, which he quit with three credits left.

No mention of Keaton or Alpha Wolf. They lived in the same town. Went to the same school. I'm amazed at how little he's actually told me in the time we've spent together.

Why is Keaton Bridge even in the United States?

Deeper isn't the way to go. I need to search wider.

I set my VPN to London and do a broad search. I'll take anything. A picture. A school. A birth announcement. He was born just as social media was, so I didn't expect much from that, but what does come up surprises me.

—A Facebook profile with a picture of a handsome boy who looks exactly like the Keaton Bridge I know. Three posts. Fifteen friends from every corner of the UK. None with mutual friends outside the circle.

—His name and photo listed in London's Dagenham School. No clubs. No interests. No quote. He's facing slightly left. All the other students face right.

—A crystal-clear birth announcement in a small local paper.

I'm in the process of looking up William and Phyllis Bridge when Frieda pokes her head into my office.

"I'm on my way out to Springfield," she says. "You're not coming?"

"Working Mr. Smirkypants."

"Always on it." She looks over my shoulder. "Is that his birth announcement?"

"Yeah."

"Are his parents famous or something? Rich? Old money?" She leans farther, squinting at the screen. She sees what I see. Crisp digital lines from an analog age.

"Not that I can tell."

"Kind of odd to have a birth announcement then," she says.

"Yeah. Everything about him is kind of odd."

"Sister?"

"It's fine," I say.

"You know how much I admire you."

"Hush."

"Don't let him mess you up. Please. I want to call you my boss one day."

Her faith in me has eclipsed my own for as long as I can remember. She's my biggest fan, and even when I pat her hand to reassure her, I fear she's headed for disappointment.

CHAPTER 21.

CASSIE

I'm exhausted when I get home. I feel like the cat not only dragged me in, but toyed with me for hours beforehand. I feel wrung out, hungry, tired. My jaw aches at the hinge from pounding at crossed t's and dotted i's, coming up empty, and starting over again.

I figure I'll sit up with Nana for a few hours and do some puzzles. She'll tell me I don't need a man out one side of her mouth and talk about diamond rings with the other.

But I can't take another conversation about men. Not with the fresh memory of Keaton's fingers in me and the desperation in his voice when he said he was scared for me. My God, I must be tired— because not only am I ranting and raving to my grandmother in my head as I step in the door, but when I see Keaton next to her on the couch, I'm so suddenly awake that by contrast, I must have been near walking in my sleep.

He's not the only one there, but he's the only one I see. Molly's there with her knitting. Fredo, who still has a head full of hair, silver though it is, has a glass of wine swirling. Carol sits next to the box wine, filling her glass. They're all laughing like old friends, which they are. All except Keaton, who seems perfectly comfortable with the geriatric crowd.

When I see him laughing with my grandmother's friends, I feel as if I'm alive for the first time since he walked out of the little hospital office. My face nearly cracks when I smile.

And he's not just sitting. No, nothing that simple for Keaton Bridge. His legs take up half the room. They're the length of a shotgun. Nana puts a hand on his knee and pushes it because whatever he said is so damn funny, he needs to be pushed.

I close the door, and Nana cries, "Well, she's finally here!"

I'm greeted with a chorus of my grandmother's cronies.

Keaton slaps his knees as if the whole conversation is finished, finally, and he can get on with his business.

He looks up at me when he stands. "Are you ready?"

"For?"

They all laugh again as if they share a joke I'm not privy to. I don't feel left out as much as I would like to know what I'm supposed to be ready for. I give him the side eye and he winks at me.

"Did you know what they call cigarettes in England?" Carol says.

Keaton snaps up his jacket and bows to my grandmother, then each of her friends. "I have much to learn." He takes Grandma's hand and kisses it in an obsequious, British, and charming way.

Not shockingly, she loves it. She's one batting eyelash away from full flirt.

"Nana…" I hear the scold in my voice and swallow it.

"Where did you find this one, Cassandra?" Molly asks. "Have you been hiding him?"

"He does quite a fine job of hiding himself."

"All the best ones do," Nana interjects. "Now you two just run along."

Keaton can take a cue. He holds the door open for me, and with Nana & Co smiling and waving, I have no choice but to step outside with him.

I speak when we hear the dead bolt snap shut. "Don't turn around. I happen to know for fact that she's still looking out the window."

His hands are in his pockets. I suspect that's a gentlemanly show. "She's a very interesting lady." He walks me to his car. "Have you ever talked to her? She has a few choice words for your grandfather. I pity the motherfucker."

Motherfucker is Nana's pet name for my disappearing grandfather.

I point at Keaton's Lexus. "Did she see the car you drove up in? She's from Detroit. She wouldn't appreciate the Japanese make."

"She mentioned that." He opens the passenger side door for me. "The factory's in Tennessee."

He almost has me. I'm almost in the goddamn car. But I stop myself.

"I didn't agree to go anywhere with you. You can't just show up here. One, people talk. I haven't told them my source, but now you just appear on my couch, pretty as you please, and expect no one can put two and two together."

"Most people can't."

"You're not understanding me. I'm trying to protect you."

"Thank you, but I have this."

"And how did you know where I lived? Do you know that's weird? You could have called, not that I ever gave you my number."

"Is this any worse than you pickpocketing me? Or tracking down my best friend's girlfriend to get intel on me?"

"My reasons are clear."

"So are mine. I couldn't keep away. The more I learned about you, the more I wanted to see you again. And this morning, everything changed for me. So maybe it's me. Maybe I'm the one with the problem. I figure there's only one way to find out. I was going to suggest this over dinner, but since you're such an insistent little git, I'll bring it up now. I need to find out if this is my problem or your problem."

I blink at him. "Are you asking me out?"

"Apparently. I also need my wallet."

"I was supposed to return it tomorrow night."

"I need it today."

"You could've just called."

"I'm hungry now, so I'm taking you to dinner."

"Something like that."

He touches my cheek with his thumb. It's tender in the way I've never experienced. Sure, men have touched me before, and they have been gentle. It's been fine. But his thumb on my cheek is more than the results matching the intention. It's more than a simple touch. He has a complexity that is encapsulated in the place his thumb meets my cheek. He's been charming, chivalrous, and deferential. Tenderness is the revelation of another plane in a stone that seems to have more facets than I can count.

"I have never met a woman so deserving of everything being better than normal for her. And I'm sorry if my attempts to do better for you are actually worse. I'm breaking new ground with you"

I don't expect this. I'm not only surprised, I'm a little bit liquid right now. It's the danger-dash-unknown-dash-taboo-dash-dash-dash. But more than any of that, it's him. I like him. I like his confidence, but I also like the thread of unsurety that runs through it. I like his competence, and I also like the way he lets my grandmother tell him how to do puzzles.

"I'm going to have to forgive you." I take his wallet out of my bag. He holds out his hand for it. "After all, when a girl kisses a hacker, she shouldn't be surprised when she's hacked." I place the wallet in his upturned palm, and we rest there with his long fingers curling to take my hand as well as the wallet. "Just leave me something to tell you over dinner."

He steps away, pulling the wallet with him. He runs his finger over the worn circle, checking for the cert kwon. It's there as expected.

"Thank you for that," I say. "For letting Harper tell me."

He smiles and indicates that I should get in the car, which I do, letting him close the door and realizing I've hacked him as surely as he's hacked me.

CHAPTER 22.

CASSIE

He's taken me to one of the the nicest restaurants in Doverton. It's late, so we're seated right away. And it's a good thing too, because I'm starving. The host hands us menus and takes our drink order.

"Red wine," I say. "Just something dry is fine."

"Ginger ale," Keaton says.

The host spins off to fulfill the order. This is the second time I've seen Keaton order a drink, and it's the second time he's ordered something without alcohol.

"Do you not to drink at all?"

"Driving." He smirks as if he knows this is half an answer. "And I still need my wits around you."

I've never been more flattered by a compliment. Once my mother went away and my grandmother started raising me, I was homecoming queen, captain of the cheerleading squad, and voted most likely to be on the cover of a magazine. I've been called a long-stemmed rose, a tall drink of water, and a handful of adjectives that all meant "attractive."

But this brilliant guy saying he needs to keep his wits around me is the nicest thing a man ever said to me. I smile into my water glass, trying to swallow my gushing satisfaction.

He's reading you.

Obviously, he knows how to flatter me.

The waitress is fresh out of high school, and tucks her hair behind her ear when she talks. She addresses Keaton as if I'm not there, mesmerized by him, rattling off specials and smiling like a ventriloquist's dummy.

"I read the burgers are really good here," I say just to get her attention. "I like mine rare. And I mean rare."

"Okay, and sir?"

"She'll have the filet mignon."

"Wait." I hold up my hand.

"You want a burger more than the filet?" he asks as if what I want is an issue.

"Well, no. But it's…" I run my hand over the length of the menu. I'm saying *it's at the bottom* without saying it, which is code for *it's forty dollars.*

"Delicious!" the waitress chimes in.

"Fine." I hand over my menu.

"What do you have without meat?" Keaton asks.

"We have a chicken cacciatore that's really nice."

I'm as surprised by his question as I am by her answer.

"How about an eggplant parmesan?" he asks gamely.

"Sure thing!" She pencils it in, asks a bunch of questions about sides and drinks, and takes off with the leather-bound menus under her arm.

"So," he says, folding his hands on the table and pressing the full weight of his gaze on me. I'm distracted by the arch of his eyebrows, how perfect and expressive they are. How they seem to hint at all the facets of the stone.

"So," I say. "How long were you hanging out with my grandmother?"

He shrugs, holds his answer until the waitress is finished giving us our drinks. I suddenly wish I hadn't ordered wine.

"She has quite a story to tell," he says. "Working her way up at the plant, taking care of her daughter all by herself."

"My great-grandmother was also a single mother. Grandma understood what it would take for her to make a life."

"You must come from a long line of extraordinary women."

"We don't make it easy on ourselves." I don't want to talk about me or my mother, the kind of person she was, how she raised me, or how I wound up taking care of my grandmother. I want to talk about him. I want to see how many facets of this stone I can uncover over one dinner.

I swirl my wine. A basket of bread and a bowl of butter appear between us. I wonder if I'm in over my head.

"There are two reasons people become vegetarians," I say. "They either believe in animal rights or they do it for health reasons. Which is yours?"

"How binary of you."

"If you have a third reason, I'd love to hear it."

He regards me, the room, his bread, me again, for what seems like an hour, but is actually two Mississippis. He's leisurely about it. I can see the wheels turning as he calculates what to tell me. I hope it's everything.

"I grew up in London, right in the middle of everything. Small row house with flowers in the windows. We had a cat to kill mice and a dog to keep the cat in line." He pulls out his stirrer and finishes his ginger ale. "I had an extraordinarily ordinary childhood."

He waits, as if testing for what I already know, and I take a second to weigh the fact that he's Alpha Wolf against how his hand felt under my skirt.

"In the interests of full disclosure," I cut in, "I'm still an FBI agent. So you might want to be careful about what you tell me."

Mr. Smirkypants is in full effect. "Tell me then, what do you think you know?"

"I know the shape of a fat goose egg. Your UK records were completely fabricated."

"How so?"

Does he not know?

He knows. He has to know. He wants to know how I know, and I decide it's a fair question.

"Your school records are impeccably average for someone so smart. Your elementary school photo faces the wrong direction. Your birth announcement has the clearest edges I've ever seen in documents that predate digital inputting."

"You have a real nose for bullshit, don't you?"

I tip my glass toward him. We click, and I sip my wine.

"So," he says, leaning forward, "do you have a fact to share? Any theories? Wishes? Dreams? Who would I be if I could be anybody?"

"Dreams and wishes aren't things I waste a lot of time with. I do, however, have a hypothesis."

He leans forward even farther, as if he wants the table to fold away and disappear. As if, given the choice, he would twine his body into mine to hear what I had to say. "Spill it now."

Such is my desire to obey him that I nearly tip my glass. I blame his dead serious tone of voice, but the fact is, I've heard this tone before and not reacted this way.

"If I put together your story about decamping to New Jersey, which is a known asylum state for the United Kingdom, and if I look back at what was going on then in the international community, it's all pretty clear."

His left eye squints just a little. He's not exactly smiling. But his dimples crease a little more, as if a smirk is waiting just behind his mouth.

"I had to look it up," I say. "NATO *did* have a sort of agent protection program during that time. You went dark. Your identity was wiped clean. A new one was created for you."

He leans back. I feared, even as I told him what I'd discovered, that he'd be angry, or afraid, or worried, or that he'd act aggressively in confirmation or denial. Instead, he seems pleased. Is he pleased that I'm so very wrong? Or that I have such a vivid imagination?

It's neither of those. He's glad that I'm right. I can see it in his face, in his deepening dimples, in his relaxed smile and posture.

"I still don't know why," I add. "I can't find your father or your mother anywhere. I guess that should be a clue itself. But without something to go on, I'm not going to assume."

"Did you manage to uncover the reason we moved?"

"Your dad was in MI6 and pissed off the wrong person."

It's a shot in the dark, but he nods, finding my answer acceptable. "I'm going to tell you things I haven't told too many people. I may live to regret it. But it may also relieve me of the burden of these ridiculous secrets."

Secrets are indeed a burden. I want to relieve him. I want to be that person he can tell things he won't tell anybody else. The badge in my pocket weighs four hundred pounds at that moment. For the first time in my career, I wish I wasn't a federal agent, and I make a promise I believe I can keep.

"It's between us," I say, twisting two fingers in front of my lips and flicking my wrist as if I'm throwing away the key.

With a short nod, he accepts my guarantee and puts his elbows on the table, getting close enough to me that he can speak softly. "I haven't eaten meat since I was fifteen. Our last morning in London. Our last hours. My father was home, which was always my favorite time. He often took me out of school on a Friday for a weekend trip.

We'd packed to go camping. We always brought Baron, a sheepdog and the sweetest animal you ever met. It was morning. Crack of dawn. We had a little alley behind the house with a car park. I open the door to start loading the boot. I stepped…" He stops and closes his eyes for a second, then opens them. "I'm not a squeamish man. We hunted and dressed deer and fowl. But this was different. You might not want to me to continue before dinner."

I lean forward on my elbows and hiss, "Finish the story or I'm going to give you something to be squeamish about."

He laughs softly then looks away as if checking the room, before turning back to me. "All right. I'm carrying my rucksack in my arms, so I can't see where I'm stepping. Then…" He flattens his hand, palm down, and draws it horizontal across the space in front of his body. "I slide. My feet go out from under me and I'm arse over tits in Baron's guts."

"Ugh. I'm sorry."

"I was quite fond of him."

"Do you know who did it?"

"My father had…" He pauses, wheels clearly turning. "His job made him enemies."

"Was he a prosecutor or a spy or something?"

"Yes and no. But to the meat of the question—"

"Good pun."

"Thank you. Baron was special. His insides, however, looked exactly the same as packed meat, and I thought any animal could be Baron. I was put off it completely."

"Wow." I say it with real awe, just as dinner arrives.

"Wow, what?" He flips his napkin open and drapes it over his lap.

"You really have a heart." I push my knife into my steak and twist so I can see if the restaurant understands what rare means.

"Maybe. Let's let that be our secret."

My meat is deep pink inside. Just the way I like it. I look at him. He's watching me with his dark blue eyes.

I point my knife at my dinner. "Does this bother you?"

"No. Does it bother you?"

"Actually, kind of. I feel sorry."

"It's fine. Really." He points his form at my plate. "Eat. You're going to need energy."

"For what?"

"*Bon appetit*, Agent."

CHAPTER 23.

KEATON

Taylor knows Baron's story, as do a few relatives I contacted when it was safe to do so. I don't see the harm in telling her, and I like her. I like the way she bites into the bloody steak after I tell her I was swimming in dog guts one morning. I don't tell her I was in those same clothes all the way to America, on an unregistered military flight. I don't tell her that I didn't want to take the clothes off because I didn't want Baron to be gone forever. I don't tell her I love dogs but can't bear to get another.

Maybe later.

Right now, she's wiping her mouth, looking away, eyes flicking to the exits out of habit. Her lashes brush her cheeks when she looks down at her food, strategizing the next bite. She's gorgeous, but that's a small part of her charm. The rest is inside her, and all I want to do is dig it out.

"What?" she asks, noticing that I'm staring.

"You came with me. To dinner. I thought you were going to hand me the wallet and send me on my way."

"I was hungry too."

"After everything I said, you could have eaten out of your own fridge."

She spears a green bean. "It had a ring of truth."

"Really?"

"Because…" She takes a deep breath. "I don't understand myself either. Why I feel like… I don't know, like you take up more space in my mind than you should. Whenever I'm in a room with you, I feel like you press against the world. My world. My attention. That makes no real sense, but you make no sense."

I reach for her hand, but she pulls back.

The effort required to tell her things she's not ready to hear is monumental. Crime is folded into the fabric of society, sure. I could argue that, but it misses the point, because so is crime-fighting. Also, we're past intellectual posturing.

"Where is your mother?" I ask gently.

"She died in a prison fight." She says it as if she's trying to cast off the pain of it. As if it's nothing. But she holds onto it at the same time, like a buoy of righteousness in an ocean of uncertain morality.

"I'm sorry. How old were you?"

"Sixteen. And there was a part of me, an awful part that I'm ashamed of, that was relieved to not visit her every other Saturday anymore. God, I'm a terrible person. I wouldn't blame you for walking out right now."

She can't look at me. Her self-abuse lights a fire under my already hot sense of protectiveness. I want to protect her from her opinion of herself, but if I jump across the table and shout her doubts away I'll make them worse.

"A sixteen-year-old girl probably wants to do fun things on Saturdays. Probably has to make up a story for her friends every other week about where she's going."

Cassie nods and bites back a quiver in her lower lip.

"The part of life when we define ourselves isn't a fitting time to be lying about who we are." I take her hand, and she lets me. "Trust me. I get it."

"It was awful there. Dirty. Someone always yelling. And the last time I saw her, I was so mad at her for leaving me, even though she wouldn't have if she could have helped it. But I was so sick of those visits and her stupid advice…" She wipes her cheek with the pads of her fingers. "I didn't know it was the last time, so I was kind of a bitch. Why am I telling you this?"

"Because you think I'm an amoral criminal." I hand her my handkerchief and she presses it to her eyes. "You don't have to impress me."

She doesn't respond to the charge, but carefully wipes away her tears and dabs her nose like a lady. I wonder if her mother or her grandmother taught her manners. I wonder if she learned them from observation or a desire to distance herself from her humble beginnings.

The waitress slips a fake leather folder in front of me and slinks away as if I might bite her. If she'd interrupted, I might have.

"Are you all right?" I ask.

"Yeah. This was kind of purging."

"You look…" I search for the right words. "Unguarded for the first time since we met. Your real self is beautiful on you."

"For now, at least. I'm emotionally disinfected."

I laugh as I open the folder.

"I have that." She stretches for the bill, but I snatch it away.

"Thank you, but I have it."

"Half then."

"I appreciate you wanting everything to be even." I reach for my wallet. "But I owe you."

"For what?"

I close the leather folder. I'm about to do something I said I wouldn't do when I walked into her house, but knew was unavoidable from the time she came through the door. "For what I'm going to do to your body tonight."

The crackle and tingle of her skin is practically audible.

CHAPTER 24.

CASSIE

He helps with my coat, and we walk out to the parking lot.

The last time we walked out to his car, he tried to steal a kiss and I flipped him for it. Wondering what he's going to do is as far as I get, because he's quicker this time. There's not a millisecond for a defensive move before his lips are on mine and his hands are on my face and his body is so close, all my thoughts basically melt into a warm puddle.

"All night," he whispers in my ear. "I want you all night. Now until the sun. You promised me I wouldn't sleep with you, and I plan on helping you keep that promise."

Which I want. I want it badly, and I want it before I lose my nerve.

Keaton kisses my cheek. His lips pull electrical current over my skin, crackling gunpowder sparks down my spine until they all land and ignite between my legs.

I don't push him away.

"I can get into trouble." I say it because I want him to talk me into it. Give me a single, simple reason to risk my career to feel his body against mine.

"One night."

That's his single, simple reason. Odds are good we can get away with a night, but can we keep it to just that? Won't it be worse? If it's good, how will I control myself?

I can wonder about the future all night. I can regret the past for the rest of my life. His voice and his scent are a hard call to *now*. His hands are a demand that I be *here*. I can't ignore it. I can't turn away from it. In the parking lot outside a Doverton restaurant, there's not a dream or ambition I ever had that doesn't involve Keaton Bridge.

"Not my place," I say. "And not your room at the club."

He leans away. Even in the ugly light, he is beautiful, scruffy-cheeked, angular, lupine in his appetite. "We'll take my car. I'll drop you off in the morning."

It can all be solved. I can have this. I can fold into tonight and disappear with him. In the morning, I can unfold back into my life.

I give myself the opportunity to change my mind, and decide I'm going for it. I don't want to go home. Something happened over dinner that needs to be consummated. No more unfinished business.

He takes out his phone and says one word. "Yes?"

"Yes."

He taps something into the glass while we wait for the car. When it comes, he puts the phone away.

"All arranged," he says beside the open car door.

I get in, and he pulls onto the highway.

"Where are we going?" I ask, trying not to knead my hands together. They make their own sign language. Only I can understand it. They're saying, *It'll be all right. It'll be all right.* When I clamp them still, they say, *You'll regret it if you don't.*

"Somewhere so secret, I bet you don't even know about it."

"I bet it's crime-scene perfect."

He flicks his signal and leans into the turn off the next exit. "I promise no one will hear you scream."

It's pitch dark on the service road. The cone of the headlights drown out color and movement, rendering the world in two dimensions. A two-lane strip cutting through flat, overgrown trees and bushes. No one will hear me scream, that's for sure.

My nerves are dumb and blind, humming hard in the frequency of arousal when they should be generating a rational fear that will trigger a plan to get the hell out of here.

Fear of being seen in this little archipelago of towns.

Fear of being taken to the unknown.

Fear of being left for dead.

He reaches for my hand, turning long enough to look me in the eye. "You all right?"

Should I lie? Should I tell him I'm not afraid of the fact that

I'm not afraid? That my confidence in him is what frightens me? "I'm good."

"Good." He slows by a sign with nothing more than the Doverton Country Club logo. It's so small I wouldn't notice it in broad daylight. He turns into an invisible driveway.

"What's this?" I ask.

"The club keeps a bungalow behind the nature preserve."

He slows before we reach the white-and-yellow gate.

There are cameras. I find them without even thinking about it. The little red lights glow like single eyes. They don't make me feel safe from Keaton; they make me feel exposed to the conflicts of my decision.

He stops the car and reads my mind. "Do you want the cameras or no?"

"No."

"Good." His phone rests in his palm. He gestures to the camera to the left and taps his phone.

The red light blinks out. To the right. Same. The camera dies.

He pulls up to the gate and keys in a four-digit code. The arm goes up. I turn as we pass. The red lights flicker back on. I face front again, breathing easy.

A cute bungalow with a short porch and garden lights appears as we turn. He parks at the front door.

"Before we get too involved," I start.

"Yes?"

He shuts the engine. It's quiet. Dead quiet. Forest creatures are hibernating, and the crickets and insects are in their winter cycles.

"I don't have any condoms or anything." Which means I insist on them, and in the time it would take us to get them, I could change my mind. I might need that space to come to my senses.

"I have some."

I'm concurrently relieved and discouraged.

He opens my door, and we walk up the steps together. The little porch is outfitted with two chairs and a table, with potted plants in the corners. The pots have the club logo engraved on them. A little home in the middle of nowhere.

Keaton unlocks the door with a code. "Are you sure you're all right?"

"If I wasn't, you'd be on the floor with your arms behind your back."

"Indeed."

He shoves the door open and steps aside. A lamp is already glowing by the couch, illuminating comforting florals and homey paisleys. Behind me, Keaton shuts the door and yanks the cord on the blinds so they close like a stack of eyelids.

We are alone.

I've never done anything like this. I realize that when the door closes. I lost my virginity at seventeen to a "nice guy" named Mark Wayburn, who I stayed with for five years. Boring sex with a boring guy had been all I'd known. We broke up when I went to Michigan Law. He was afraid I'd make more money than him. That was an actual argument I was supposed to sympathize with. Then he couldn't stand the idea of being with a federal agent because he didn't believe in the federal government. I'd dodged a slow-moving bullet with that one, and I'd never looked back. I slept with a professor for a few months, a fellow student for a year, a seven-night stand with a guy I met in a bar. That was it, and it was never great.

Since entering the Bureau, I'd been too busy, too distracted, too ambitious to date. The few boyfriends I had after law school didn't last more than a few weeks. One-night stands don't suit me. The whole process is boring and unfulfilling.

I've never just gone to a hotel room for a night. And here I am, turning so a man can see me. Unlooping my coat's belt while he watches. His eyes run over the center of my body, where the placket opens as I unbutton. The rush of fluid between my legs is so fast it hurts.

I let the coat slip down my arms. He takes it and hangs it on the wooden coat hanger by the door. I swallow. I'm not wearing anything special, just trousers and a blouse. Work clothes. The way he looks at me makes me feel as if I'm in black lace.

"Go on." He takes his coat off efficiently, popping snaps and jerking it over his shoulders. "Take it slow."

He hangs the coat, then pulls the cuffs as if he has no intention of taking it off right now. He leans on the dresser and crosses his arms, nodding as if I can start any time now.

Where is the blind passion that inspired him to kiss me in the factory parking lot? Why are his folded arms and leisurely commands even more arousing? I'm a rule follower, but I'm not blindly obedient either.

At least, those are the things I believed about myself.

I unbutton my jacket. I want to rip it off, but I'm trying to go extra slow because I'm wondering how turned on I can get. My underwear is touching sensitive skin. I feel like a bullet the moment the hammer hits the primer and the gunpowder ignites.

I reach for the fabric stretched over my hips, ready to pull down the skirt.

"Your blouse next."

His voice reaches my ears just fine, but that's not where it has the most effect. It vibrates everything below my waist, and my obedience comes not from the mind but from my bones. I fumble with the buttons. Undo two. Pull it over my head. I toss it away.

When I look at him, in my pale pink cotton bra, his arms are still crossed and the bulge in his pants is unmistakable. It's then that I know I don't need to drown this in kisses and unconscious decisions. I'm here for the night.

"You're very sexy, Agent Grinstead." He leans hard against the dresser and crosses one ankle over the other. Mr. Casual with a boner the size of a Glock 44.

"Thank you."

"Have you ever been properly fucked?"

"Can I get back to you tomorrow on that?"

"Get that skirt off and we'll see."

"Are you getting undressed?"

"In good time."

I pull down my skirt and kick it away. I have no idea what underwear I put on this morning and I can't get my eyes off his erection long enough to check. When he takes a fast step toward me, I hold out my arms and get ready for a kiss. My lips are disappointed, but my mind is too busy to register the fail, because the floor disappears from beneath me as he scoops me in his arms. My lungs empty in one gasp.

Then he kisses me, laying his lips on mine as if asking for permission. With my fingers running through his hair and the movement of my mouth, I give it to him. His kiss is languid, patient, grateful. It's the prologue of the night, telling me what's inside these hours together.

The story is about us. About the outside world's irrelevance. We are two bodies existing in a time outside the troubles of our choices.

He carries me through the living room to a closed door. He opens it with the hand that's under my knees.

It's a closet. We laugh.

"I'm an idiot."

"You haven't been here before."

I kiss him, and he kicks open the next door. It's the bedroom, and he lays me on the floral duvet. Slipping his arms from under me, he drags his fingers over my belly, my underwear. I put my hands on his chest as he bends his fingers around the ends of the panties, to the crotch, where he slides them underneath. I'm so wet and bursting, I nearly come when he touches me.

His breath is hard when he feels it. "My God." Curling his fingers around the crotch, he pulls down, exposing me. "I don't know where to fuck you first."

"You looking for suggestions?" Everywhere. He can fuck me everywhere.

Taking his finger from between my legs, he puts it in his mouth, curving his lips around it. He sucks me off him, then he kisses me. I taste myself, the sex, the arousal, the flavor of my musky tingling thighs.

I sit up on the bed. He undoes his belt. I quickly slide off my underwear. When I look back up at him, his cock is out in its full glory.

This erection is mine. I move his shirt tails out of the way and take it by the base.

"Have you ever been properly sucked?" I ask before running my tongue along the length of him and kissing the dot of salty juice off the tip.

He smiles down at me. "We'll tally that tomorrow too."

I hate to overpromise and under deliver. So I take him with my tongue, then lock my mouth around him, and suck on the way out. Slowly. I work him deeper and deeper into my throat, opening it for him, breathing and going in again. He pulls his shirt over his head, and I reach up with damp fingers to touch his flat stomach and grip his hard waist as I pull him in.

He groans, whispers to God, then jerks away with a gasp.

"Votes are in," he says, letting his pants drop. "I was never properly sucked before tonight."

He crawls on top of me and kisses me. My pussy can sense how near his dick is, noting its placement like a flower turning toward the sun. He pushes up my bra, kisses my tits, moves down, and now the placement of his tongue on my inner thigh is the sun and my body is a garden, focused on a moving source.

When he runs his tongue along my seam, my back arches.

"That's my girl," he says before he slides two fingers inside me and runs his tongue over my clit.

I dig my fingers into his hair, crying out when he sucks the tip. He opens my legs so wide, they hurt in the best way.

"I'm—" I can't finish, but I want to tell him I'm close.

He reads my mind, saying, "Give me what's mine."

I come in his mouth, pumping and squirming, digging my fingers into his bare shoulders. When I push him away, he kneels above me and wipes his mouth with his wrist. A condom packet sticks out between two fingers. I have no idea where he extracted it from or when he did it, and I don't care.

"I'm on the pill," I say.

His expression is a question as his hands freeze over his mouth.

"I'm not with anyone, at all," I add. "It's just that I don't want to be the latest single mother in my family."

"An abundance of caution is something I admire in a woman." He rips the packet open. "I hope you can admire it in me."

"Your hope is my reality."

In the seconds it takes him to slide on the condom in his abundance of caution, we connect not over how interesting our differences are, but in the values we share.

"Can you remember something for me?" he says as he wedges his hips between my legs.

"Do I look like a reminder app to you?"

He arches over me. I spread my legs wider for him, sighing when his weight and force press against me.

"You are the sexiest reminder app I've ever tapped."

I laugh, but I'm cut off when he enters me, and my giggle turns into a groan. I just came three minutes before, but my body responds as if it's already hungry for another. My fingers dig into his biceps. I have to be taking skin. He has to feel it. But he's controlled and slow, running his lips over my face and neck.

"Dee-seven-four-nine,' he says into my ear.

"What?"

"Repeat it, love. When you know it, I'll let you come."

"Dee-seven-four-nine." That was easy.

"Ex-four-two-two-eye."

"Ex-four—"

"From the beginning." He drives in harder, and the pleasure across his face is unmistakable.

"You're joking. I..."

The words die on my lips when he stops and raises himself so we can see each other. His bemused smirk is more telling than a hundred status reports. He wasn't joking. Not at all.

"What am I memorizing?"

"What's the fun if I tell you now?"

I'm irritated, but also turned on by his little game. I like his control, and I like his attention. He could just blow his wad, thank me, and walk away.

"Dee-seven-something... I forget." I run my hands over his chest, over the patch of hair in the center, scratching downward.

"From the top then." He relishes my forgetfulness, thrusting into me with each character. "Dee-seven-four-nine-ex-four-two-two-eye."

I repeat after him, and he gives me a push with each syllable. By the time I get to the last one, the pressure between my legs is massive.

"You're very close," he says. I nod with heavy lids. "That won't do."

He leans forward and gets his arms behind me, lifting me. When he places me on my feet, his dick frees itself. I'm not disappointed long. Gently, he guides me to the dresser and kicks my legs open. I bend over it. My face is inches from the mirror when he enters me from behind. He's deeper and I'm wider. The discomfort quells the arousal, which must be his plan.

He puts his hand on my lower back and repeats the sequence, driving slowly inside.

I get to "Ex" before descending into grunts.

"Finish."

"Four-two-two-eye."

He cups his hand under my jaw until I'm facing the mirror. "Again."

I repeat it, not knowing what or why, but loving every minute of it.

"Good girl."

"Do I get the prize?"

He fucks me hard enough to push me to the edge of the dresser. "Maybe. Keep your eyes on us, and repeat it before I tell you the rest."

I repeat it over and over, realizing he can add as many random numbers and letters as he wants to as I realize my memorization of them is the only thing between that moment and an earth-wrecking orgasm.

In the mirror, he looks down at my ass. His hands slide along my sides, my outer thighs, and work inward. He uses both hands to reach around and spread me apart.

"Very good," he says after I finish it for the third time. "Tee-six-zero-twenty-four-twelve-el."

On the third to last, one of his hands finds my clit.

"I can't," I gasp. "I-I-I…"

"Tee. Not eye."

He repeats it, and when I don't answer, his finger and his hips stop.

"I hate you," I tell him in the mirror, meaning something completely different.

"From the top."

I can barely breathe. I'm totally under his control and mad as hell. I also love it.

I start with "dee" and he pounds me, stopping when I stop. Rubbing and fucking when I continue. When I stumble, he pinches my clit and I scream in pain and pleasure.

"Six," he says, and I finish all the way to "el."

"Again."

I know he'll let me come if I keep repeating it, and I'm right. I'm in a cyclone of pleasure, with the number sequence in the center cone, anchoring me. I say the number and letter sequence over and over. Far away, I hear him telling me how good I am. How sexy. How I've overwhelmed his senses.

I hold back until I finish a sequence and let go, shuddering under his touch, filled with him. My knees bend until my toes are holding my weight, and Keaton has to hold on tight to reach around me. I'm an automatic weapon, discharging over and over, hot in the hand, until I'm spent and empty.

"Thank you," I say.

"My pleasure." He kisses my back and holds my chin up again. We're two faces in the mirror. "Watch me."

"Yes. Okay."

I get up on my elbows. In the mirror, he straightens and takes my hips in his hands. He strokes twice, as if taking aim, then fucks me in a rhythm meant for his pleasure alone. I watch him in the mirror. Our eyes meet as he slams deep inside me. His jaw tightens. His eyelids droop. I watch him push as far inside as he can go, grabbing the flesh of my hips, pulling me toward him. He's lost control. His refinement is gone. He's lost all sense, making himself completely vulnerable inside me. There's nothing scary about him now. He's not a threat or a nemesis. He's not an asset. He's helpless.

That feeling lasts for a minute as he curves his body over mine and catches his breath.

"I think I forgot the numbers," I say.

"No, you didn't." He stands and lightly slaps my butt. "Try it."

I rattle them off.

"Brilliant." He kisses my back and steps away from me.

I turn, stand. My body aches in the most delightful way. "I'll never write the number twenty-four again without thinking of you. You might own the letter D."

He twists the end of the condom into a knot and drops it in the little pail under the vanity. His naked body is long enough to reach across half the room. "The night is young. I can give you feelings about the entire alphabet."

"That's some kind of access code, right? To the Third Psyche forum?"

"Nope." He wraps his arms around my waist and kisses my shoulder. "But you should remember it anyway."

"Dee-seven-something-something-ex-something?"

He pinches my side, and I squeak. He tickles me until I writhe, giggling onto the bed.

He kisses my lips. "Let's start over. Shall we?"

CHAPTER 25.

CASSIE

The bathroom light makes a tinny sound when it's turned on. The fan whirrs. Soap, shampoo, deodorant sit on the counter in single-use containers.

Like me, stuffing feelings for Keaton into a single-use container.

I look like a hostage. I haven't slept more than an hour. I'm sore. Sticky. My hair is a rat's nest.

I've been rendered stupid and dull by orgasms. Even though I can barely put together a string of words in my head, I remember the code Keaton gave me. I turn on the shower, stretch my arms over my head to crack my shoulders and spine. Check the water. Ice cold. I get in quickly and I'm shocked awake.

That's better.

I don't rush, forcing myself to get used to the cold.

Best sex you ever had.

The clarity of the thought comes as I'm cleaning between my legs. I've been sore before, but never so happily sore.

I let the water soak my hair, freezing out the disappointment, washing away the desire for more, for things to be different, for our options to sunset later in the day.

One: He's a hacker. The FBI can't prove it today, but everyone knows it. I could lose everything I've worked for.

Two: My feelings are irrational, and I know it. I don't trust them.

Three: There is no three. Two is enough.

I stay in the shower until I'm shivering.

Three: You don't even know his real name.

I shut off the water. I don't regret last night, but I might regret it being our last night.

I get out and wrap a towel around me. It's soft and warm. The door is open a crack. I can see the front of the house through the opening. The blinds glow with the dark blue of sunrise's beginning, and the end table light is still on.

The front door opens, and I clutch the towel tightly around me. I'll let it go to spring at an intruder, but it's not necessary. It's Keaton with a tray. He's fully dressed, and nothing about him makes him look like a hostage. He looks like a man who has had a full night's sleep and just decided not to shave because the scruff made him even more handsome.

He slides the tray onto the table and smiles when he sees me peeking through the bathroom door. He crosses the bedroom and leans in.

"Does the hot water work?" he asks, not looking at my legs or my bare shoulders. Right in my eyes, like a gentleman when it's time to be a gentleman.

We'd agreed that he'd take me home right away so I could change for work, but now I want to call in sick.

"I don't know," I say. He raises an eyebrow, not understanding the answer, so I continue. "I didn't try it."

"It's freezing in here."

"I made you break your promise. I slept, but I'm awake now."

"Indeed you are." He smiles, and only then do his eyes drift. "Hurry, then. No puttering about. I got breakfast."

I quickly put on yesterday's clothes and go into the small dining room. It's ringed with tall windows overlooking a little yard and the forest that surrounds the club. One of the hotel's golf carts bounces down the driveway, back to the main house.

Eggs, bacon, toast are set up on the table.

"It's nice that they send room service out here."

"Anyone will do anything for a price." He pulls out a chair for me. "You were in there a long time. I'm surprised you didn't catch your death. Sit. Please."

I sit because I'm hungry, and because I don't want to leave this idyllic little bungalow just yet.

Keaton sits kitty-corner from me and puts eggs and toast on a plate. "I'm afraid the eggs might be cold."

"That's all right." I take the plate. While he makes his own, I peek into one of the two hot pots. Tea. I pour for him.

"Cheers," he says instead of *thank you*. Before I can get the second pot, he pours me coffee.

"Cheers," I say, instead of *I want you.*

The air is thick between us. I work backward from when I'm expected at the office and calculate Keaton and I have twenty minutes to eat.

I want to tell him he was wonderful. I can do that in twenty minutes. Outside, the winter wind flexes its muscle, knocking tree branches against each other, sending long-settled leaves clicking over the ground.

I want to tell him I'm conflicted. He's risky. *We're* risky. I don't trust him, but I want him. That code he made me memorize and won't define—it intrigues and scares me. I want him to soothe me, reassure me, clarify his feelings if he has any.

I can't do all that in twenty minutes.

The eggs are cold. I don't mind. His presence is warm enough for a few dozen cold eggs.

"So." I stab a lump in the scrambled eggs and put it onto a triangle of toast. "How long are you in town?"

The question is absurd. I feel as if I'm in a bad movie. He does me the favor of ignoring it.

"I want to see you again."

He utters the sentence as if it had gotten impatient at the back of the line and shoved a dozen other sentences aside. Yet when I look at him, he's not trying to cover up or choke back what he said. He means what he says and says what he means.

I go for the least emotional but most honest form of the truth. "I don't know how to make that happen." I'm about to take another bite of eggs, but I put down my fork. "When you gave me that Post-It, you became a federal asset."

"You mean a snitch?" He's smiling as if the word doesn't bug him at all.

"Call it whatever you want, but there's the issue of payment."

He leans back, laughing. "Please keep the taxpayer dollars."

"Not all payment is in cash."

The air goes out of the room. I can't look at him. My eggs suddenly look like yellow snot and the bacon fat is gathering in my throat. He's silent. All I can hear is my heartbeat and the *click* of the leaves in the wind. When I swallow, it's with effort.

He needs to say something, anything. Give me an opening to tell him I'm in this bungalow because I want to be, not because I'm selling myself. But my jaw is glued shut. I'm locked by inertia. I can't deny it out of thin air. I can't explain without a push.

"I'll wait in the car." He gets his jacket and bag. His movements are graceful and unaffected by anything I might confuse with tension or offense.

Does he care that I implied I had sex with him as payment? Did he even catch the inference?

Does it matter? We're a one night thing for a reason. I won't sabotage my life by getting involved with a man, only to be left by a man, but that doesn't mean I spent the night with him for any other reason but desire. If I run out there and explain that I'm with him honestly and that my concern with payment was no more than a concern about appearances, what will I achieve? Nothing. Another turn around the hotel when he comes again, more worries about how to fill out the forms, and I have to face the fact. If he gives me another piece of intel, I may not actually be sleeping with him for information, but it'll feel like it.

When I get outside, he's standing by the passenger side of the car. He opens the door.

"I didn't mean what it sounded like." I can't get into a car with him without addressing this. I'm not made of stone.

"I know."

I get in, and he closes the door. He gets in on the driver's side. He knows, but nothing's changed. By the time we're on the highway, he hasn't said a word and I'm on round three of beating myself up.

It's a TKO on the interstate.

"You know what's really stupid?" I say finally.

"What?"

"I've given you more trust than I've given any man. But you..." It would be great if I could organize my thoughts coherently. "I don't date a lot because I don't like wasting my time. If I don't like a man right away, I don't bother, so believe me, there's not a lot of bothering happening. And don't get me wrong, I didn't like you. But then I did and now I do, but the obstacles are real and that's all I'm saying."

He gets off my exit. "And I told you that I know."

"So?"

"So. You're right."

Right. I'm right. He knows I'm right and I know I'm right. He'd wanted to see me again, but in the front seat of the car, he's just a guy driving and talking. He's not looking at me. He's not reassuring me. He's not saying he wants to see me despite all of it.

So.

I'm right.

"Should I drop you on the corner?" he asks.

Because of the context, that question hurts more than anything anyone ever said to me. It means he's heard me, understood me, and agreed with me. I should be happy. I'm not. My lips have been kissed raw, and I'm so sore, I can't cross my legs. I can't shake the feeling that I've lost something I would have treasured. My mother missed only a few marks in her day. The amount of loss she felt was related to how close she came to making the catch. She said there was nothing worse than having the fish on the boat and letting it slip off the deck, unless it was already in the bucket and it tipped and slid back to the sea.

"The corner's fine."

He pulls up to the curb at the end of my street.

How close are Keaton and I to being fish in a bucket? Are we even caught? Were the muscles in my cheek ripped from the metal barb? Or had we both seen a lure and run away before getting bitten by the hook?

"I'd let you out," he says, "but that defeats the purpose of letting you out on the corner."

"No. You're good." I pull the handle and let the door swing halfway while I take a second to look at him. The perfection of early morning has worn off. He seems tired. Confident, handsome, and assured, but tired. "I enjoyed myself last night."

"I know." He lets the two words hang in the air. "I did too." There's nothing left to say, but as I shift my weight to get out of the car, he grabs my forearm. "I have to go back to California on business. When I get back, I'll be in touch."

"Is that a good idea?"

Say yes. Say yes. Say yes.

"Don't assume I care about the Federal Bureau of Investigation. Or the government. Don't assume I'll ever let the *law* come between us. I don't give a bugger about it. I don't give a shit how it looks or ethics or any of it."

"What do you care about?"

"Those things, but only because you care. I won't be the man who makes your life harder. I want to tell you something, and I'm tired enough to tell you the truth."

I lean against the back of the seat, but keep one foot on the asphalt. "Okay."

"No matter what happens, never, ever believe I abandoned you. You can forget me. I can go into the dustbin with every other man who wasn't worth you. I don't care. No matter what happens, I didn't desert you. Say you understand."

"I understand." I only say it because he asked me to, not because he's making sense.

"Say you believe me."

"I believe you, but I don't know what you're talking about."

He runs his hand along the length of my arm. "You will."

I say it because behind his words lie his intentions. He cares what I think of him. He wants me to think highly, and I do.

"When? Because you're freaking me out."

"Not today or tomorrow. Possibly never. Remember the promise that this was for one night?"

"Yeah."

"I lied to you. I never wanted this for one night. You're talking about a transaction, and I'm telling you, I've been around the world and I've never met a woman like you. You're cop and criminal. You're subtle and direct. Everything I know about you is the opposite of something equally true. You're a coin flipping in the air and I never know if you're coming up heads or tails."

"What if I have to hurt you? What if it's heads and you called tails?"

"I'm infatuated with your head and your tail, darling."

The stupid pun deserves an appreciative laugh, but it comes out sad and broken.

"I promise you," he says. "I'm going to disappoint you. I'm going to hurt you. But not today."

He kisses me, but it's not the kiss of a man who will never see me again. It's the kiss of a man promising more. I don't want more, but I do. I was lying to myself from the beginning. I was both the architect and the mark of my own long con game.

"I'm not dropping you off at the corner next time."

I nod. "Next time then."

I get out of the car and walk home in last night's clothes.

When I open my front door, I turn around, let the screen door shut, and watch his car drive away.

CHAPTER 26.

CASSIE

*—Be ready 5pm on Friday. We're going
on a short holiday—*

Keaton's text comes in the late morning. The geographic tag puts him
in Uzbekistan, where he couldn't have gotten to in the last few hours.
He's cloaking his whereabouts.

There's a guy you can depend on.

I sit at my desk with a deep feeling of sadness. My life hasn't
changed one bit from even twelve hours before. But I've changed. I've
gotten stupid.

His text weighs on me. Every sip of coffee, every answered email,
every time a bird chirps outside, I'm aware of the minutes that pass
without me responding.

I don't know what to say. I don't know what he intends. I'm
afraid that if I answer him, I'll discover another facet to him and I
won't have a choice but to see if that's the last level of complexity to
Keaton Bridge.

I want him. I know that. I don't know how to want him. I don't
know how to let myself make it possible.

I write down the letters and numbers he made me memorize. I
try a few things that fail, but after that, I don't know what to do with
them, and to be honest, if I did know, nothing would change. Once I
use whatever information he gives me, he's an asset and I'm cutting off
the possibility of a relationship. There would be paperwork and ques-

tions. Until then, he exists in the netherworld between a problematic tryst and an ethical lapse.

—Be ready 5pm on Friday. We're going
  on a short holiday—

My chest is a balloon filling, squeezing the walls of my heart tighter and tighter. I'll touch something—a piece of fabric, the silicone grip of a new pen, the smooth glass of my computer monitor—and wonder if he's thinking about me. Does he feel the creases in his bedsheets, the damp warmth of a coffee cup, the yielding inside of a loaf of bread and think of me? Because I think of him. I want to stop, but I can't. I text him back and hit Send before I think too hard.

—You're going to make it all the way
                      from Uzbekistan by Friday?—

—An ocean cannot separate us —

"You all right?" Frieda says as she passes my desk.

"Fine." I put my phone facedown.

"The pay grade packet's going to be late. Coming on Monday."

"Maybe they were waiting for Ken to get mobile. He'll get his transfer when they announce, I guess." I look up at her. She's clutching her coffee cup, and her one eyebrow is shorter for being knotted in the middle.

"And I'm sure you will too. One hundred percent. You earned it."

"We should have some preemptive champagne this weekend." My voice is flat, because one, I'm not getting promoted, and two, making plans with her means I'm not going to have a bag packed on Friday at five.

"Nope." She thwarts all my quickly laid plans. "I won't jinx it."

Sometimes, I wish Frieda wasn't so superstitious.

Now isn't one of those times.

CHAPTER 27.

KEATON

Get a handle on yourself, man.

I tell myself this about every fourteen seconds. I feel unglued. I blame this feeling on the fact that she and I have unfinished business, but I fear it's *her* I miss.

I flew into San Francisco for a simple meeting with an agenda that had been set, but I needed to change everything. Every step into the stone courtyard and every click of my heels on the marble floors of the British consulate is a punctuation in the paragraph of my revised intentions.

By the time I'm in the waiting room, I'm dissatisfied with what I have done for her and with her. I'm dissatisfied with what I've taken, what I've given, and what I've sacrificed, and I don't know what to do about it. I only know I need more time to do it.

Betty, the receptionist, has a master's in political science. She knows me. She knows I'll refuse tea, but she offers it anyway and goes about her work. The leather chair squeaks under me when I shift. I don't know what to do with my body. It wants to be inside Cassie, smell her, taste her, feel her texture from the lining out. I start to consider crazy things, then stop myself.

I'm not here to ruin her life, but if I keep thinking about taking her with me, I most certainly will. She'll be separated from her grandmother, the only family she has. She'll be torn away from the job she's dedicated her life to. All the work she's put into separating herself from her mother's criminal past will be wasted.

This is not about me. This is not about what I want. This is about her. And I hate it. I hate it with a bloody rage I can barely contain. I tap my fingers on the wooden arm of the chair, cross about leaving without her, panicking about staying with her.

I remind myself that I don't panic. It's not in my repertoire.

All I ever wanted was to go home. That's all I've been driving toward for the past three years. And now I've added another contingency to something that is already nearly impossible to plan.

I'm a patient man. My plans are incremental. Long term. I am not a child.

But she makes me want to throw it all away.

"David," the ambassador says as he shakes my hand. He's a greying man with the friendly mask and calculating eyes of a diplomat. We walk toward his office. "How's the factory coming?" He closes the door behind us. "On schedule, I hope."

His office has been the same since I was a boy, with leather books, leather chairs, deep-green wallpaper, and a Persian carpet his father brought home from his days as a Field General.

I can tell he does not have good news. I sit.

He snaps a glass off the bar. "Whiskey?"

"You ask me that every time."

"This time you may need it."

"Are Mum and Dad all right?"

"Right as rain, far as I know. You should call them." The bottle clicks on the edge of his glass. "Tell me about QI4."

I sit in the leather chair I always sit in, and he unbuttons his jacket before sitting across from me.

"You know Taylor," I say. "He's not building a factory, he's building an empire."

"I trust he can take care of it."

"He can."

"Good." He folds his hands in front of him. "Because we have a change of plans."

Hope races with fear and wins, taking a victory lap before I utter the first word. "How much so?"

"There's chatter. It may be nothing. The bureau and some white supremacists got in a row?"

"With guns, apparently."

"Right. Chatter's about your involvement."

"Mine?" I press my fingertips to my chest as if I can defend the idea that I had nothing to do with it.

"Kaos thinks it was you."

With the simple utterance of a boastful Internet name, the sparks of hope sputter out and the fear catches fire. I know the real identity behind the avatar. I know that I have alerted him to the fact that I'm not who he thinks I am, or for that matter, who anybody thinks I am. This is why I'm so careful, and this is why looking for Third Psyche must have opened Kaos's eyes to what was in front of him all along.

"He's paranoid." I'm stating the obvious.

"Indeed. But you knew once you went visible with Taylor Harden, they'd stop trusting you. And now that we know Kaos runs Third Psyche, we can see just how paranoid he is."

Kaos is very dangerous. I've worked with him, so I know. But I want to get this discussion over with so I can tell the ambassador I need another month or two. I can't disappear so soon.

"The fact that I didn't sell him out to the FBI is irrelevant, I presume."

"Well…" The ambassador takes a swig of his whiskey and clicks his glass down. "It wasn't anyone. He mucked it up himself and needs someone to blame."

All I can think about is the positive. All I gravitate toward is the hopeful. In no time at all, I've become a little boy in the park throwing sticks with his dog. Everything is just roses and honey cakes. The future is all possibilities.

"Is everything still in order?" I ask.

"Yes, but we have to move the timeline."

"I need more time," I say before he can tell me where he's moving it. I don't even recognize my voice, it's so calm, so flat, so businesslike in its denial of my actual emotions. "I need to stay another few months."

"You're leaving in two weeks."

I don't have extra weeks or months or years to spend with Cassie or anybody. I won't be able to set Taylor up completely, but he doesn't need me. Not really. And if I'm being honest with myself, Cassie doesn't need me either.

What I need has changed. My hope illustrated that a little too clearly.

It's as if I've learned nothing since the morning I slipped in my dog's guts and MI6 relocated us for our safety.

"What?"

"You'll have a fresh passport. New name. Bank account. Everything as planned, but sooner. You're going to die in a fiery crash instead of drowning, if it's all the same to you. Your parents are looking forward to seeing you again."

"I need…" I drift off. I miss them.

I need more time.

I need to see if what I feel for her is real.

"You need to make sure you've done what you wanted for Taylor."

Taylor? Shit. He'll be fine.

The ambassador leans over and folds his hands in front of him. His right middle finger taps the wedding band on his left hand. "We have moles in Kaos's operation telling us he feels particularly betrayed by your new habit of doing the FBI's bidding. It's a damn near obsession."

"He and I had a lot of good times. He's leaning on them."

"If you're defining 'good times' as moving money and guns, then I don't think he's leaning on any actual warm feelings."

"Funny how I was never actually the mole."

"Maybe he's realizing what you actually were." He picks up his glass again, rolling the bottom edge on the table before taking a sip. "Be that as it may, we're working on neutralizing him."

"You haven't been able to neutralize him in twelve years. What makes you think you can do it now?"

"He's after you, and that creates a vulnerability. A sniper has to stick his head out to see his target. That's our opportunity. The plan is, you disappear for a couple of days. He'll try to find you, we grab him."

"And if it works? We push my timeline further out?" That hope again, glowing like the last coal in the dying fire. The ambassador is discussing life or death, and I seem to be guided by the unpredictable dictates of my dick. But that's not fair, not even to my dick. It's my heart that's doing the hoping.

"If you like," the ambassador replies, opening his drawer and taking out a black thumb drive. "But you know these people are like roaches behind the cupboards. Just smash one against the counter and forty more will come out when you shut the lights."

"And here I am, thinking you grew up in Kensington."

He slides the drive across the desk. I pick it up, flipping it between my fingers. It's completely nondescript.

"We've been invested in your safety since you were a lad, and we protect our investments. You have a room booked in beautiful Las Vegas for two nights."

I groan. "My God, man. Vegas?"

"Lay low. Eyes open. When you're back, we'll discuss the timeline."

I'm about to leave when something occurs to me. "Are you working with the Yanks on this one?"

"Of course I can't say, but I can tell you what you already know. Keyser Kaos is targeting agents."

I know what he means immediately. He means the shootout, but he also means future tactics. I've never seen anyone on the dark web takes things more personally than this fucking crew.

"Ruthless, these fellows. Ruthless but not reckless. We'll get them. Don't fret."

Fret. He says it as if I'm worried the milk might be a little off. Or that Manchester United might choke at the last minute. Indeed, it's his job to make everything seem as though a stiff upper lip was a cure, rather than an attitude. I'm not in the mood. I want to get back to Doverton. I never thought I'd say those words, even to myself. But I need to look at Cassie. Make sure that she safe. And not just safe, but happy.

I'm going to fret long and hard until I know that any threats against her are neutralized.

"If you don't get them, I will." I stand and pocket the black drive. "Mark my words. I know I promised you that once I was gone, I wouldn't resurface to pay any old debts or get vengeance. I wasn't dishonest but if he's a loose end, I might turn myself into a liar."

"Trust us. We'll clear this up."

We shake on it, and though I trust his intentions, I don't trust that faith, luck, or some combination of incompetence and overzealousness won't leave Cassie Grinstead exposed.

That will not do. That will not do at all.

I text her from the building lobby.

—Be ready 5pm on Friday. We're going
on a short holiday—

I need to figure out Cassie before I go. I need to see her away from everything. To give us time to be us, then I'll know what to do.

I check my texts.

*—You're going to make it all the way
from Uzbekistan by Friday?—*

She noticed my VPN server's geotag. Clever, clever girl. How long will it take me to get to the end of my fascination with her?

— An ocean cannot separate us—

• • •

She has a black leather bag that she holds in one hand. Jeans, trainers, a V-neck T-shirt that shows just enough of what I'd love to get my lips on.

I get out, pop the boot, and take her bag. "You ready then?"

"Where are we going?"

"Las Vegas."

She claps three times and almost jumps up and down. She's on tiptoes when she stops herself.

"I take it you like Vegas?"

"Never been." She's smiling like a Cheshire cat.

"Don't get knocked up!" Her grandmother waves from the front stoop in lavender polyester pants and white turtleneck with a teddy bear on it. She's wearing a down coat, slippers, and telling her granddaughter not to get pregnant.

"Not on my watch!" I shout back.

"Nice boy." She wags her finger at her granddaughter as if Cassie had told her I wasn't nice. Grandma obviously knows best. I could be brilliantly nice.

I slap the boot closed. "Your grandmother is a wise, wise woman. You should take her advice more often."

"I'm so sure." She waves at Grandma, who sits on an aluminum chair at the top of the steps. "I never asked what you guys talked about the other night," Cassie continues. "Or, actually even last night. What time did you get to my house? What did she tell you?"

"Aren't we curious?" I give her bottom an affectionate swipe as I pass to open the passenger side door.

She stands still in front of the door for a second, meeting my eyes before getting in. "We are. Mostly because you're a puzzle."

"She told me about your grandfather and how she wanted you to do better."

"I've already done better."

I have nothing to say to that. When she sits, I close the door, wave to her grandmother, and we're off.

CHAPTER 28.

CASSIE

"You can stay through Monday, no?" Keaton asks.

I can. I have a personal day I haven't taken from last year. "Y—wait. How did you know that?"

"Oh, please, Agent. You had your fingers all over my data. To wit—the direction of my school portrait and my results, which were quite adequate, thank you. If you can use your privileges as a federal agent to see if I am who I say I am, then I can use whatever methods I have at my disposal."

"I'm not a career criminal."

"Is that so?"

With three words, he shut me right up. My point was meant to land like a hammer but fizzled like a fuse without a firecracker at the end. I'd told him about my years of training in the arts of the long and short confidence game, and I was sure he hadn't forgotten the incident that ended with me sliding his wallet across a dinner table.

My ideas about who I am and who I was raised to be intersect where Keaton Bridge and I connect.

"Point in fact." I hold up a finger. "You're hiding something from me. I can't tell what it is, but there's something going on with you and that database. You're withholding. Omitting. Both. You can tell me now. Or I can figure it out. If I have to figure it out, I'm going to be really pissed off."

He turns toward me at a traffic light. Are his pupils dilated because it's getting darker? Or have I said something that causes a physical reaction? My skin tingles at the tips of my fingers and in the crevices between my legs. It's that dangerous side. The side I've challenged to speak truthfully. The side I've threatened with my anger. I fear this, and I like it. I want to scoop it up like a palmful of fresh water and drink from the heels of my hands as sheets of him spill down my forearms.

"Do not threaten me, my artful dodger." His voice is a little lower and as serious as a gunshot wound.

I am not afraid.

"You think you can take me in a fight?" I'm only half joking. I can take down bigger and better trained men. But I know he's not talking about hand-to-hand combat.

"If there is ever a time I don't tell you something, the omission is for your own good."

"What's that code you made me remember?"

"What code?"

I rattle it off.

"That code is everything you need to know," he says.

"Keaton!"

"Let's make a deal, love. You tell me everything that you have failed to mention. And I will tell you things you have no business knowing."

"You know I can't talk freely about my job."

"I can't talk freely about mine either. You know what you're involved with here." He taps his middle finger on his sternum. "And I'm pretty clear about what I'm involved with." He reaches for me, glancing over so he can place his fingers on my sternum.

The touch isn't sexual. It is unexpectedly tender. The startling nature of it makes my own hand react by joining his over my heart.

I'm in this too deep already. I slid down a muddy ravine into a surging river before my brain even registered that the dirt was loose. I don't even know if I ever had time to hold my breath before I was pulled away in it.

He puts his hands back on the wheel. "I have a list of things I want to do your body this weekend, and if I don't start ticking them off soon, we're going to be fucking deep into Tuesday."

His words seem heartening, but they're not. They suck. I'm not a "live for now" kind of girl. He knows that. If he doesn't, he's going to find out, because I can't visualize walking away from him, and I can't strategize a way to make it work unless he's fully forthcoming.

"Is there something wrong with fucking on a Tuesday?"

"I have a separate list for then." He winks.

I hate it when guys wink. Winks are ways to assure me that I'm not seeing the whole picture and everything's taken care of. But he's different in this too. His wink is a devilish hint, not a way to shut me up.

When Keaton Bridge promises mischief, there's a good chance mischief will occur.

I'm satisfied for the moment that I'm not going to have to walk away from him after Vegas. I'm also confident that I can chip away at his secrecy if he gives me enough time to do it. Maybe enough time to figure out if he's been in the FBI database out of more than curiosity.

As a woman—not a federal agent—I want to know where his interest in me lies. I don't know if I can ever make him believe that painful truth.

CHAPTER 29.

KEATON

The commercial airport is one hundred sixty miles away. We'll get into Vegas late.

We're almost on the highway when she plugs her phone into my dashboard. I stiffen as if she's pulled a gun on me, then I try to hide it. I never plug my devices into anyone else's without the explicit intention of stealing information from it. I want to scold her for being so careless, but I don't want to start the trip on a bad foot. I also wouldn't mind acting like a normal person for a change. I wouldn't mind trusting someone. With her phone plugged in as she flicks her hands along the glass of her phone, this feels more intimate than what we did in a bungalow in the woods, or the time she threw me against the side of the car because I tried to kiss her.

What about that time she picked your pocket?

The connection between her phone and my stereo is like a mosquito bite I can't scratch. It's against every protocol I've ever set for myself out of necessity, but an equally urgent necessity drives me to shut the fuck up about it.

"I made a playlist of driving music," she says. "Actually, two playlists. One with old stuff and one with new stuff. Which would you prefer?"

I admit to being a little enchanted about the idea of driving music. Of course, I went to high school in New Jersey, where one takes long, short, and intermediate drives to Bon Jovi and Bruce Springsteen. It's not a foreign concept. But I've never actually taken a long drive to actual driving music.

The stereo is controlled by a pane of glass in the center of the dashboard. She taps it.

"Which ever one your lovely hand is stroking right now."

"You're a scoundrel, my good sir!" She says it with probably the worst accent I have ever heard in my life. No one would confuse her for British. "You get the new stuff. Cheerio!"

An anthem of guitar and vocals get the star treatment from my speakers. With the playlist going, she should be leaning back and looking out the window or making small talk. But she's not. She's playing with the screen on my stereo. What the hell is she looking for? The nuclear codes? My bank account number? At seventy miles an hour, I glance at her and she glances back for a second before I put my eyes back on the road.

"What do you think you're looking at?" I ask as casually as I can.

"I have never heard of any of this music. Is it music? You listening to books or something? Spoken word poetry? What the hell? Is this even English?" She mangles the pronunciation of an Icelandic band, and I know, just know for certain, she isn't trying to hack my car.

"I'll have you know most of the music produced and released in the world is not in English."

"Well, fancy that!" Her British accent, if at all possible, has gotten worse in the past minute. She gobbles up her vowels like a multisyllabic glutton, sticking her Ts as if there's glue on her tongue and flattening the tones with an aural steamroller.

Yet I am more than charmed. I don't want to hear her British accent ever again, as long as I live. But having heard her hideous rendition, I appreciate her natural American steamroller-vowel-gobble. I want her to talk more. I want to hear her history in her voice. All the words, but not the words. I want to hear the fingerprint of who she is inside of what she says and how she says it.

"Have you ever been to London?" I ask, stopping myself before I tell her I want to take her there. I can't guarantee her anything, but I want to promise everything.

"Nope. I haven't been much of anywhere. Virginia, Quantico for training. Ann Arbor. Dipped into Canada twice… uuh…Washington, D.C. I'm pretty boring."

"Do you want me to tell you that you're not boring? I don't usually invite boring women out for more than an hour for a quick shag."

She runs her hands along her thigh, smoothing out her jeans.

I grab it and squeeze. She runs her thumb along the ridges of my fingers. This feels nice. This companionship with her on a drive.

"Where do you want to go?" I ask. "If you could go anywhere."

"Anywhere?" She looks out the window. "Like as a tourist?"

"Sure."

"I read about this place in Edinburgh. It's a whole city under the city."

"Mary King's Close?"

"That's it! I've seen pictures, and it's like a parallel universe, right under the streets. Have you been?"

"No."

She twists in her seat, forgetting about the stereo. "It's got huge rooms with stone arches and little rooms with beds where people died of plague, and a room full of dolls people leave for this little girl who's a ghost."

"You believe in ghosts?"

"Of course not." She sits straight. "But the idea of a room full of dolls underground is kind of cool. I loved dolls when I was a kid. That would have been heaven."

"I bet you were very cute with a dolly under your arm." I rest my hand in her lap and she takes it.

"When I was a baby, my mother used me to distract people while she robbed them."

"You must have been quite an adorable child."

"Yep. People literally paid money to coo at me. I was that cute."

I bet she was, and I wonder what her children will look like. A dangerous path, because there was a good chance they won't be mine.

CHAPTER 30.

CASSIE

I start by telling him the safest stories, and slide into the things I don't normally talk about. The years away from Nana were the hardest because she kept Mom honest, watching me while Mom was "working." She made sure I went to school, did my homework, ate and slept at regular times. But between the ages of seven and eleven, my grandmother lived on the other side of town. This was by design. She and my mother weren't speaking for reasons that had to do with an old boyfriend, my grandmother's unwillingness to reveal my mother's paternity past the name "Barry the Motherfucker," and probably plain old daily personality conflicts over the breakfast nook.

I don't often talk about those Nana-less years. My mother didn't abuse me in ways that were discernible. I never had a bruise, I was never raped by one of her boyfriends, she never neglected my basic needs. But there was one winter the furnace broke and she couldn't afford to fix it, so we slept in our coats. Another Christmas when she kicked her current boyfriend out for the way he looked at me in my pajamas. He tried to beat her, but she got lucky and cut his face open with a letter opener.

She's the reason I never assumed women were weak, but she's also the reason I want to fold between moments and disappear. She's the reason I came into adulthood with sins to expunge.

I try to make it all sound funny and interesting. I sprinkle in funny adjectives and make faces Keaton can't turn around to see. He doesn't judge or expect me to be ashamed when I tell him how a nine-year-old goes about picking a pocket or leading a mark to a con. He seems to appreciate that there are things my mother taught me that I never would have learned in a normal household. How to read people. How to understand the criminal mind. How to find backdoors and loopholes.

No, he doesn't "seem" to understand. He's a master at backdoors and loopholes. He's the king of not getting caught. He's a ninja at cleaning up his messes and covering his tracks. He doesn't have to tell me that, but I know it and it's more than an assumption. It's a common thread between us.

Two thirds of the way to the airport, he pulls into the rest stop to go to the "loo." It's not a bad idea. We meet on the outside of the convenience store attached to the gas station. He cracks open a fresh bottle of water and hands it to me.

The lights flood the parking lot. Everything looks yellow-green, and Keaton's eyes are a clearer shade of blue in this light. They move down my body as I drink and back up when I finish the bottle.

"Never seen a woman drink a bottle of water before?" I ask as I hand it back.

He chucks it in the recycling. "Not with such purpose."

He puts his hand on my lower back as we walk. I usually find this gesture infuriating, but I like the feel of him, the weight of his hand on me. Is this what chivalry really is? All the things that I can't stand, but from the right person? That doesn't seem quite fair, but if I tell him that I don't need to be guided across the parking lot, he'll move his hand, and I'll lose the warm security I feel when it's there.

I want to give him something for listening to me, for not judging me, for taking care of me in these small ways. I want to give him a gift.

When we're in the car, he locks the doors before kissing me. Together, we taste like water. Fresh, cold, new. He slides a hand under my shirt and I put mine between his legs. He's rock hard, sucking in a breath when I put pressure on it.

"This can't be comfortable," I say, pulling his belt through the buckle.

"It's not a big deal."

"I bet I can suck you off so quick we still make the plane."

"I don't—"

"Have to do a thing."

I have his dick in my hands. Thick, ridged with veins, so hard the skin is tight around the core.

"Suck it then," he moans, shifting low in his seat.

I bend over his cock, licking the salty drop of pre-cum away, replacing it with moisture from my tongue, sucking the end. He gathers my hair away while I work my way down him, opening my throat on the way in, giving him my tongue on the way out.

He whispers my name. "My God."

His pleasure inspires me to suck harder, picking up speed. I give my breathing a break, sliding my tongue along the length of his shaft, then with a sudden move, I take him as deep as I can. He releases a sharp *uh*, pushing down my throat.

Having him under my control, being solely responsible for his pleasure, drives me wild, and my consciousness drives to my own pleasure, where the seam in my jeans meets my core. A groan vibrates my throat.

I take his shaft in one hand and use my saliva to move it up and down with my mouth.

"Cassie." He's shuddering. His hands have stilled and now just press down. "I'm going to come."

I groan onto his cock again and come down on it, sucking on the way out.

"Wait. I'm. Going. To."

He's trying to be a gentleman, but I got this. I'm going to suck it right out of him.

"Fuck." His surrender has a beautiful sound. The sound of the wind in your ears during a freefall. The sound of jumping off a cliff with no guarantee of a net.

The base of his cock pulses under my hand as his balls empty into my throat. I taste him, bitter and sharp, sticky at the back of my tongue. I swallow and take more. All of it. All of him.

When his last drop is spent, I pick up my head. He strokes my hair reverently, pulling a single strand from the corner of my mouth.

"That was lovely," he says.

"Thank you." I sit straight.

He fishes a napkin from the glove compartment and wipes my mouth.

"Do you kiss a girl after she's had your dick in her mouth?"

He takes me by the back of the neck and kisses me deeply.

CHAPTER 31.

KEATON

As we drive from the airport to the center of Las Vegas, I feel Cassie's excitement in the seat next to me. She squirms a little, leans forward as if she wants to see a little farther over the horizon.

Here's something we do not have in common. She's excited by this mess. Well, I can see that's not going to work. I can hang on that. I can engrave it into a plaque and nail it on the wall. Quote: "She likes Las Vegas." There we have it.

"I hear there's a fake Eiffel Tower," she exclaims. "And a big, fake Statue of Liberty."

"Yes. All that. And they're building a Big Ben."

"Oh! We can pretend we're in your hometown."

That is absolutely the last thing I want to do. Nothing feels less like London than Las Vegas.

"I should take you down to the shops under the Bellagio," I find myself saying. "They're quite nice. Quite posh."

What the hell am I doing? Las Vegas is hell, yet I want to give her tour. I want to show her all of the abominable sites and watch her find whatever happiness in it that she can. I just want to see her happy, full stop.

"Well, you can show me, but I'm not buying anything."

Maybe she won't, but I make no such promise.

CHAPTER 32.

CASSIE

The Strip is amazing. I've seen crowded places and cities, but though I've seen pictures and videos, I'm totally unprepared for Las Vegas. I can barely keep in my seat. Everywhere I look, I see something I want to point at. The big stuff, sure. But it's the little things that are the most fun. The little bits of lights, the little details in the façades, the way people dress as if they're all on a permanent red carpet.

I can tell Keaton thinks I'm just adorable, and normally I'd want to punch him in the face for his knowing little smile. But he's driving, and also? The way he smiles isn't condescending. He's smiling because he can't help it. I've always tried to impress people with what I know, but here I am, charming somebody with what I've never seen.

He makes a right into a long circular driveway. Over a line of trees, an arc of water lifts into the sky as if borne by angels. Lights from underneath it renders it into a sparkling silver, and another one joins it, then another. They fall back under the tree line, surrendering to gravity.

I tap on my window. "Can we go there?"

"The fountain?"

"Yes."

"Your wish is my command."

I spin in my seat to face him. "Really?"

"I suspect I'll be sorry I said that."

Behind him, a valet in a burgundy jacket opens his door. The dome light goes on, and behind me, my door opens.

We're at the head of the circle, in front of a wall of glass doors leading into a massive golden lobby capped by multicolored glass flowers.

I get out. The crowd is a living thing with a controlled pattern of chaos. Clicking stiletto heels, sequins, silk tuxedo jackets with sneakers, cheap tourist sweatshirts fill a scene of mosaics—flowers—huge rotating glass doors in constant motion. I turn back to Keaton to share my delight, and he does. I can see it all over his face.

Our bags are already on a brass trolley being pushed by young bellmen.

Keaton leans down to whisper in my ear. "I got us a room overlooking the fountain. I'm going to fuck you while we watch it."

CHAPTER 33.

KEATON

I walk slowly with her under the ceiling of multicolored glass flowers. I enjoy watching her that much. The way her eyes flicks from flashing light to flashing light, the slight smile, the way the exhaustion of the long drive falls off her body like a jacket in a warm room.

There's no way to get between the rooms and the outside, or restaurant and the bathroom, or between the parking lot and the show, or between heaven and hell without going through the casino first. The design of Vegas hotels is infuriating except when I am with Cassie. She slows down when she sees something, which is every fifteen seconds. Her lips part as if she wants to ask questions, but before she can, she moves onto the next thing.

"What's this?" she asks indicating a poker game.

"Have you never seen poker before?" I admit that I almost wish she'd never heard of the game, but it's unlikely.

"Of course I've seen poker before, you idiot."

"Sorry then, what was the question?" She looks at me slyly as if she doesn't believe that I didn't understand her. "I think your beauty has deafened as well as blinded me."

"Keaton Bridge, you are utterly full of shit."

She's right, of course. I am utterly full of shit under just about every other circumstance.

"This one." She indicates the small low-limit table to our left. I'm not off the hook to explain the game. "They remove their bets every time he shows a card. You're supposed to put money in, not take it out."

I put my arm around her and pull her close so that I can whisper in her ear. "It's for people with a soft stomach." The scent behind her ears is a garden of flowers. "You're not asked to bet on what you think you have. You show what you have and you take money away as you proceed to lose your nerve."

"What is wrong with people? Where is the fun in that?" She looks as if she's just eaten a rotten lemon, or swallowed a half a cup of cheap white vinegar. For a woman who seemed overwhelmed, amazed, enchanted, and even out of her depth, she is the mistress of this con game. She is the most artful of dodgers.

My lips linger at her throat, brushing the skin, tasting her as she tries to figure out who would want to sit at a poker table and not increase their risk. She tastes like a good bet, made at the right time, with a straight royal flush.

"What do you play?" I nip at the edge of her ear. "I'd like to know before I play you. I want to know how much of a risk-taker you are."

She turns halfway, looking at me with a sultry tilt to her head. "I like blackjack, but I wouldn't make too much of that. The hands are usually short and unsatisfying. And only a couple of cards can end the game."

A quick upward jerk of her eyebrows punctuates the entendre, and though a minute ago I wanted to watch her play cards, all I want now is to watch her come.

I slide my fingers down her arm and grasp her hand. "The tables are open all night."

"I might be as well."

That just about does it for me. I'm not waiting another second. I pull her to the lift.

CHAPTER 34.

CASSIE

We get out on the top floor. There are six penthouse suites with doors at the far corners of the hall.

"I've never stayed in a penthouse," I say.

"First time for everything," he says as we step into the hall.

My skin misses him. The waters go still again, but they crave the rippling wake of his touch.

There's a door at the end of the hall. He drops behind a step, watching me as I walk in front of him. I feel his gaze appreciating me, wanting me as much as I want him. The door seems so far away, and I know that once we get to it, that look will turn into his hands and his body.

When I get to the end, he's on me from behind, pushing his body into me, his breath in my ear, his hand wrapped around my waist pressing against the fabric between my legs. "Are you ready?"

"For what?" I say playfully.

"To see the fountain from the penthouse, of course." He waves his card in front of the lock, and it clicks open. Then reaches around me and opens the door.

He slams the door, and I turn to face him.

I've seen Keaton look hungry before, but framed in the hotel doorway, he looks ravenous. Feral. Like a man with a single thing on his mind. And it's me. It's the barrier of my clothes and his. It's the space of the few feet between us. He looks as though he wants to tear those obstacles away and shatter them under him.

He's frightening, but I'm not scared. Maybe I am scared, but the fear doesn't make me want to run away. The fear makes me want to be captured.

I back up a step, and he steps forward. I realize I'm smiling. He must realize it too, because a mischievous grin spreads across his face.

From the window, I hear a boom and the first notes from an orchestra.

He unbuckles his belt and says, "That would be the show."

I turn my back to him and walk to the floor-to-ceiling window where the sound is coming from. The suite isn't dark, lamps are on, but I don't see a thing yet. Just the rectangle of the window overlooking the Las Vegas strip. I feel him behind me, those eyes, that feral look that has a physical presence, and hear his belt slip around his waistband.

Down below, the fountain is huge, and the jets of water stream to the sky in sync with Brahms' hallelujah chorus. It's beautiful.

The water jets boom with pressure, and his body presses against mine. He takes my hands and lays them flat against the windowpane. It's cool to the touch.

"Just stay still," he whispers, sliding his hands along my ribcage and hooking his thumbs in my waistband. "Enjoy the show."

I'm immobile only by his command, and I want to be. I want to watch the water fountain, and I want him to touch me as if I'm a pliant statue.

Reaching around to my front, he unbuttons my pants and pulls down the zipper. My stillness lets me feel every single brush of his fingers as he wedges his hands under my underpants and slides them to my mid thigh. I can barely breathe. He does it so slowly that I feel impatient, yet every single moment is a morsel to be savored.

I let out a whimper just as the chorus down below reaches its apex. The water drops to the surface in a mosaic of ripples and splashes. "Is it over?"

"Hardly."

Before he's even done speaking, another classical piece rises. I recognize it but don't know the name. A jet of water so powerful it almost reaches the top floor makes me gasp. Or maybe it's his hand running along my stomach and just barely touching the skin between my legs.

"My God, Keaton. I don't think I can really watch this if you do that."

"Believe me, there will be another show." He slips his middle finger between my folds. I almost lose my footing, and my hands slide down the glass a few inches. "You're pretty wet for a girl who wants to watch the fountain."

"Yes, I —" There's no end to the sentence, because two fingers slide from my opening to my throbbing nub and rest there.

A crowd has gathered around the fountain. They lean up against the gate on the Strip and on the hotel side. The suite is dark enough that I'm sure they can't see us, and we are on the thirtieth floor. But I like seeing them below. I like knowing that I'm doing this and they can't see me, but I can see them.

The skin of his dick pushes against my bottom. He's hard, thick. There's a brutality to his erection and how he pushes it against me that makes my eyes nearly flutter closed. The rush of blood between my legs drains the feeling from the rest of my body.

His hands run up my belly, under my bra, pushing it up until my breasts are free. He runs his hands back down and presses my lower back. "Take your bottom up, my dodger."

I do what he asks, watching the water explode with the rhythms, exposing myself to him. I feel as though I'm begging. And when he pulls my thighs apart until I move my feet, I feel as though my pleas have been heard.

"Are you ready?" He runs the head of his dick along my wet seam.

I jerk toward him as if that will make him enter me sooner. I should know better by now.

"Please." I don't know if I sound as needy as I feel, but if I do, he ignores me.

"I'm a patient man," he says, running his hands all over me, letting his thumbs fall into my crack as they make their way along my upper thighs, slowly, maddeningly, until I groan with frustration. "This is quite a lovely piece. Beethoven. 'Ode to Joy.' Do you see how they've programmed the fountain to go slowly higher as the piece gets more intense?"

He slides two fingers into me. This satisfies nothing. It makes my anticipation even greater.

"Yes." Yes to everything. I can barely keep my eyes open. My head drops when he strokes my inside wall. With his other hand, he pulls my hair back gently yet forcefully until I'm looking out the window again.

"You're so beautiful when you're like this. You, hovering between two worlds. Your mind doesn't know whether to pay attention to what you're seeing or what you're feeling. One has to win. Which one is it going to be?"

"Feeling. I'd say feeling, in about five minutes."

The music swirls. The jets of water fly upward, and as they hit a finale, he enters me.

When I cry out, it's not in pain or pleasure. It's the anticipation leaving my body all at once.

He presses his hands against mine, pushing them against the glass, which is no longer cold but warm from my touch. He thrusts powerfully and slowly. Every movement is calculated. Another concerto rises from the speakers, and like the fountain that is programmed to explode with the rhythm, so is his rhythm programmed to my body.

The music rises again, but I can barely hear it. The jets of water have turned into a blur and my attention can only focus on one thing. Him. The way our bodies slam together. The way my orgasm is about to take over my entire body. He finds my clit and rubs it for three strokes before my toes curl, my back arches, and a long, hoarse vowel spirals from my throat.

A million miles away, his voice says, "yes,yes,yes," in a drumbeat of affirmation.

He pulls out, and I'm left empty and wanting. His hands on my hips push forward left and toward him right, turning me around. My hands leave the glass reluctantly, because he told me to leave them there, and when I'm facing him with his shirt half open, his pants around his ankles and his fist around his cock, I see his hunger yet again.

He pushes toward me, and with my back pressed against the newly cold glass, he spurts onto my belly, leaving a warm trail of thick pleasure.

Below us, the music falls, dies, and the last jets of water drop to the pool's surface with a splash. The crowd applauds, and Keaton and I catch our breath.

He puts his elbow on the window behind me and runs his fingers over my hair. His hand drifts to my waist, through the semen he has left on me, spreading it over my belly. Marking me with it.

He moves his hand downward again and lays four wet fingers over me. "You make me want to come inside you."

"I told you I was on birth control."

His hand runs over me from back to front. "I know."

I wait for him to continue, but no more reason is forthcoming. He slips three fingers inside me and I suck breath through my teeth. I don't know how I'm still standing. Maybe he's holding me up. But when he presses all of those fingers against my nub again, I lose all feeling in my legs and fall into his arms, sliding to the floor. He guides me to a chair. I fall over the arm of it, sideways, legs spread—one over the back of the chair with one set of curled toes leveraging against the floor—as he brings me to orgasm again.

I can't move. Can't think. I can barely get myself to a more comfortable position as he stands over me, one hand up with his wetness and mine glinting in the flashing lights of the Las Vegas strip.

He kneels by the chair, that mischievous smile back in spades, and puts his thumb to his lips and sucks it clean. I open my mouth just a little and flick my tongue over my bottom lip. He reads my mind and puts two fingers in my mouth. I suck us off him.

"You are a filthy little girl." He removes his fingers. "Let me get you washed up."

With that, he gathers me in his arms and lifts me.

I put my arms around his neck. I can finally see the room, with its flower arrangements, plush furniture, mirrors, and fireplace. He carries me into the bathroom, popping on the light with his elbow. The tile is glistening white, there are four sinks, a deep bathtub, a glass-enclosed shower, and Keaton Bridge.

My Keaton. Whatever his name is or where he's really from, for this weekend, he is mine, secrets and all.

I sigh softly.

CHAPTER 35.

KEATON

I get my money's worth out of the penthouse by fucking her in every room, on every piece of furniture. I tell her about the fog in London (it's real) and the law that allows pregnant women to have a wee in a policeman's hat (that's false). I feed her room-service strawberries, and she washes my hair in the bath.

She is foggy weather, when the air gets so close you can feel it around you like a skin. She is the crowds flowing around Trafalgar Square with their own purpose and predictability that is comforting. She is the smell of the sea air unexpectedly coming from the south, bringing the sting of salt to the city. She is an unexpected reminder of where I stand in the world.

She's none of those things. She's not even British. She's an American woman through and through. She probably wears American flag underwear as she eats apple pie on July 4th.

I've been drifting too long. I'm fed up with drifting. It's that irritation that brought me here. It's that discomfort that led me to the ambassador's office to assure him I was ready for something different.

"I want to gamble," she says on our last morning. "Do we have time before the flight?" She's fully dressed in a flowing skirt that seems quite unlike her. I like this new, casual look. Will I ever get a chance to truly know all of the ways she can be?

I zip my bag closed. "You don't want to give this bed another workout?"

She slips her arms around my waist and looks up at me. "I'm sore."

"Giving up, are you?" I kiss her temple. I'll kiss anyplace I can reach. "Never took you for a quitter."

"I'll teach you how to count cards."

"You count cards?"

"For blackjack. I know how, but I'm not great at it." She pulls away. "Come on. Let's have a couple of hours of dumb fun."

Gambling is money wasted on manufactured risk, but I want to see her in the bright lights, doing something I can't imagine her doing. I want to revel in her competence and unexpected skill.

A call comes in, and though I've ignored my phone all weekend, I take it from my pocket and check the caller as she rests her head on my shoulder.

It's the ambassador.

"I have to take this." I hold it up with the glass facing me so she can't see.

"Do you want to meet downstairs?"

"Sure thing." I tap her backside. "Don't talk to anyone. This place is loaded with hustlers and scammers."

"I can handle it." She sticks her tongue out and slings her bag over her shoulder.

I tap the phone to answer it as I watch her go. It occurs to me that this could be a mistake. I shouldn't let her out of my sight. But nobody knows we're here, and she's a federal agent for fuck's sake.

"Hello?" The ambassador's voice comes from the phone.

I'd forgotten I answered it. Now I have to deal with time and the fact that it's slipping away from me. "I'm here."

"I'd ask you if you're having a good time, but I don't give a toss."

"Fancy that."

"There's been some chatter. I don't want to alarm you, but I want your caution."

I sit up straight, foot on the floor, leg tense so I can bolt if I need to.

"Kaos says he's coming after you personally. Got on a plane, apparently."

I'm heading for the exit before he even finishes. "When?" Jamming feet into shoes.

"This morning."

"Where did he say he was going?" I'm out the door. Down the hall. Shoes softly shushing on the carpet. The lift is light-years away.

"He didn't," the ambassador says with not a single ounce of shame. "You should go, and not back to California. Certainly not back to Barrington."

I slap the button for the fourth time. Why don't these fucking lifts show you what floor they're on so a bloke can get on the stairs if he needs to? Fucking Yanks.

I hang up as the lift arrives. He can just bugger off. If this is how he's going to manage my transition, then maybe I should just transition my own fucking self.

In the two minutes it takes to get to the casino level, I'm painfully aware of the fact that I let Cassie walk out of that room without me. Fucking stupid. So easy to get careless when I feel comfortable. She's making me soft. I liked it, but now I hate it.

The casino that delighted me because it delighted her is now a cacophony of lights, sounds, smells, vying for my attention. But Cassie isn't at the blackjack tables she promised she'd be at. I text her.

—Where are you?—

I clutch my phone at my side and wait for the buzz while my eyes scan the casino. It's designed so you can't see across it. If you could see across it, you'd know how to get the fuck out. But the twists and turns are devised to create smaller spaces that loop passers-by into machine-lined corners and dead ends. I can't see across the room. I can't see past the next bank of glitzy machines. I don't know where she is and my phone isn't buzzing. I look at it. No message. No surprise. The signal sucks. It's intentional. It shuts out the world. Casinos are big Faraday cages.

I could be walking in the opposite direction. I check the blackjack tables, but there are blackjack tables everywhere. I check the poker tables for the low-risk gambler, but she's not there either.

Finally, a message comes in.

—I don't know—

The text is like a cold spear through my gut. She doesn't know. Does that mean she doesn't know which end of the casino she's in? Couldn't blame her for that. Does it mean she's been led away? Or taken away?

I call her, but the lines won't connect. I text again.

—What do you mean you don't know?
What are you close to?—

I continue scanning the casino. I walk from one end to the other, considering the possibility he knows I'm here, calculating the distance from McCarren to the Strip, how long it takes to park, whether he was a passenger on a chartered flight which means he would just have to get from the plane into a car, or if he flew the plane himself which means he'd have to park it, check in.

If he landed thirty minutes ago, he could be here by now. He could be in my room, looking for me. I hope he is. One, because I'm not there. But mostly because she's not there.

I walk from the bar to the other bar, from one stairway to another. I'm losing patience. I send another text.

—Cassie?—

The cold spear through me expands, turning my body rigid and cracking my heart.

CHAPTER 36.

CASSIE

I decide to hold off on blackjack until Keaton comes down. Wandering around, I sit at a poker table. I buy some chips and nod at the other two players at the table, a couple in their fifties. He's wearing a cowboy hat and bolero. She's in a Vegas sweatshirt and hairspray. They smile and nod. Nice people. I don't feel bad when I win the first hand.

A man slides in two seats down from me. He has soulful brown eyes and a nose that's been busted. He's not much older than I am, but they seem like they've been hard years. I smile at him, and he smiles back. One of his front teeth is a little chipped. I've seen chipped teeth look worse.

"How is this table running?" he asks with a vaguely Eastern European accent. His blink is hard and long. A tic.

"I'm batting five hundred," I say, mixing my sports with my games. The couple doesn't give him the same warm welcome.

"I'll take those odds." He throws a few hundreds on the table, and the dealer changes them for chips.

We play the next hand in silence. I end with a pair of nines, which doesn't get me far. The couple leaves with a tip of a hat and a nod.

The next hand is dealt. I watch Chipped Tooth. He reacts to every card. Extra blink. Tap of the corner of the card. Shifting the cards quickly means there's something there to organize. He doesn't move any of them.

"Did you see that kid over back that way?" Chipped Tooth jerks his thumb back in the general direction of… I don't even know. His hairline is deeply receding, and he scratches right where the hair meets the edge of his forehead.

"I didn't see anything," I say, tossing ten into the pile. "I just got here."

"Young girl, couldn't be more than eight years old, caught with her hand in a lady's purse. The cops cuffed her. Can you even believe it, a kid that young?"

This has nothing to do with me. But it has everything to do with me, and I can barely finish the hand before I talk myself into getting up and taking care of whatever it is they're doing to this girl. The psychology of it is so cheap that I should see right through it, but I don't because I am justice. I was never caught, but I was lucky, and I can make another girl like myself just as lucky, and maybe one day she'll be an FBI agent too.

It's not that simple. It doesn't go through my head all that clearly. It's too fast, it's too bright, and it's too loud. But I'm standing and collecting chips before I can work through the sound, the light, or the speed.

I win the hand with three of a kind.

"Where was it?"

He scratches his head again. His fingernails are manicured. "I guess… um… I think it was by the bathrooms."

Of course it was by the bathrooms. I could have told him that. I take a few steps away from the blackjack table, scanning for the walls… are there any walls? Is there an end to this room? A boundary line along which the bathrooms would be situated?

"Hang on," Chipped Tooth says. "I'm sure I can get you there if I'm actually walking it. She your kid or something?"

"No, but I have some experience with this."

"Okay. Okay, I can take you there, but she may be with security already. Are you a social worker or something? Work with troubled kids?"

"Sure." I don't want to say I'm an FBI agent. That's just silly.

"I'm a doctor myself," he says. "I have a practice in Texas. San Antonio. Have you ever been?"

"No."

He leads me in one direction, then another, then around the bend and down a wide indoor boulevard lined with stores. The text comes in. It's Keaton.

—Where are you?—

— I don't know —

I look at Chipped Tooth. Who is this guy with the European accent? What kind of weirdly specific story is he telling? Suddenly, my instincts kick in like a stalled lawn mower engine. He's asked all the questions and every single one put me on the defensive. Something's wrong. Very wrong. Keaton warned me about con artists and I thought I was too smart to hear it.

"What's your name again?" I ask.

"John."

"Cassie!" Keaton's voice comes over the din of bells and whoops. I turn toward it and wave to him.

When I turn back, Chipped Tooth is gone.

CHAPTER 37.

KEATON

She's standing there in one piece, not a hair out of place. Panic drops off me, leaving a relief so profound, I'm left breathless.

"Hey," she says. "I'm sorry I got lost."

I kiss her long and hard. I don't have to tell her I was being overprotective, or that I thought I'd put her in danger by leaving her alone. Nor do I want to describe the sense of panic I'm still shedding. She'll want to do something about it, and I don't want to put her in danger.

I just want to kiss her. Surround her. Worship her wholeness and her well-being. I want to feed her my relief without defining it.

"What's with you?" she asks when I let her get a breath.

"Just glad to see you."

"Well…" Her eyes scan the room as if she doesn't know what to say next. She looks as if she's hiding her own secret. "We should go."

"Did you want to play a few hands?" I stroke her arms, still appreciating the solid reality of her life in the world when I was convinced it would be snuffed out.

"Nah," she says. "Let's just go if you don't mind."

"Did something happen while I was gone?"

"I won fifty bucks at poker."

I don't know if she's off or I'm off. But something's off. Maybe she's embarrassed to win money at a low-risk game. Maybe she's put off by how relieved I was to see her. Maybe, since I thought everything was getting turned upside down, my view of the world is still sideways.

I assume it's me and take her home.

• • •

By the time we board the plane, she's back to normal, from what I can see. She's lively and bright, thanking me for a wonderful weekend. I kiss her and thank her back, but my thoughts are caught in a net.

With her head on my chest and a book in front of her, I pretend I'm asleep on the plane. I need to think. I need to not just decide my future—that was done weeks ago. I need to acknowledge the decision and do something about it.

Vegas was the proof.

I can't leave her behind. Even without Kaos in the picture, for better or worse, Cassie Grinstead is a part of my life. Pretending otherwise is a fool's errand.

I'm going to have to neutralize Kaos myself.

CHAPTER 38.

CASSIE

Orlando stands at the front of the briefing room that morning and makes an announcement. It's over. One little Nazi in the Springfield cell had a cert kwon, and once the Cyber Crime division used it to confirm his ID, he flipped like a pancake. Federal authorities all over the country were banging on doors six hours later in secret night time raids.

And all because I told them about the little hacker coins.

Ken's shaking my hand as well as he can with a bad shoulder, Frieda's fist-pumping, and everyone at the field office is clapping.

"All right, all right." Orlando's at the podium, tamping enthusiasm by bouncing his palms at us. "You can thank her later. For now, we want t's and i's crossed and dotted, in that order. We caught these guys because of the exceptional work of one agent"—he indicates me in the crowd of agents and staff—"but we won't get them put away without the careful work of every other individual in this office."

We disperse. I shake more hands, feeling a curious emptiness. I wanted this, and yet it's not what I need.

"Grinstead!" Orlando calls as he goes into his office. I follow. "Close the door behind you."

I do it. He sits behind his desk, and I stand in front of it.

"They have psychics over in Quantico," he says.

"Sir?"

"You put in for a transfer to division?"

"CID, sir."

"That's what I nominated you for."

"Thank you, sir."

"You're being sent to Cyber Crime."

I open my mouth to tell him that wasn't what I wanted. I wanted criminal.

"I have to be honest," he says. "This is the right call. You have a razor-sharp sense of that world. And someone over there doesn't want you in CID."

"But I can't get into a division I wasn't nominated for."

"Apparently you can." He stands and holds out his hand. "Congratulations, Special Agent Grinstead. You are to report to the Division Office in San Francisco in two weeks. Case dossiers will be on your desk in a couple of days, if not sooner."

I shake his hand, eyes wide in disbelief, gratitude, and utter bafflement.

• • •

It's midnight when I get home from the best day ever. My feet hurt, my hair is scraggly, and my suit is wrinkled, but I feel expanded, lit from within, tied to the earth and filled with helium.

—We need to talk—

I send this without thinking that it might sound as if I don't want to see him again. But I figure I can clear it up quite quickly once he's in front of me. I don't know if he's in California, New York, or a mile away at the club.

When I pull into my driveway, I check my phone. Still nothing back from him. I'll compose something more inviting once I'm inside.

The flickering blue light of the TV tells me Nana's up, but when I open the door, I find her sleeping on the couch with a blanket over her, wine glasses on the side tables, and a half-complete kitten puzzle on the card table. I'm a little disappointed. I want to tell her about my reassignment. She's always wanted to go to California; now I can take her there.

The sound of creaking floorboards startles me, and I almost reach for my gun when I see Keaton coming out of the shadows, drying his hands with a dishtowel. I'm surprised. He's the last person I expected to see and the first I want to tell.

"Hello," he says.

He starts to say more, but I can't wait another second. I leap on him and smother his face with kisses. He's all leather and rainy London mornings.

"I'm so pissed at you," I say between kisses. He's holding me straight as I climb him. The blue light flickers on his face.

"Why?" He pulls my leg around his waist.

"Just showing up here? Presumptuous."

He's hard already. I feel him against me as we kiss and drag each other to the kitchen so we won't wake up my grandmother.

"Not cool," I whisper. "Bad form."

He pushes me up against the kitchen counter and I'm absolutely wild with sensation. The TV light flashes on the open door and the teacups hanging under the cabinets, drowned out by the stars I see when I wrap my legs around him.

"I needed to see you," he says. "You took the air out of the room with you."

His needy, clutching hands push up my shirt, under my bra. I don't even feel the corner of the counter biting into my back. I don't feel a thing but his lips and his fingers. I think I'm grabbing his shirt. I think I'm kissing him back.

But his softly spoken words fill the sound range. I can only hear him and feel his body where it presses against mine. "Everyone else looks flat and grey now. There's no life in anything. You carved a place in my world and everything else fell into it."

We thrust our hips together in a rhythm, the length of him flush against me, end to end.

"I think I can come like this," I say.

"What's stopping you?"

The blue light disappears and we freeze. A rustle of blankets. A creak of the couch.

"Nana?" I say.

"Where are you?" she calls.

Keaton and I look at each other. We try not to laugh. He could let me go so I can deal with my grandmother. Instead he presses me into the counter.

"I'm home." I try to sound normal.

"That nice man was here looking for you."

"I know, Nana."

There's a long pause. I wish I knew where she is, but I can't see her.
"I'll be going to bed then." She says it more loudly and deliberately than normal. I hear the floor creak and her bedroom door
snap closed.

"She knows," Keaton says.

"She's old, but she's not stupid."

"Then she knows I'm going to fuck you senseless."

"Let's not confirm it for her, okay?" I whisper so low I can barely
hear myself.

"The only thing that's going to be holding you straight is my
cock." He bites my lower lip.

"My bedroom is past her door. She's a really light sleeper."

He takes a breath, looks around. I'm thinking a quick dash to a
hotel. Maybe we can fuck in the car or something. But he opens the
pantry door and leans over to check it out.

In half a second, we're crammed inside between the unbleached
flour and the serving trays. The only light's coming through a tiny
window above us. Below it sits a little stool for getting to high shelves.
He closes the door behind him, knocking over a bowl of Halloween
candy. We stifle laughter.

He doesn't waste a second, pulling his belt out of the loops and
looking at my pants as if I should know better than to be wearing
them at all.

I take the hint and wriggle them down, getting one leg out.

"What were you so happy about today?" He says it while he's fishing his dick out of his pants, which freezes me in place for a second.

I'm happy because I got a pay raise, a promotion, and a new title.
Special Agent. Cyber Crime division.

And here I am, in my pantry about to fuck a cyber criminal.

"Cat got your tongue?" he asks.

"There's been a change."

"What sort of change?"

He doesn't seem particularly concerned. Maybe he thinks there's
a guy in my life who he's going to have to vanquish, or maybe he
thinks I have my period or something. I hate doing this to him, but
more importantly, I hate doing it myself. I want him. I want to peel
away his layers like an onion and find the center. Or never find the
center and just die trying. I can't decide this now. It's all too big to

figure out while I throb between my legs and my knees feel like butter on the counter, keeping their edges while slowly softening.

"I don't want to lie."

"What an intriguing way to begin," he says, drawing his hand up my shirt, under my bra, squeezing away a few more IQ points until I am half dullard.

My brain is mush. My mouth is dry.

Keaton cups my jaw, slides his hand back, and pulls my hair until I buckle. "Maybe you'll tell me on your knees."

I drop to them. He steadies me with the hand that's not yanking on my hair until I'm looking up at him with the spot of moisture at the tip of his head an inch from my nose. I flick my tongue out and lick it off. He breathes through his teeth.

I did that. I made this beautiful man tilt his head back and suck on air as if it's a drug. And I know there's no going back. From this point on, it's only going to get harder to tell him. I shouldn't care. If he's a criminal, then he's on my radar and it doesn't matter. My job is to hunt him and people like him and my job is my life. But it's not. I don't know what my life is anymore. I care about this man. I crave his attention and his approval. I want to get to know him, and now I won't be able to. How can I not be honest with him about that, or give him the opportunity to prove to me that he won't be on the wrong side of the law while it is my job to defend it?

"I got reassigned," I say. "I'm moving to San Francisco in two weeks."

"Well done, my artful dodger!"

He seems too happy. The obvious reason is that I haven't told him the division. It seems crazy to tell him with the hard, heavy weight of his erection an inch from my nose, the glistening drop of pre-cum begging for my tongue's attention.

"Cyber Crime division." I choke it out before I can think too hard about it.

I'm ready for him to step back and thank me for my time. I'm also ready for him to fuck me as though I'm his enemy, which might not be the worst way to say goodbye.

"You think you'll be chasing after me then?"

It seems ridiculous that I'd ever chase Alpha Wolf, or that I'd ever catch him.

"You tell me."

I'm giving him a chance to assure me that he is just an investor. I'm giving him the chance to surgically remove everything he has admitted and insert a same-shaped lie.

He doesn't.

He draws two fingers over my cheek and slides them into my mouth. I take them, closing my lips around the webs at the base.

"I'm going to tell you something, all right."

He smiles and puts his fingers back in my mouth before I can ask him for his reassurances. He puts them far back, as if testing my abilities. I take them, locking eyes with him above me, sucking on the way out. I want his cock. I want to show him how deep I can take it, but he only gives me his fingers. With his other hand, he reaches onto the shelf with the spilled Halloween candy and grabs a lollipop. The kind with bubble gum inside.

"I'm going to tell you when and how to take whatever I put in your mouth."

He unwraps the lollipop with his teeth, spitting out the shavings of paper like confetti. When the deep red ball is freed, he removes his fingers.

"Open up." He taps my lips with the lollipop. I open them and he slides it against my tongue, to the back. "Say *ah*, Special Agent Grinstead, and take the lolly."

Something about being called Special Agent, or maybe just *special*, floods me in arousal. I want more than anything to please the man who said it. I open my throat and the lollipop goes down it.

"Brilliant," he says softly, twisting the pop out then back in. He leaves it on my tongue, and I close my lips around the white stem. It's strawberry.

"Yum," I say around the pop.

"Indeed." He takes it away and puts it in his own mouth. "What are you going to do when they tell you to get Alpha Wolf?"

"I get him."

"I like that answer."

"Thank you."

Why isn't he worried? Why isn't he reticent in the slightest? Why isn't he denying who he is or anything he has done? He seems delighted.

"You're going to go far in Cyber Crime, dodger." He squeezes my cheeks until my lips part. "Again. Say *ah*."

My mouth is barely all the way open before he has the head of his dick in it. I take it, groaning deep in my throat when I can, breathing every few strokes. His skin is slick and soft, throbbing underneath. The lollipop is jammed into the side of his mouth, teeth tight on the stick. When he jerks away with a gasp, I know he's close.

"Bloody hell."

"What?"

He plucks out the lolly and bends to give me a strawberry-and-sugar kiss.

"You almost had me," he says, pulling me up. We're both standing, looking onto each other's eyes. "I'd love to come in your mouth, on your body. I want to mark you with me, but I can't."

"Why not?" I sound like a petulant child because I feel like one. I desperately want to be marked with him, by him. Yet I know what's stopping him. "You're legit now. Right? That's what you said."

He drops his gaze, pressing his lips together. I can sense he's keeping himself from saying the first words that come to mind.

"I know you," he says finally. "Better than you think and more than is fair. I know what I am to you. I'm a thrill for a woman who forgot how to seek thrills. But you're not that to me. I don't just fancy your ass in a tight skirt. I want you to have everything you ever dreamed, and you can't if you're with me. You understand that, right? I'll sabotage everything you're doing. I won't mean to do it, but I will. How can I live with myself? How can you live with it?"

He takes my chin and tilts my face up to his. I can smell the strawberry sweet on his breath. It matches my own. "You think you can because we're in a bloody pantry with our trousers down. How long will it be before I'm a liability? You'll be asked to hunt me down or I'll be your informant. Or someone I know will feel you breathing down their neck. And here's the rub, darling. I'll do whatever I need to to make you happy or to protect you, and they're not always going to be the same thing."

"What if I didn't take the promotion?"

Did I really mean what I was saying? Would I really refuse the transfer to stay in Doverton? I hadn't thought about it enough to know for sure, but it was a very real possibility.

For me, it was an option. The idea made him chuckle.

"What's so funny?"

"You think I'd allow that?"

"I can wait for a spot in CID."

He kisses me, but it's a consolation prize.

I gently push him away. "Don't you do this. Don't you use this as an excuse to run away from me. If you don't want me, then just say so."

His expression flares into anger and his grip on my jaw gets tight. "You think I'm standing here with my balls out to fuck with you? I want to fill your mouth and your tight little cunt with me like I want nothing else, but I can't lie to you. I can't fuck you now and listen to you talk about quitting afterward."

"I'll do as I like, Alpha."

He's as much as admitted to being Alpha Wolf, but I've never acknowledged it by using the name, and we both stiffen as if I dropped a bomb.

Clarity is a powerful thing. Clarity put into words is a sawed-off shotgun two inches from a target. It blows resistance away. It turns barriers into hot shrapnel.

"I want you to fuck me, Alpha Wolf. I want you to fuck me like you've wanted to kill every fed that ever got close. Fuck me like I'm reading you your rights."

He yanks my hair so hard, my lungs empty in a single breath. "That's a lot of saucy talk from a special agent."

"You have the right to remain silent." It's hard to say that without a smile, but I manage.

He indulges in what I deny myself, letting an evil grin spread across his face. "I have the right to fuck you unconscious."

He pushes me into the shelves. Two cans of beans clop to the floor as our hips meet. His cock is pushed up against my belly. I wrap a leg around his waist, and he holds it there with one hand while he guides himself into me with the other. I stretch, angle myself, push into him until he's buried inside me. He pulls out halfway and thrusts forward with a grunt. More cans fall. Pumpkin pie. Artichokes. Pitted black olives. The cabinets shake as he pounds me. Paper towels fall. I'm pinned against a shelf of pasta and crackers, his fingers digging in my ass cheeks. It hurts. God, it all hurts and feels so good.

"This what you want?" he growls.

"You have the right to fuck me harder."

He obliges, wrapping my other leg around him and thrusts slower and harder. Another stack of cans rattles, falls, rolls off the shelf. I'm too blind to see what they are. My body swells around him, hungry for more, more, more. I want him deeper than physically possible. So deep he wipes me into the ether, into invisibility, into nonexistence.

When I come, he covers my mouth. I scream into his palm, shaking over and over, completely lost. Invisible.

I'm made of jelly. My limbs have lost the will to function. My tears fall over my cheeks and onto his hand. He slides it away.

"Hang on to me."

I wrap my arms around shoulders, sharing the weight between them and the legs I have curled around his waist. He pulls out and with one hand, he fists his throbbing cock; with the other, he lifts my shirt. In three strokes, he's exploding all over my belly, and I think this is me. I've done this. He's so beautiful when he comes that I feel like an artist stepping back to see a finished masterwork.

He breathes his last orgasmic breath and kisses me, putting his arms around my lower back to hold me up.

I reach behind him, grabbing a horizontal roll of paper towels that's half hanging off the edge of the shelf. He sets me down, snaps the paper towels away, and unspools a few sheets.

"Thank you," I say as he cleans me off.

"The pleasure is all mine."

When I'm clean I let my shirt drop, and we both pick up our pants. The floor is littered with groceries, like flowers in a nonperishable garden. I pick up a can of beans in each hand.

"You knew," I say.

He slides a box of pasta back onto the shelf. "Knew what?"

"Don't play coy."

He doesn't play coy. He plays silent. He plays with a knowing smile. He plays a long pause punctuated with the sounds of shelf-stocking like a musical instrument.

"Keaton."

"Cassie."

He looks down at me, lit by the street light coming through the tiny window. It's a little blue in the depths, a little yellow at the highlights, cutting to black at his dimples and the ridges under his eyebrows, tilting a box of Cheerios against the edge of the shelf. He knew. He fucking knew.

"You knew I was going to be sent to Cyber Crime."

"You don't trust me?"

"I trust you. But I don't believe you."

"I came here to tell you I'll be away for a few days. Maybe a week." He slides the box on the shelf until it pops against the back wall and bounces back a quarter of an inch, then he picks up crackers and a half-eaten bag of tortilla chips. The plastic crunches at a billion decibels. "There's nothing else going on."

I take the chips and put them on a low shelf. He puts the crackers where they go with a flawless sense of order. I scan the floor. There's nothing left to pick up. There's nothing left to do in this tiny room but leave it.

He puts his arms around me, and I sink into the warmth and solidness of him. I shouldn't. I know that. But he fits into me, and I fit into him so easily that it must be law of physics that draws me close to him.

CHAPTER 39.

KEATON

I said I was going to be away for a few days as if it was nothing. As if I had some easy business to manage, not that I was going to Salton Sea to track down Keyser Kaos. Not that the success of this mission would determine whether I could stay with her or not. Not that I could be killed.

All I want her to know is I won't be around, not that I'm leaving in the hopes that I'm protecting her and whatever we have together.

This woman means more to me than the goals I've been reaching for, and after the lie of omission in the pantry, the lies about her promotion won't stand. I have to relieve the pressure.

She's walking me to my car as this unravels. It's like a net coming loose. Or ropes that bound me suddenly unwinding themselves until I can move, then breathe. Soon they'll be so loose I can walk away.

Which is why I can't continue the lie.

"About the promotion." But I can't finish so fast. I've stuck my foot in it now. It's the truth, or nothing.

She is calm when she responds, closing her jacket around her, waiting a full two seconds before opening her mouth. "What about it?"

"They weren't going to put you in criminal. They weren't going to put you anywhere. And before you ask me how I know, trust me, I know because I know people. You deserve to be where you are, and you need to go where you're going. And don't look at me like that. Don't look at me like it's cheating. Because it's not. This is the way the world works for everybody. Everybody."

She opens her mouth to say something, then snaps it closed, waiting another two seconds before speaking.

"What exactly did you do?" Her breath makes clouds in front of her face, giving me the impression that she's breathing fire.

I have to answer. I'm trapped now. Trapped on this street, trapped in her gaze, and trapped in the truth.

"I know you think that you never got caught lifting wallets and being bait for your mother's con jobs. And it's true, you don't have a record. But they know. They know about your mother, and they assume that you've inherited some of her art. Criminal justice and counterterrorism is full of Boy Scouts. You'd never get in. Cyber Crime is a totally different game. All I did was move your application from a place where it was toxic, to a place where it would be seen by people who would appreciate it."

The air has gone from heavy, to heavy and wet. Cold dewdrops collect on her cheeks as she looks at the ground with wet lashes, thinks a good long time as the mist gathers on the ends of her raven hair.

"How did you do that?"

"Someday I'll tell you."

"You just hacked it and moved the application over?"

"More or less. There were other steps. You got the job based on your qualifications."

"I'm uncomfortable with this."

"You said you trusted me, but you didn't believe me." She turns away, billowing a breath, then turns back so I can look her in the eye when I answer. "I want you to believe me, but it's your trust I treasure."

Her sigh is long and profound, with a deep, sad resignation. "Will you be back before I move to California?"

"Will you be here for me?"

"Yes."

"Then I'll be back before you know it."

I expressed my hope rather than my certainty.

CHAPTER 40.

CASSIE

Nana took the news quite well. She seemed more excited than I was, opening her closet as if she was throwing open French doors after a month of rain.

"Everyone was moving to California." She throws clothes on her double bed and tells the same story I've heard a hundred times. "All the girls. They thought they'd find nice boys in California, and maybe they did. I had Barry the motherfucker and your mother in my belly. So we went where the jobs were. Detroit, Michigan." The story took on a new, never-heard-before emphasis on the Golden State. "All the other girls were moving to Los Angeles, but me? If I had my druthers, it definitely would've been San Francisco."

Whatever druthers are, they must've been in short supply back then, and I must have plenty. I may not always be happy and I may not always get what I want, but taking her to California with me gives my life meaning.

She starts packing almost immediately and backwardly, putting the mementos away first, piling unidentifiable knick-knacks into the middle of the room.

I almost trip on a box of old bills. "We can hire movers, you know."

"Why would you do that? Something wrong with your arms?"

Midwesterners. Defining do-it-yourself for four generations.

"I don't want you straining yourself." I try to get a box out of her arms, but she won't let it go.

"It's heavy."

"Fine if you want," she says. "Put it over there and grab that red box on the top shelf if you don't mind."

"I do mind. That's the problem. Are these boxes of puzzles?" I hold up a box with a bowl of fruit. "Are you bringing boxes of puzzles you've already done to California?"

"That one's important." She snatches it away. "It's the one I was doing when you got into the academy. It goes in the keep pile."

"You moved puzzles from Flint to Doverton? How did I not notice this?"

"You used to not question me this much."

She puts the fruit bowl puzzle in the stack under the window, then attacks the pile of puzzles in the corner and slides one out of the middle with enough dexterity to keep the tower from falling.

"This one too." She hands it to me, running her finger down the stack.

I take it. It's a generic mountain landscape. "Why?" I'm practically whining.

"That's the one I was doing when you broke up with that idiot. Mark the idiot." She pulls out a slim box and hands it back. "This was the day you fractured your elbow playing volleyball."

I take it. Wild horses running over the plains. I worked on it with one arm in silence with her, passing the time I wanted to be out with my friends on small victories.

"Junior year." I run my fingers over it. Every piece snapping together made me a little less miserable.

Grandma's stacking them in my arms now. Pumpkins. Orange leaves. A cold blue Autumn sky.

"What's this one?"

"That time you weren't pregnant."

"Jesus, Nana, I was eighteen."

"And you almost killed me." She hands back a swirling mandala. "The last time we visited your mother."

As I take the mandala puzzle, my sinuses fill and my lungs squeeze tight and release, forcing out a sob. I say something I didn't know I believed, but it exits me with the same uncontrolled velocity as the sobs. "I miss her."

Grandma lays a family of bunnies on top of the pile in my arms. "I know, sweetheart. I do too. But I have you and you have me. So we have her."

She squeezes my shoulder and looks me in the eye. Hers are clear, grey-blue, darker than mine and lighter than Keaton's. They're clear. I think of her as old, but she's not. She's just got years on me.

"She taught me so much."

"She did."

"She was teaching me how to survive without her. She was doing her best."

The puzzles aren't heavy, so I let Grandma take the stack from me and lay it next to the keepers.

She hugs me as I cry. I hold her as tightly as I can, putting my head on her bony shoulder. She understands me. She believes in me. There's no replacing her in my life.

"All right," she says when I pull away and wipe my eyes with my wrists. "Let me get to work here."

"Keep them all," I say. "Every one of them."

She picks up a puzzle of the White House. "This is the one that nice man did with me."

"He's not so nice." Correcting her is completely counterproductive. Why shouldn't she think he's a nice man? The fact that she's completely wrong notwithstanding, it doesn't make a damn bit of difference, except it feels as if she's stealing from me what I find most attractive about him.

"I'm sure you're right, not such a nice boy. I was a young woman once. I understand the appeal. But I'll tell you the same thing I told your mother."

I move all the puzzles to one place. "What did you tell her?"

"I told her not to get knocked up. Fat lot of good that did."

I laugh. She loves me. I'm the product of my mother not listening to a word Nana ever said, and I know she's glad of it. We both are.

CHAPTER 41.

KEATON

The trailer stinks of men. Three of us in an enclosed space, the processor tower set inside the shower stall. We're in the deserts of the Salton Sea in January, home of survivalists, meth cookers, and fugitives. We got lucky when we found Keyser in this little trailer park, but the conditions are terrible. No wireless for miles. Below freezing at night. Fuckhot in the day. Cassie's a thousand miles and a week away. I'm tired and dirty. We haven't left this tin can in six days. With Keyser and a handful of cronies in the next trailer over, we don't risk being seen in the daylight.

"I don't think we're close enough," Hodgekins grumbles, crouched at the base of the four-foot-wide, five-foot-high antenna, twisting two wires together. He's the antenna guy. Jackson's managing the satellite connection. I'm the one who knows how tempest emissions work.

I'm not here for my comfort. I'm here for my life and Cassie's. But my God, we just took the cabinets out to get the antenna closer to the trailer wall.

"We could just put it outside," I say without looking away from the monitor. Tempest emission decoders pick up delicate signals from machines in range and feed the contents of a neighbor's screen onto the hacker's, no matter the encryption or security. They're always wonky, and this setup is no different.

"Or knock on Keyser's fucking door and ask him what's on his screens." Jackson's monitoring the satellite connection, which is shite. His voice is muffled past the headphones I'm wearing to catch the aural peaks and valleys of the emissions.

"Fuck you both." Hodgekins slides out from under the antenna.

"Fine. Tonight you're my bitch," Jackson replies.

"Again?" I say. Something's coming in, so my retort isn't as sharp as it should be.

The screen sparkles with smears of color. Hodgekins and Jackson look over my shoulder.

"Is he watching...what is that?" Hodgekins asks, referring to the pristine landscape and dancing humanoid monstrosities on the screen. We don't have sound and the picture is incomplete, but there's no mistaking the show.

"*Teletubbies*," Jackson says. "The antenna's pointing at the wrong trailer."

"It's not."

"Fix it," I command.

Hodgekins gets back under the antenna.

With the satellite connected, my phone dings.

It's Taylor on our secure channel.

*<Did you hear about Cassie's
grandmother?>*

The computer screen flickers, changes with the speed of my mood. Code and panic. C++ and trouble.

<What happened?>

"That's him." Jackson seems in awe of what we've just done. Hack one of the best hackers in the world.

My awe is put to the side when Taylor texts back.

*<Harper says she's in the hospital with a
broken hip>*

"He's flipping to a forum," Hodgekins reacts to the change in screen. "Fuck. We're doing it. He's laying out the whole plan."

<She's sending flowers>

I'm breathing, but my lungs feel pinched and hollow.

Keyser is laying it out, right on the screen. He thinks I'm in California. He's got my apartment wired.

Bugger the flowers. Bugger the plan. Bugger the broad daylight. Cassie's alone. Maybe not exactly alone, but I'm not with her. I haven't been needed many times in my years, so this feeling that someone I care about is calling me without saying a word is new. It's fresh, and it's a physical urge, like hunger or exhaustion calls for food and sleep, this yearning calls for me to go to Cassie.

But if I leave now, we lose Keyser, and he's still a threat. We may not have an opportunity like this again.

The only choice is to stay and finish the job. My only option is to take the long view. Neutralizing Keyser will ensure Cassie's safety and give us the possibility of a life together. Going back to Doverton to sit next to her won't make her grandmother any better any quicker.

I simply can't go.

She'll understand.

"Gentlemen," I say, taking off my headphones, "I'm sorry, but I have to leave."

"What?" they cry in unison.

"We can't maintain the connection without you," Hodgekins complains.

I crack the door. The light hurts my eyes. We all hold our arms in front of our faces like vampires.

"I'm going for the car." I put on sunglasses. "Give a shout if the bastard leaves his tin can. And if he threatens to come to Barrington, Doverton, or anywhere near there, give a shout."

I leave them and run in broad daylight for the car. Quite possibly, I've traded my singular goal of the past few years for a few hours of comforting and supporting someone in her time of need.

For her, it may be a worthy trade.

CHAPTER 42.

CASSIE

If something happens to my grandmother—and by "something," I mean if she dies—who am I?

Who cares about me? Who do I care for? Who do I love?

I understand that these thoughts are selfish. I understand that it's not about me, my feelings, my needs, or my life. But I need to wonder these things to block out the knowledge that I'm sitting in a hospital waiting room because I wanted to move to California.

If she'd been sitting around watching QVC like she's supposed to, she wouldn't be in a hospital bed. She'd be telling me to get married to break the cycle of single motherhood in my family. She'd be worrying about me, hoping for the best, pushing me toward my future while she held onto my past.

I have never felt so alone. The hospital waiting room is empty and decorated like a meal with no salt. It's so bland, so completely inoffensive that it leaves me no choice but to use my thoughts as weapons against myself.

My friends are working, what little family I have is far away, and if I lose my grandmother, I won't be uprooted so much as unmoored.

I finger my phone. Frieda is going to come by after work. Unless some new emergency pops up. Then she'll have to stay to cover for my absence. I appreciate her. She's a good friend. If I move, I lose her.

I hope Nana isn't suffering. I hope they give her all the pain medication she wants. I hope I can see her soon. I've brought a bunch of puzzles and some junk food that they probably won't let her eat.

I can't pay attention to a book. The news is depressing. There are no granola bars left in the vending machine. If Nana dies, is it my fault?

I say things to myself that make me anxious, as if anxiety is a drug that I need extra doses of. Why do I do this to myself? I'm helpless to stop it. Helpless to stop the self-bludgeoning about my responsibility and my loneliness.

I don't cry. Not until he shows up. When Keaton walks in from the hall with his travel bags and unkempt scruff along his jaw, the water main funneling my emotions cracks. When his eyes land on me and he smiles with those damn dimples, the crack snaps the pipe and I flood.

I don't know if he rushes toward me, or saunters, or jumps, or runs. All I know is that I'm blind with a sadness that I'm now allowed to express, and a joy I don't feel any guilt for. I'm in his arms, held tighter by him than by my own skin. He squeezes sadness from me, drop by drop. With sweet words, he gives me back what was hurting me, and takes away the loneliness that kept me from feeling it fully.

He leads me to a chair, snapping tissues from the dispenser on the coffee table. He presses them to my cheeks and eyes. This hacker criminal who cares nothing for anyone is caring for me. I let him put a fresh tissue under my nose and wipe away the snot.

"I'm sorry I'm so gross," I say with a sniffle, taking the tissue from him.

"What was she doing?"

"I came home from work, and I was two hours late. And I'm sorry I was two hours late, but I didn't know. She was on the floor. She's only seventy-three. She's not at the 'I've fallen and can't get up' phase. But there she was and she didn't even know how long she'd been there. But she was lying on the floor, helpless. They say she fractured her hip. So I'm glad she can't remember it, but I feel bad. This wouldn't have happened if I came home on time."

"Pretty good chance this would have happened even if you were on time."

"She's so young for this. Do you know that women who have a fall like this are five times more likely to die within the next year?"

"Do you know anything about how statistics work, Cassandra? If one woman usually dies under normal circumstances and five will break their hip and die, that's five times more likely. Something can be five times more likely and still not be statistically significant."

"My grandmother is not a statistic."

"Agreed. She will not be a statistic because she has a wonderful, competent, caring granddaughter to watch over her."

He really seems to believe that I'm instrumental in saving my grandmother's life. He makes me want to believe it as much as he believes.

"I really wish I'd been there for her when she fell."

"I know." He brushes away the hair that sticks to my cheek, kneeling dutifully on one knee in front of me as if he's at my beck and call. Maybe he is, but it doesn't even matter. "Business first. Are you thirsty? Hungry? Horny?"

"Honestly, sex is the last thing on my mind. Though you do remind me of sex."

He gets up and sits next to me, sliding down the seat a little and crossing his ankle over his knee. "Well, I'm at your disposal. We're quite good at a quick shag in the closet."

"Everyone has talents." I take his hand and squeeze it, half turning toward him so that I can look him in the eye. "Thank you for coming. I can't tell you what it means to me. No, I can. The reason I was comfortable picking up and moving across the country was that I have no one here. I have no one anywhere. I've only ever had my job and my grandmother, and the thought that I would have to choose between them made me feel like I was getting ripped in two. It still feels that way. And I may still have to make that choice. But you coming… I don't know what you had to do to get here, I don't know how you found out that I was here, and I don't care. You being here makes me feel…" I choke back another sob. "It makes me feel less empty. I feel like I belong to something, and I know I shouldn't say stuff like that this early in a relationship, but I don't know how to not speak the truth right now. I might not feel whole ever again in my life, but sitting with you here instead of alone makes me feel, damn, I don't know, half full? Five eighths? This is a crummy way of saying thank you."

I slide down a little in my chair as well, and I squeeze his hand, looking away so I can gather my thoughts. They won't come together. I'm just a mess of feeling where words should be. He's not asking for my thoughts, he's not asking for my feelings. He's not asking for anything.

I settle in with the possibility that this is exactly what I need.

CHAPTER 43.

KEATON

I wish I knew how I could help her. I offered her food, water, affection, comfort. I didn't have anything else after that. So I just sat with her until the doctor came out in her knee-length white jacket and reading glasses as she flipped through papers on a clipboard.

When the doctor first appears, Cassie stands with her hands fidgeting at her sides, then folded in front of her. I don't want to impose, so I let her stand by herself, but she looks back at me expectantly as if I have a place in her family, collecting family news and sharing a family experience. Maybe she wants some water, or she wants me to bugger off. I'd get her water and bugger off at the same time, but she waves her hand a little by her hip and there's no way to misinterpret what she wants.

She wants me to come stand by her, and it still feels funny to do that even after she takes my hand. Funny, but right.

The doctor smiles and pokes her reading glasses up her nose. "So, I have some good news and some bad news."

Cassie squeezes my hand so hard, I'm sure she is cutting off the circulation.

"The good news is the surgery went fine." The doctor pauses. "The bad news is she won't be one hundred percent mobile for a while."

Cassie squeezes my hand until her arm relaxes and her exhale is so deep, her shoulders drop an inch. "I can live with that. We can do that. Yes. That's okay."

She doesn't sound as if she's trying to convince herself of something; she sounds as if she's working herself up to believing it. Digging herself out of her hole of despair. I can't help but smile.

They discuss physical therapy, prescriptions, some other shit I don't care about because the endgame is that her grandmother will be okay for a while.

"Would you like to go see her?"

"Yes." Cassie sounds as if she's been offered a chance to drive a Lamborghini.

The doctor heads toward the hallway, and Cassie follows. She tugs me along.

I resist out of surprise. "I'll wait here."

"Are you kidding? You're gonna cheer her up."

She yanks on my hand, hard, until I have to follow. On the way to her grandmother's room, I wonder if this has been wise. She's counting on me, and she won't be able to do that for much longer. She's also smart, well-connected, and curious. She'll look for me. The closer I get to her and the more I offer her, the more likely this diligent and ambitious woman will seek me out, and not only will she find me… I will want to be found.

CHAPTER 44.

CASSIE

Why's he freaking out on me? He just stands there as if he doesn't know whether to do what I'm asking him to do or not.

"I don't know why you would come all the way here so that you could be with me and then stand in the hallway. Are you afraid of sick people or something?"

I thought of it as soon as I said it. Maybe he has some kind of sick person phobia. Maybe hospitals freak him out. In which case, he can stand in the hallway all he wants.

He shakes his head for a second as if getting cobwebs out. "No, no. Let's do this then."

"Keaton, really. You've done a lot by being here. If this is too much for you, you can wait in the hallway. Or in the waiting room."

"Get in that room before I pick you up and carry you in there."

I turn slowly and walk in to find my grandmother in a hospital bed with a My Little Pony twenty-piece puzzle that she should be able to do in thirty seconds splayed out on a tray in front of her. She isn't even looking at it. She's gotten half of one edge finished and seems to have lost interest.

"Nana," I say. "How are you feeling?"

"She's very tired," the doctor said. "She might not be able to talk much."

I point at the puzzle.

The doctor takes my meaning right away. "I grabbed one from the children's wing."

I sit by my grandmother and take her hand. She looks at me as if she doesn't recognize me. Or as if I actually exist somewhere in her mind but she can't place me. This is scaring the shit out of me. Have I lost her forever? I'm overwhelmed by the horrible possibilities, all the stories I've heard about grandparents who had an accident and never came back from it. Then her eyes flick over my shoulder and suddenly become awake.

"Ah," she groans hoarsely. "You're back."

I follow her gaze over my shoulder to find Keaton standing behind me with his hand on the back of my chair.

"You never finished the story about moving to Michigan," Keaton says. "I still want to kill that guy you were with. What was his name?"

"Barry. The motherfucker." Her eyes flutter as if cursing my mother's father took a lot of effort. But she's called him a motherfucker at least a thousand times in my short life.

The doctor laughs a little. I smile. Keaton puts his hand on my shoulder, and I put my hand over it. I feel as though I can get through anything with his hand resting on me.

"That's kind of how the story ends," I say. "My grandfather is a motherfucker, like the rest of them."

"He gave me you," she says, turning her head toward the window. "Even your mother, who was a huge pain in my ass. He gave me her."

"Motherfuckers can be a necessary evil." I hear Keaton smiling behind me, as if smiling had a sound. His does.

"So are you feeling all right?" I ask.

She nods ever so slightly but says nothing. I wait. We all wait. But there's nothing else. She's breathing. I see her chest rise and fall under the sheets. I look at the doctor, a little worried.

"Let's let her rest for a while," the doctor says.

When the three of us get to the hallway, the doctor seems more cheerful than I feel.

"I know this can seem worrying," she says. "But this is as good of a result as we can expect so soon. I'm actually surprised by how vibrant she looked after such an experience."

I take a deep breath. Yes. Of course. Who would want to have an extended conversation after that? She was lucid. She recognized a man she'd only seen twice. She called my grandfather a motherfucker. What else did I expect?

I put my fingertips to my mouth as if they can hold in my relief.

I didn't realize how tense I was until I sensed the doctor's confidence.

"So you mean she's going to be all right?"

"She's not a young woman," the doctor says.

I cut her off. "I know."

She's not a young woman.

She's going to stop existing soon.

She won't be in my life anymore. But for now, she's okay.

My breath hitches again. Crying is like drinking a bottle of wine. You can get drunk, and you might have moments of lucidity, but when you try to stand up, the room spins a little bit. So yes, I stopped crying before I went into the room. Hearing that she was going to be all right was like standing up. The tears came back like a drunkenness. Tears of relief for the present and fear for the future.

Keaton's arm is around me, tightening me in a protective vise. I hitch again, swallow, have an intelligent conversation with the doctor about my plans to get my grandmother home in a few days, sign some papers, and it's all over.

But it's just beginning.

"Keaton," I say as we sit in plastic chairs lining the hall, "I don't know what I'm asking you for. But don't leave me. Or, if you're going to leave me, can you do it right now? If you just turned the plane around to fulfill some sense of obligation or because you thought I was interesting, I totally get it and I won't think worse of you if you bail on me right now and say no thank you. Because it would be the right thing to do."

He shakes his head and *tsk*s as if I'm totally out of line. He's a good person who doesn't want me to suffer unnecessarily in a hospital hallway. But that's not what I want. I don't want to be a good person right now. I wanted him to be the bigger person.

"I don't want reassurances," I say. "I don't want promises. I want to not worry."

One-Mississippi-two-Mississippi.

"What have I ever done to make you worry?"

How funny, the pause before he answers my question with a question. Maybe I should worry that this is a technique, or maybe this is just who he is.

"Besides the usual?" I say with a smirk. "Nothing."

"There you have it."

This time, I do the counting.

One-Mississippi-two-Mississippi-three-Mississippi.

I'm not going to say a damn thing. Inside, I'm smiling from ear to ear. I can see his discomfort in the way he looks around the room and in the way he strokes my fingers.

Four-Mississippi

"You've gotten a bit under my skin, Agent Grinstead. If that surprises you, imagine how I feel. There aren't many people who can do that. And certainly not any women I've had before. But there's something about you. Maybe it's the artful dodger in you. Maybe it's that badge. Could be the way you threw me against my car. I don't pretend to know, but I can promise you..."

He presses his lips between his teeth as if he's stopping himself from saying more. He's so sexy when he does that. The scruffy hairs around his lips stand up like porcupine spines when his skin bends to the new curve. He was so cocky that first day in the interrogation room. I can't believe this is the same man.

"I can promise you that no matter what happens, I'll never leave you willingly." He shakes his head once as if knocking a pinball in place, then stands and holds his hand out to me. "Let me get you home. You must be tired."

I am tired, but I'm also alive and exhilarated. I want to find out more about this man, who he is, and what I'll find when I peel away the next layer. I don't think I'll ever run out of layers. I don't think there are a limited number of facets to the diamond of Keaton Bridge.

CHAPTER 45.

KEATON

I've stripped her down and laid her on her bed. She already has things folded, piled, packed. Her room has the look of something completely lived in, with its knick-knacks and attention to detail, but the dresser is moved a little away from the wall and the wardrobe's been half emptied.

But my focal point is her, naked on her stomach, toes pointed, the arches of her feet calloused and hard and facing the ceiling. Her eyes are closed, and her hair is splayed across the sheets. I haven't fucked her yet. First, I want her to feel as safe as I don't feel. I run my hands from her shoulders to her lower back, pressing against the skin and releasing tension from the muscles. She groans in release.

"I'm going to drive you to and from work for the next few weeks," I say.

"You don't have to do that," she grumbles sleepily.

"I know."

The fact is, I'm lying. I do need to do that. I need to make sure she's safe. I need to see her walk in and out of her office. If she leaves during the day, she'll be with other agents. I can't do more than this. Not without alarming her.

"I want to," I say, running my hands along the backs of her thighs. She's warm between them, and soft everywhere.

"Thank you for coming to the hospital." Her voice is barely a breath. She didn't sleep at all the night before.

"I will always try to be there if you need me." Again, I'm a liar. I'm voicing my desire, not my reality.

"I'll always need you."

She's killing me. Her dependence is a sugar-coated knife twisting and twisting and twisting, spooling my guts around it.

I slide my hand between her thighs. Her skin and muscle yield under me when I slide toward her core. When I touch her, she groans, already wet for me.

"Hush, my love."

She makes a satisfied hum, opening her eyes for just a second. I pull her ankles apart, not more than enough to give me access to her. I don't want her to be uncomfortable. Not this time.

"Just stay still and relax," I say. "Let me take care of you. Just for now."

Gently, I touch her and stroke in a way that isn't aggressive or forceful, but soothing. With my other hand, I hold her down between her shoulders, giving her something to push against. When she comes, her toes curl and her knees bend. She groans from deep in her throat.

I get my pants off, then her eyes flicker open, a smile playing across her lips.

"Keep smiling. I'm going to fuck you right to sleep."

I only pick her hips up as much as I need to angle myself inside her. I move slowly and deliberately, wedging my arms under her and holding her tight. I don't want to jar her out of her stupor. I don't want her to worry about her grandmother or us. I want to surround her with my love.

She grips the sheets, and when she's close, I come inside her. I want to fill her with everything I have. I want to mark myself on her soul.

I fall on top of her and let my weight press against her body. She can't see my face, and I'm grateful. Because she would see regret and loss.

I let her sleep, but I can't fall into it. My deception keeps me up.

CHAPTER 46.

CASSIE

When I put in for two weeks to move, and I got it, I figured the timing was tight but I could manage. Now, with Nana in the hospital, I'm not sure if I have enough time to make sure she's well enough to even go back to the house we already live in.

I enter her hospital room and drop the toiletry kit she asked for on the table next to her, bending over and kissing her cheek. Her skin is warm under my lips. She's getting better.

"It's about time you showed up," Nana says, taking the puzzle from me. It's an idyllic seaside scene with palm trees and a beach chair. She's never interested in the picture as much as the process, but now I'm realizing I just handed her a box of California.

She hands the box back to me, and I slit the tape that holds the top to the bottom. She looks better, she sounds better. I'll be stunned if she dies in a year or ten.

"I had to find one you hadn't done already." I hand the box back to her. It's only a hundred pieces, but it's better than the twenty-piece My Little Pony puzzle she's been taking apart and redoing for two days.

"When are we leaving?" She pokes through the box for the edges.

"You have a week of inpatient physical therapy, and then—"

"They have physical therapists in San Francisco, don't they?"

"I don't think you should move," I blurt. "I don't think it's safe for you."

Her fingers hesitate for a moment in the soup of puzzle pieces, then continue as if nothing important has been said. Anyone who ever said that a hospital stay dims the mind of an elderly person never met my grandmother.

"Thank God," she says. "I can turn your room into the sewing room."

The fact that she hasn't sewn a goddamn thing in years notwithstanding, she has never shown an interest in my bedroom before.

"You're not getting rid of me that easily."

"I'll put a guest bed in there. I'll make it a queen, so you can invite that nice boy over."

"I'm staying. I can get a promotion another time."

She pushes the puzzle box away to the other edge of the tray. It's only two inches, but the statement is clear. "You will do no such thing, young lady."

"I am a grown woman and I can decide what's important to me. You are the only family I have. I'm not leaving you alone, I'm not moving a thousand miles away, and I am most certainly not going to put your life in danger by taking you with me."

"How is my life in danger?"

"You can't move with a broken hip. It's bad for you."

"Then you can just move the hell out of my house."

"It's my house! Give me a break."

She jerks the puzzle back, sending pieces flying. I pick them up off the blanket and put them into the box, flicking an edge piece onto the tray.

"You know," she says, "you're the first one of us who had a chance to be something."

"I am something. I'm your granddaughter."

"That's very sweet, but stupid. You know I'm not that old. And I'm not some crotchety old biddy that can't get around."

"I know, I—"

"Just go. I'll meet you there." She deliberately picks a piece out of the box and lays it flat. Tapping it twice. "You missed an edge."

I know my grandmother. My mother didn't come from nowhere, and I inherited a bunch of genes from the both of them. She's manipulating me. She's reverse engineering the whole argument to get me to leave her alone. Or she has a point. I have no way of knowing. She's too good at this.

"I don't want to leave you." I have more to say, but they're only illustrations of those six words. "I was fourteen when you took me in.

You were supposed to have a life then. All you did was make sure that I was taken care of. I didn't make the same mistakes that you made and that my mother made, my great-grandmother made. Why did you have such faith in me? Why did you love me so much?"

She rests her hands on the tray, covering a bunch of pieces we laid out. "I always knew you were special. I knew you could do anything you wanted if you just had someone to love you and teach you the right way. When I got you, I knew I could make you the best thing that ever happened to me. And you are. I'm so proud of you. So proud to know you. If you stay here because I fell like a fucking fool, you're going to ruin all of that. So go for me. Get the hell out of here for me."

I pinch the bridge of my nose, hoping she can't tell that I'm crying. But she's way too sharp for my pathetic obfuscations.

"Can you reach that little makeup kit for me?" It's the one I brought from home for her. When I pick it up, she says, "Open it."

I unzip it. Inside is a collection of old powders, blushes, eyeshadow from the 1980s. And a blue velvet box.

She points at the box. "Open that."

I snap it open and inside is a diamond solitaire. "Nana! How did you get this?"

"You mean with the Fisher-Price credit card you gave me?" She raises an eyebrow. I'm starting to think that breaking her hip has actually made her smarter. "That there is a gift from a man named Jack. He was okay. Or I thought so. When your mom went to prison and I told him I was gonna raise you, he gave me that ring. He said he'd marry me but he didn't want any children. Can you believe that? I told him to take that ring and shove it up his ass."

My jaw drops. "Wait. You could have gotten married? But you took me in instead?"

"Nothing like a crisis for a man to show his true colors. Mark my words, once he gave me that ring, he showed me who he really was. Being married is not worth that much. In any case..." She waved as if the whole thing is water under the bridge. "He told me to keep it, so I did. I kept it for you, so you wouldn't have to wait for a man to get one."

It has to be a carat and a quarter. What kind of man tells a woman to keep a ring that big?

A rich man. A man who could have made her very comfortable. A man who didn't want to take in a stray.

"Thank you. For everything."

"Might want to see if that nice British guy wants to give you one of his own before you start wearing it around."

I slowly close the box and cocoon it in my palms, one on top of the other, as if it is a powerful talisman.

Keaton is a mysterious and probably dangerous person. I haven't given much thought to him wanting to spend his life with me. It's too soon and there's too much going on, but for the first time, I allow myself to hear her suggestion.

I want him. I want him now, and I want him in twenty years. I want to know all of his mysteries and peel back the danger, the sharp edges, the puzzles, until I find the raw vulnerable place that makes him who he is. I know it's there, and I know I'm going to love it.

"Can we make a deal?"

She's poking through the box again. She's a real piece of work. My mother was more like her than I ever understood. My grandmother conned me into being my best self when I was on the path to becoming someone completely different.

"I will go to San Francisco without you. But as soon as you heal, I'm coming to get you."

"We'll see."

"We will, Nana. We sure will."

CHAPTER 47.

CASSIE

Two weeks off work isn't actually two weeks off work, apparently. Not when there are dossiers on the desk.

I let him drive me to work because I like him. I like making him happy, and he's a nice guy to be around in the morning. He cooked me breakfast, washed my hair, took care of me in a way that is surprising, comforting, and delicious. I'm pretty confident that whatever happens with my new job, we'll figure it out. No one's proving a damn thing against him, and look, he's a legitimate businessman. Anyone can see that. I practically whistle my way into Orlando's office.

"Good morning, sir," I say. "I heard the dossiers came in."

"Live cases and assets." He hands me a thick accordion file. "They're going to expect you to hit the ground running as soon as you get there. I told them you can do undercover work."

"I won't make a liar out of you."

"I know you won't." He smiles and pats my shoulder.

I take the dossiers to the viewing room. They're on paper, which seems counterintuitive for the Cyber Crime unit, but there's nothing more secure than pencil and paper. I leave my phone at the guard station outside the door and go in, making myself comfortable at the empty desk.

The first surprising thing I find in the dossiers is that Keyser Kaos is two people. The first folder is for Keyser, who's a tall man with a round face and little glasses. He dresses as if he's seventyfive, but he's probably not older than thirty. Romanian. I memorize the rest of his stats and the particulars of the photographs of him.

The next dossier belongs to Kaos. There's much less known about him. His general age, fifties or so. Home country is Romania again. He claims to be a doctor, but it's never been proven. The only photograph is from behind. There's something surprisingly familiar about his posture, but it's hard to say.

The next surprise shouldn't have been a surprise. I should've seen it coming like a high-speed train at the end of the tunnel. Or an anvil falling from the fifth floor, set to drop on my head exactly as I passed underneath.

The presence of Keaton's dossier should have been cartoonishly obvious to me, but when I open it and see his face, I almost want to throw up. Looking straight at me with desaturated eyes and a mouth that accuses me of willful blindness, he freezes me. It's not a mug shot, but that doesn't matter. The notes swim. The details aren't sentences; they're meaningless boxes and dots. A code I can decipher if I can just push through this wall of panic. My instincts scream so loud, I can't hear myself think.

I shut the folder, gripping the edges as if I want to tear it in two. I should want this. I should read it from cover to cover to find out who he is. Every lie he ever told me is right there, and every tiny truth might be exposed.

But it's not what I want. I don't want the truth. I want reality. Reality is his touch. Reality is his voice. Reality is him showing up when I needed him. Reality is my trust in him.

What is this folder full of paper going to tell me about Keaton Bridge, or whatever his name is, that I need to know?

I shift it aside and go through the last two dossiers. Sure, sure, sure. Catch this guy, he's done terrible things. And this lady, she's stolen more money than I'll see in my lifetime. And what about Keaton? Where does this money come from? Who can afford a penthouse at the Bellagio in Las Vegas? Or to invest in a new kind of computing? Can't be cheap. What did I sign on for? What am I asking of myself?

As I put the folders back into the accordion and figure-eight the string to close it, I know I can be told all the truths, I can have all the facts, but I also know that what I have with Keaton is real. I love him, and it's real.

I will never trade reality for ambition. Ever.

CHAPTER 48.

KEATON

I left Cassie in hospital with her grandmother to make a quick visit to the factory. Taylor's about to leave the office. I push him back in and slam the door behind me.

"What the hell, Keaton?" He takes half a step back, which gives me enough room to get by him.

"Sit."

"I have a plane to catch."

"It's a private plane. It'll wait."

"Harper's meeting me at the airport in San Jose. I don't like making her wait."

"I'm sure she'll be devastated, mate." I snap the chair around and wheel it toward him. "Or she's an adult and she'll manage."

He's going to say something, some little clever quip that'll make me want to punch him in the face. I know it. I'm girded for it. But instead, he sucks his cheeks, glances out the window, and shuts his mouth.

"You almost gave up everything for Harper," I say. "Why?"

Taylor smiles a little bit, shaking his head, giving up the fight over the next ten minutes. "I can't believe it took you this long to ask me that." He throws himself into the chair as if he's staking his claim on it.

"I figured it was your business."

"You're a strange fucking guy, you know that?"

I guess I do know that.

"The whole thing that happened with us? QI4? She broke me. I mean, she really did a job on me. And I was pissed off, but then she changed me. I saw things differently. And… I'm not trying to be a pussy, but I couldn't go on doing things the same way once I got to know her. Once she showed me who I really was and who I could be… a better guy. Okay, I'm a pussy. But I could be who I always wanted to be, all right? I could be even better with her. It really wasn't too much of a choice. Can I go, asshole?"

"Are you saying she made you a better man? You're a prat."

"I prefer it when you call me a cunt."

I can't help but laugh at him. "You know a lot of things about me. More than anyone else, but you don't know it all."

"I had a feeling."

"I'm not who I always said I was, but you were always a friend to me anyway. So I'm going to tell you something else because you really are a cunt."

"Can it be covered in a phone call?"

"That time we almost got rich together in high school? When the FBI was waiting on your couch when you got home from school? You covered for me, and I appreciated that. But it didn't work. They came to my door too, but I was still a British national."

"Are you serious?" He sits straight as a rod, the plane forgotten. "What happened?"

"I can't tell you exactly. But what I can tell you is that everything I've done since then is the result of that stupid little exploit." I take a deep breath and lean on the desk, gripping the edge. "And now all of the chickens are coming home to roost as I found my own Harper. She's changed the calculus completely. Everything I assumed I would do, every calculation I've made, every shit decision is landing in my lap. I would do anything to be with her, and I don't know how. I don't know which decision to make to have her or if having her is the worst decision I can make for her."

"You're being a little cryptic. I can't help you if you don't tell me the specifics."

"I'm not asking for your help. Not today. But if she asks for your help, I need you to give it to her. You'll do whatever you have to."

"Is this the FBI agent?"

He's not asking me about QI4. I know he cares about how my decisions will affect the company he's built his life around, and maybe before Harper was in his life, he would be demanding answers for the sake of his dreams. But now he looks as if the gears are turning in a different direction.

"Yes. You need to take care of her."

"I'm not saying I won't, but where are you going?"

I stand straight. "I'll leave it for you to figure out."

"If I put Harper on it, she can hand you your ass."

"Good luck with that. Just know that you're a fucking cunt, and I should have kicked your arse fifteen years ago."

"I love you too, dickhead."

"Go fuck yourself."

I leave before I tell him too much.

CHAPTER 49.

CASSIE

Frieda can't believe her ears. I slide my folders into my briefcase, shaking my head just as she is right now. I'm shaking it because no one understands me. She's shaking her head because, yeah. She doesn't understand me.

"I can't leave my grandmother. She means everything to me." I try out my half-truth to see if I can make it sound like complete honesty.

"You've wanted this forever." Frieda is practically stomping around like a three-year-old.

But I'm confident I'm doing the right thing. One, for my grandmother. Two, for Keaton. But I can't tell her number two. I can't tell anyone. Not even him.

"I know." I shrug as if it's nothing. It's something, but not everything.

"You've wanted this forever. What did you think you were going to do if you got sent to CID? Not go to Quantico?"

"If my grandmother had broken her hip, I wouldn't go to Quantico either." I snap my bag shut. "How does it feel being GS-12?"

"Same as being GS-11, but with more money. You know, I really admired your ambition. So I think I'm taking this kind of hard. Personally."

"Yeah, look, you're not the only one who's disappointed. I really think my grandmother is going to be completely impossible to live with now. She's trying to kick me out the door. She keeps telling me that she'd have a boyfriend already if I were gone."

"Maybe she wouldn't be the only one who had a boyfriend."

She waggles one side of her eyebrow, then her expression grows dark. Almost angry. "Unless you're staying for Mr. Smirkypants?"

Of course I'm staying for Mr. Smirkypants. I'm staying to protect him, not to be with him. I could be with him from the San Francisco office just as easily if being there didn't mean he'd be the object of my investigation.

"Think about it," I say. "You and I can still hang out together. We can go have champagne every time there's a pay raise. When we catch some lawbreaking douchebag."

"Sisters-in-the-law." We bump fists.

I sling my bag over my shoulder and walk out. My heels clack along the sage-green hallway. Every time I walked that hall in the past, I assumed there would be a last time. One day I'd move past this little field office. One day I'd fulfill my destiny and remember this linoleum fondly, the shade of green with warmth, the buzzing fluorescence by the utility closet with some kind of nostalgia. But none of that is going to happen. I'm here. I'm here for the duration.

Am I okay with that?

I can't say that I totally am. I'm a little sad, a little broken, very disappointed. But what choice do I have? I will not be pitted against Keaton. Truth be told, I'm not sure how long I can even stay at the Bureau and have him.

I won't give him up for anything. Not to be the director of the FBI. Not to have that silver badge linked to my name and my ID for the rest of my life. Not for all the approval in all of the world.

I only want his approval. I only want him.

There are some choices that aren't really choices. Some are really tests. This is one of them.

Out in the cold, in front of the long circular driveway between the federal building and the parking lot, I stamp my feet. It's snowing, and my shoes are completely inappropriate for the weather.

I'm five minutes early, that's how eager I am to see him.

The parking lot looks especially dismal under the cloud cover and the slapping wet snow. I pace, my heel slipping on icy crust. I right myself by grabbing a pole. It, too, is slick and cold with new ice. It's going to be a hard commute home.

When my phone rings, I'm not surprised it's him.

"You should wait inside," he says. "The bridge is covered in ice."

"Be careful."

"Winter is crap."

"Yeah."

"You won't have this in California. Not even in San Francisco. It gets cold and rainy in June, but never like this."

His excitement carries over the squeak of the windshield wipers. He wants what's best for me, to the exclusion of everything else. He has to know we have a dossier on him. He has to know he'll be a target for me once I move. He doesn't seem to care.

The snow is getting thicker. Horizontal.

"I have to talk to you when you get here."

"Tell me."

"Not while you're driving."

"You're on speaker. It's safe. I do need to talk to you as well."

"I'll see you when you get here."

There's a long pause. The wipers squeak. The rain pats his windows.

"Hello?" I say. "Keaton?"

"I love you, Cassandra."

He hangs up before I can tell him I love him too.

Ten minutes pass in the break room. I make hot chocolate and look out the window while I sip it, burning my tongue. I open the fridge and grab milk to cool it.

Outside, the wail of sirens is muted by the snow and wind. Their flashing lights move across the open fridge door. The squawk of radios, the jingle of keys and equipment, stomping feet all come from the hall, and one of the security guys pops his head in.

"You seen Nelson?"

"No. What's going on?"

"A Lexus skidded off the Winnetaka Bridge."

I drop the milk.

• • •

I don't have my car. There's not a cab in town. No one should drive in this. No sane person would.

Apparently Nelson and sanity have not made acquaintance. I find him getting his boots on by his desk.

"Can you take me over to the scene?" I ask, not panicking at all.

"Sure. Give me half a shake. I'll be out the west gate. Green Sierra."

There's no need to run to meet him there. He's still in his office, but I hurry so I can do my very best waiting and, despite my claims to the contrary, my most efficient panicking.

I head for the west gate, which exits onto a smaller service road, and trudge through snow-thick air, turning my face against the biting wind.

What if it wasn't Keaton's Lexus? What if it was some other Lexus, or another make, or the car in front of him? What if he's coming around the front and I'm sitting at the west gate?

I call him. No answer.

I text.

> —*Hey, are you all right?*
> *Text any response*—

I wait. The signal's pretty good, even in the storm, and the message is quickly marked as delivered. But there are no twinkling dots to indicate he's typing something back. He's driving in a blizzard. If he has half a brain, he's ignoring my text.

My fingers are getting cold. I pocket the phone and put on my glove.

I'm going to quickly check the front gate and see if he's there, then he can drive to the service gate and tell Nelson we're good to go.

It's a plan.

I walk across the lot as quickly as I can in these stupid shoes, head bowed against the snow, hands in my pockets, thinking it'll only take me a minute. A minivan pulls astride me. Is it a Sierra? Green? Covered in snow, with only the dark arcs of the windshield uncovered, it's hard to say. The side door slides open.

I get in.

"Can we roll by the front first?"

The side door closes, and the driver turns to me. A scarf covers the lower half of his face and a hat covers the top.

My relief at being in a warm car is swept away by the sight of a crumpled up Burger King bag on the floor and a mini baseball bat in the driver's hand.

My defensive move comes a split second too late.

CHAPTER 50.

CASSIE

I hear rain first. I'm not fully capable of feeling my body outside the pain in my head, my shoulders, my hips.

I'm not quite sure I can move, even if I want to. My skin wakes. My clothes are damp. The floor against my cheek is dry. Even warm. Even soft. It's not a floor. It's a bed or a sheet or a blanket. But it's dry, belying the click of raindrops. I wonder how this is possible.

The sound of the accident is in my head, not my ears. Bangs. Whooshes. A shout from Keaton.

Keaton. Where is he?

With that panic, the rest of my senses wake up. My awareness of my body becomes fuller, surrounding the pain with the feeling of tightness in my arms. They're boxed, wrist to wrist, behind my back. Restrained. When my eyelids flutter, they scratch against fabric. A blindfold.

Where's Keaton? I can't imagine he'd allow this, and the speculation that he's the cause of this circumstance sparks and dies. No. He would never.

Is he dead? From the accident I can barely remember, or from some other crime?

I strain against my bonds only enough to test their strength. I'm conscious enough to know that I'm too unconscious to think clearly or fight off whatever's gotten me here.

Through a wall, or door, or some combination of both, I hear a male voice. Another language. Not Keaton.

I don't know if he speaks any other languages. How can I not know that?

The sound of rain is not rain. It's a crackling fire, and I realize that I'm warm even though my clothes are damp. I feel like two hundred pounds of dead, wet weight held together by ache.

I don't recognize the language being spoken on the other side of the wall. It's punctuated by a short, derisive laugh, and no other voice joins it. Whoever it is, he's on the phone. I don't assume he's alone.

Keeping my body still, focusing on my breathing and the lines, contours, and limits of my body, I move my ankles apart just enough to determine that they are not bound. I'm on my side, a flat pillow under my head.

Whoever it is doesn't want to kill me quite yet. What does that say for Keaton's life? Will they hold me for ransom to flush him out? Or are they waiting to kill me for some other reason?

I don't know what to wish for, so I don't wish for anything. I don't think about Keaton. Speculation uses too much energy.

The voice stops. There's a bit of shuffling, a bit of clanging around the kitchen. I'm desperately thirsty.

The door opens with a creak. Needs oil. The house, or room, or whatever must usually be vacant. Nobody could live here and deal with that creak.

"Wakey, wakey." The voice that had been on the phone a minute ago is slightly familiar when it's in the same room. Not quite familiar enough to pin down just yet.

I don't move. I just breathe and listen to his movements. One step. Two steps. Three steps. The distance from the door to my side. Eight feet. Nine feet, maybe.

The creak of the chair. The flick of a lighter. The thick, earthy scent of a foreign cigarette.

My blindfold is moved away. Light shoots through the veils of my eyelids. Incandescent. Not sunlight. Maybe there are dark drapes or closed blinds, but my guess is that it's still nighttime.

"Nothing broken, lucky girl."

I open my eyes. The figure sits in a chair next to the bed, smoking. My vision is too blurry to see properly, but I can see the orange pinpoint arc to his lips and I smell the smoke as he exhales it. I blink the fog away, but it's stubborn. My arms move reflexively to rub them, but I can now identify my binding as a single loop of duct tape around my forearms.

"Who are you?" And what have you done with Keaton?

"Are you warm enough?"

I'm not answering that. Hostility won't get me far right now, but I don't owe him my comfort.

I squeeze my eyes shut and move them around. Left. Right. Up. Down. Then I open them again.

He has soulful brown eyes and a nose that's been busted. He's not much older than me, but they seem like they've been hard years. He smiles at me. One of his front teeth is chipped a little bit.

I've seen chipped teeth look worse.

"Hello, Doctor John," I say with a voice that's hoarser than I expect and a throat that burns with water and grit.

"So kind of you to remember. So like a well-trained abuser of power." He reaches his arm close to me and flicks his ashes into something out of my vision. His jacket opens and I see the shoulder holster on his right side.

He's left-handed.

There's a window behind him. The blinds are open, and I can see the deep orange of the sky reflected in the snow. The color tells me that light from the ground is bouncing off the clouds. We aren't too far from the city. But the dimness of the orange hue tells me we aren't too close either.

I open my mouth to ask him where Keaton is, then shut it. I won't let him know what's important to me.

"I'm so sorry about your boyfriend." His smile turns his sentiment into a lie, but his message holds the truth about my lover.

I've lost him. Somewhere in the blackness between those brake lights and waking up here, he slipped away forever.

I swallow what little spit I have, along with my grief. Not now. Now is not the time.

"I can't move."

"I left your legs free. There's nowhere to run in a blizzard."

The lines of water pattering and dripping on the window mean the blizzard part of the storm is over, but I don't correct him.

"No, I mean I really can't move. I can't feel my legs."

He smiles, and I wonder if I've overplayed this hand. He switches his cigarette to his left side, leans toward me again, then I feel a searing pain in my heel. I jerk away, rolling over until my hands and arms are again between my back and the bed.

John pulls the cigarette back and takes a drag. "I seem to have cured you."

Now I'm wondering what he did to Keaton, or if he's still doing it. If he was sorry about my boyfriend not because he was dead but because he has cigarette burns all over him. Now I want to take his face off.

"You're a miracle worker."

"Apparently not. I couldn't save that man you were with. So now I have to use you. I'm very sorry about that. But I have some business to attend with some people. And I need a little leverage. You, dear girl, are my leverage. We're going to get along fine as long as you cooperate."

As long as I cooperate, and as long as the other side of the negotiating table cooperates, and as long as I don't fall apart. Falling apart seems like the only real choice. Grief has a way of boiling over whether you turn up the heat or not. Grief seeps through cracks in the hardest armor, and right now, I'm all cracks. I have to hold back, pretend nothing matters to me, but my eyes burn with tears I'm not allowed to shed.

"What do you want? The FBI is not going to negotiate with you. Not for my life, at least."

"Fuck the FBI." He stubs out his cigarette on the night table behind me. The glass ashtray clinks as it taps the wood.

"You were going to kidnap me in Vegas, Keaton found me first."

"He was disloyal. You would have been a tidy way to pay him back. You're not useful for that anymore, but I can embarrass his employers."

I start to ask if he's trying to get QI4 back for something, but he can't mean he wants money from Taylor. I don't mean shit to him. If he wanted ransom from Taylor, he would have kidnapped Harper.

But what sticks is the thought that Keaton had employers at all. Imagine that. A whole other side to him. The white ceiling is in shadows, with a domed overhead light in the center. I focus on it. It looks like a breast.

God, I'm losing my mind.

"I should've taken you for every dime you had at the poker table." I lick my lips. My arms are falling asleep under my back, but the rest of me is now wide awake. "You're a mess of tells."

"Your heart is too soft to stall me long enough." He puts his hands on his knees and stands over me, eyes grazing my body in a way that's objectifying but not sexual.

I can feel my clothes pressing against my skin. I'm completely covered, yet I feel completely naked.

He takes a knife from a little leather sheath at his belt and flips it open. I'm not afraid of the knife. Dead people aren't as useful in a negotiation.

He flips me over by the shoulder, and I see the other side of the room. The fireplace has no pokers, and there's a latched screen in front of the fire. I won't be able to hit him with a brass rod or throw him into the fire.

He cuts away the duct tape. My arms creak and ache when I move them. The tape is still stuck to my arms. I rip off one side. It hurts like fucking hell, but I won't give this guy the satisfaction of seeing me get squeamish about getting a little hair pulled. I pull away the other rectangle of duct tape. It takes a piece of skin. I act like I don't give a shit.

I don't actually give a shit.

I sit up straight, bending my knees to one side then tucking them under my bottom to sit Japanese-style.

He puts the knife back in the little sheath.

"For the record, you really are a shitty poker player."

"Poker's not my game."

"Of course." I slide off the bed on the opposite side so he doesn't feel threatened. "It involves actual human interaction. Not usually a hacker thing." I wave as if swatting away trivial concerns.

"Are you trying to bait me?" He tilts his head a little, brows knotting in concern, as if I'm a monkey in a cage, palming a pile of his shit. He's asking me if I intend to throw it, and if I understand he can destroy me if any lands on him.

Sociopath.

Not all sociopaths are evil. Most lead curious but normal lives. But grouped with narcissism and sadism, sociopathy is a very, very dangerous sickness.

The sadism is apparent in the heel of my foot.

The narcissism in the lengths he will go for vengeance.

So. Here we are. Standing on opposite sides of the bed.

I have this.

I trust myself.

"I'm thirsty," I say. "I'm happy to get water myself, but you're making the rules here."

"You may go." He points at the bedroom door.

One, two, three steps, favoring the burn on my foot. By the fourth step, it doesn't even hurt and I'm out. He follows me, where I can't see him. The rustic, open living space has a kitchenette, an old couch, a larger covered fireplace with no pokers. It's a log cabin, and the horizontal lines of the logs encircle the exterior walls.

I walk into the kitchenette, watching him in shiny surfaces. The microwave door. The windows.

"Glasses over the sink," he says.

I reach into the cabinet. Plastic. Can't break and slash. I fill a pink cup with a Budweiser logo. Turn. Drink, watching him over the rim of the cup.

His fingers play with the pressed edge of his jacket.

Sensory processing disorder.

When he blinks, he squeezes his eyes shut.

A tic.

"So what's next?"

"We wait. If you behave, I don't shoot you."

"Fine." I put down the cup.

His approach is swift and stealthy. He catches me in the millisecond I take to put the cup in a clear spot, punching me in the face with mercilessness and speed. My vision explodes into a thousand points of light and I drop to my knees.

"In case you're wondering who's in charge," he says from above me. "I'm not some basement-dweller. I don't need this gun to make you comply."

"Okay." I choke out as I put my forehead on the cold floor before I tip completely. My stomach twists, but I'm not puking. Nope. Not today.

I'm not standing until I have my wits back. His shoe is right in my vision.

"You were doing your job, but I trusted him. To find out he'd been spying on us all those years? It makes me look foolish."

I look up at him. His jacket is still open. His right middle finger still strokes the fabric's edge, and when he blinks, it's so hard his nose wrinkles.

My right eye throbs. "He wasn't working for us."

"I never said he was." He holds his hand out to help me up. "You were doing your job, so I don't mean to hurt you."

Timidly, I hold out my hand, and we grab each other by the wrist.

"Thank you," I say as he yanks me up.

He blinks.

I use the extra millisecond to slip my hand into his jacket like the artful dodger I am and pickpocket his gun, pretending to lose my balance so I can unsnap the holster while he's tilted.

I have it.

Not one to waste time, I pull the trigger.

The bullet hits him in the leg, and he falls backward. I stand over him. He's got his hands up, but I'm not fooled. There's no surrender in his eyes. I aim the gun between them.

I'm going to finish this motherfucker.

The roar of engines comes from outside. The flash of lights.

"You are the luckiest man alive."

"My partner's going to find you."

"I look forward to it."

The door bursts open. Headlamps. Shouts to clear the area. Only when I see rifle tips surrounding Kaos do I take my finger off the trigger and hold up the gun. It's taken from me.

I get a pat on the back. It's Ken, arm still in a sling. When I face him, he flinches.

"That's gonna bruise up nice," he says.

I touch my eye. It's heavy and tender. Orlando joins Ken in looking at my busted face.

"I had him," I say.

Orlando nods. "I know."

Ken gives orders to forensics, getting pulled away in the chaos.

"How…?" I don't finish the sentence.

A man I don't recognize walks in. He has silver-grey hair, a long wall coat, leather gloves, and a stiff upper lip.

"Agent Grinstead," Orlando says, "this is Ambassador Brookings. He alerted me that you might be the target of this asshole."

The ambassador takes off his glove and holds his hand out to shake mine. I pin his accent in the first four words. "Sorry to meet you under these—"

"Do you know where Keaton is? Is he alive?" I leave his hand hanging.

The two men look at each other, then back at me. I've obviously shown my hand. I've told them what's important to me, who's important to me, and why I shouldn't be going to Cyber Crime. I don't give a shit. The FBI can shove that job up their ass, and this British guy can go right behind. I want Keaton. I want him now.

"Tell me." I snarl those two words. They come from deep in my throat and stop right behind my teeth

"Grinstead." Orlando uses my name as a call to attention, but I don't need to be told to focus.

There are probably a dozen agents in the tiny house. Things are getting overturned, there's shouting, barking, the squawk of radios, and I don't give a shit. I don't give the tiniest little shit. I am more focused than I've ever been.

"Let's get the scene under control." Orlando doesn't know what he's dealing with as he tries to stall me, treat me like someone with no skin in this game. He thinks this is about the job for me. It hasn't been about the job since I met that man. "You'll be briefed—"

I cut him off. "You tell me right now what I need to know, or I'm going to burn this fucking place down."

Orlando looks at me as if I have lost my mind, and maybe I have. The ambassador, however, doesn't know me from a hole in the wall. Doesn't know who I am or what I'm capable of. To be honest, I don't know who I am or what I'm capable of either, but he seems to know enough about me to know that I'm not going to sit in the back of the ambulance with ice on my eye, drinking hot fucking cocoa. Maybe he's reading me like a book. Maybe Keaton told him, or maybe I have a star-spangled tell for being a woman in love.

He slowly shakes his head, turning up his hands, one bare palm one leather-gloved palm, and says "I'm sorry."

That's that then.

You don't say you're sorry unless what you're not saying is going to break somebody's heart.

I'm not going to faint.

I am not going to faint.

I am not going to fucking faint. I am, however, going to throw up. I brush past the agents coming in, run outside, no jacket, no gloves, just enough time to jam my feet in the heels Kaos left by the door. The exact wrong shoes for an ankle-deep step into the snow as I go to the side of the house. I put my hand on the log wall and bend at the waist. All I see is the snow on the ground and the top layer of white flakes vibrating in the wind.

He's dead. They killed him. He's dead. I killed him.

My stomach lurches and I try to let it up. I try to just get rid of this loop of agony in my mind.

He's dead. They killed him. He's dead. I killed him.

I want to see the body. I never want to see the body. I want to know if he drowned or banged his head in the accident or if Kaos did it. I never want to hear his name again. I want to go. I want to stay. I want to throw up, but I can't. I can't let it up because if I do, I will be expelling him from me. He is permanent. Even if I never told him that he was permanent, he changed the shape of my heart forever. He let me trust him, molding my heart into the shape that clicked into his like a puzzle piece. No one else will fit. He custom-made my love to fit his.

I will never let him go.

"I trusted you," I say to the wind. I say it to the cold. I say to myself, and I hear it.

I trusted him.

I still trust him.

The side of the building drowns in the white lights of a car, and my shadow is a cutout on it. I am the negative space, taller in the angle of the lights, tripled in paler versions of me at the edges. As the car swings to the left, my shadow swings right and disappears. I'm still here. Only the shadow is gone.

I'm going to disappoint you.

I'm going to hurt you.

I trust him.

Had he not been hinting at this the entire time?

No matter what happens, I'll never leave you willingly.

Willingly.

But the text.

An ocean cannot separate us.

And the alphanumeric string he made me memorize.

That code is everything you need to know.

What was it? I need to know *what* it is, because now I know *why* it is.

I stand up straight, and suddenly I'm not sick anymore.

CHAPTER 51.

CASSIE

I've always been an ambitious person. I've always wanted something more. To be better. Do better. Go further. Now all of this energy is turned to one thing and one thing only.

Find Keaton Bridge.

The official story is that his body was lost in the river and they're still looking for it.

Good luck with that.

I have a different strategy. Find out what the code meant. Find out his real name, even though he might not be using it anymore.

I think best when one half of my brain is focused elsewhere. I'm at the firing range, squeezing off round after round after round. *Pop pop pop.* I don't even feel myself doing it anymore. I don't even feel the pain in my hand. I don't feel hungry, thirsty. Nothing.

The British ambassador in San Francisco does nothing but confirm lies. He's very sorry about my loss. He can go fuck himself. I have another stop to make, but I need my head absolutely clear for it. I need to know what exactly I want.

Pop pop pop.

I'm not going to get emotional. I'm going to do this job, then when I know for sure whether he's dead or alive, I'll have feelings about it. I practically have my breakdown scheduled.

Pop pop pop.

I leave my last bullet between the target's eyes and slide out the empty magazine. I'm out of bullets.

"What's on your mind?" Shadow Horse Brady asks. "Or do you have stock in a lead mine?"

I sign myself out. "Just trying to think."

"I hear you're moving?"

I never officially turned down the Cyber Crime assignment. It didn't seem wise, not when I was as likely to find Keaton from California as I was from Doverton.

"Can't beat the weather in California."

"Nice shiner on that eye," he says as I put my jacket on. "I heard what happened. Everyone's talking about what a badass you are." He winks at me.

"Just don't get in my way." I wink back at him.

CHAPTER 52.

CASSIE

I'd opened Keaton's dossier as soon as I got a clean bill of health, minus a black eye, and after the firing range, I look at it with a clear head.

I don't know if he tried to tell me all of this before and I was just blinded by him and how he made me feel. His life was spent keeping secrets. I can only imagine how hard it would be for him to hint at anything or tell me something that had been locked away for so long.

My assumptions about him were both right and wrong.

Keaton has an asset dossier, not a criminal dossier. Cyber Crime watches him closely. Both of his parents worked in military intelligence for the British government. Low level, mostly data analysts. But his father made an enemy, and I assumed correctly that the family was moved to New Jersey to protect them. So when Keaton was busted hacking, MI6 recruited him. Unlike Taylor's work with the FBI, Keaton never quit. He had been working undercover for MI6 from the beginning, and right up until the end.

There are details on top of details about his work and his relationships. None of them more prevalent than with the two dark web hackers Keyser and Kaos.

Kaos is in custody. Keyser is not.

There's no match for the code he gave me. No indication of what it might be.

I consider the possibility that he's dead and I'm in denial. I let that option sink in, but I cannot accept it until I see either the body or some other proof.

I don't have a picture of him. I don't have a memory that's physical. An object holding my hand. The photograph of him in that dossier is all I have, and Lord knows I'm not so stupid as to try to take it with me. So I memorize it. I memorize the slopes of his body as they ran under the curves of my hand. I remember the feel of his cheeks in the morning before he shaved, the blue of his eyes that is not captured in the photograph but in the beginnings of the night sky just after twilight.

"I'm coming for you," I whisper. "Buckle in, Keaton Bridge, because I'm coming for you."

• • •

I'm not exactly cheerful, but I have a purpose. I had purpose before Keaton. Get promoted. Move up. Be better.

Now my purpose is love, and if that's not happiness, I don't know what is.

The light buzzes over the door to the utility closet. The flat green is as institutional and putrid as ever. I'll see this hallway again, and one day I'll stop walking its linoleum, but it's no more than a passage from one place to another.

"Grinstead!" Orlando calls from behind me. I wait for him. "Did you get the comm from cyber? About Keyser?"

"Closing in, sir."

"I want to make sure you're not chasing him down yourself."

"No, sir."

"Good. They have it. You should be sleeping off that knock on the head anyway. You get paid downtime for a reason."

The end of the hall is a right turn for the coffee machines and a left turn for the exit.

"I'm picking up my grandmother from the hospital."

He shakes his head slowly, "Jesus, it's been a rough week for you."

"I'll be fine. Really. Don't worry. I run faster uphill."

With a light shot on the arm, he turns right and I turn left.

CHAPTER 53.

CASSIE

Nana and I are like two wounded warriors when I bring her home from the hospital. She's in a wheelchair, dying to get out of it, talking about how she's going to attack physical therapy as she has attacked nothing before in her life. I look as if I've been hit on the side of the head with a two-by-four, and I too am ready to attack my own healing like nothing I have attacked before.

I'd put a plywood ramp up the short steps, and I wheel her up it. The door's wide enough for the wheelchair, and with things all moved around, the living room is clear for her. I've already set up a bed and a chair that'll tip her in and out of it.

"I cannot wait to get out of this cage," she says for the hundredth time. "It doesn't even hurt anymore. I'm fine."

"You have pins in you. Do you want to sit on the couch?"

"When is the nurse coming? Don't you have better things to do?"

I help her to the couch and set her gently in her usual spot. "Someone's coming tomorrow to help you. I have to finish packing. They say you can move with me in a couple of weeks."

"Cassandra, I have to tell you something."

I fluff her pillows and lay a blanket over her knees. "Okay, tell me."

"I don't want to go to California."

"Nana—"

"I mean it. I want you to go there alone. I'm very sorry about what happened to that boy, and if you need me to be with you, I'll be there. But I like it here. I'm used to it. I have friends."

"You were so excited to go. Don't pretend you weren't."

"I thought if I went with you, it would make you happy."

"It was an act? Is that what you're saying?"

"I realized I was too old for the long con. I don't have the patience. And moving? I get tired thinking about it, and I get tired thinking about living with you again. I have to sit up and wait for you while you're off toting a gun and catching criminals. I have to worry day in and day out. And then I have to worry that you're stuck in a rinky-dink field office with no chance of making something of yourself. I moved here to take care of you, and maybe now it's time you take care of yourself so I can take care of myself. I'm a selfish old woman."

I sit next to her. "If you're lying… I don't want you to underestimate how angry that will make me."

She rolls her eyes at me. What seventy-three-year-old woman rolls her eyes? I laugh for the first time in days.

"Now that's the first time I've seen you laugh in days," my grandmother says. "Sweetheart, what happened to you makes me very sad and very angry. I mean, you can't even trust a man to live long enough to marry you."

I laugh again, dizzy with the release of my pain and sorrow. I want to rest my head on her lap. I want her to stroke my hair the way she used to. But she's too frail, and even after everything I've been through, she needs me to be strong more than I need her to comfort me.

"Eventually you're going to have to move in with me. I'll want you to. Can you understand that? I want you to come live with me when living alone is too much."

"Sure, kid."

Nana pats my knee with one hand and grabs for the remote control with the other, wincing with pain when she stretches.

"I have it." I turn on QVC, where a pair of sparkling earrings looks like the most beautiful thing in the world. "Are you settled?"

"Bernie and Grace are coming by."

"I'm going to run some errands."

I wheel her puzzle tray over to her. Half of the kittens are pieced together. I wonder if she'll remember her hip or my black eye whenever she sees this one. I'll think of how I started my search for Keaton.

Will I remember the disappointment of not finding him? Or finding out he's dead?

Or will he be by my side?

CHAPTER 54.

CASSIE

I learned Taylor is in the habit of eating dinner at the Barrington Mansion—Harper's family home—right across the river from the factory. It was where we first met, the day I flashed my badge and demanded to talk to Keaton Bridge. The day I met the love of my life at the factory and brought him in for questioning.

Harper's sister, Catherine, opens the door. She is the patron saint of Barrington, selling all of her possessions for over ten years to support the people of a dying town. The house has been refurnished with new things, and she has a sunny smile when she opens the door.

"Hello," I say. "My name is Cassie Grinstead. I'm with the FBI." I hold up my ID and badge. "I'm here to talk to Taylor. Is he here?"

"Come on in," she says, standing to the side. "We're eating. Can I make you a plate?"

"No, thank you, I won't be long."

She leads me into the dining room, which is richly furnished, newly painted, and populated with two men. I only recognize Taylor. The other is a handsome man in his thirties in a button-front shirt and expensive watch.

Taylor stands when he sees me.

"Cassie," he says by way of greeting. We shake hands.

"This is Chris," Catherine says warmly, introducing the other man.

We shake also, and silence follows. In the chaos around the accident, the kidnapping, the blizzard, and the search for a body that I believed was walking on the face of the earth, not at the bottom of a river, Taylor and I have given each other condolences. But seeing him, it still feels raw.

"Can we talk in private? I'm sorry to interrupt dinner, but this won't take long."

Taylor leads me onto the back porch. The backyard is spotted with garden lights, and over the evening horizon, the scaffolding and cranes around the factory are outlined against the sky.

I don't sit, and neither does he. "I'm sorry about Keaton. Again. I know you guys were close."

I gauge his reaction carefully, because no matter how many times I say it, the wound is still fresh and his expression will tell me what he knows.

The way his face drops a little and he blinks twice quickly lets me know that he believes he has lost his friend. I can't disabuse him of this until I'm sure. Hope isn't a worthy partner in death.

"I know that you've talked to some of our agents about Keaton's death."

"The other half of that team is still at large," he says, gritting his teeth. "It's taking a lot of effort not to go hunting for them myself."

"Yeah, but I want to tell you that even though I came here flashing my ID, I'm not quite here as an agent. Not one hundred percent."

"Really?"

"Well, in one sense I am. I want them to find Keyser. That's the federal agent part. But I'm appealing to you as someone who loved the same person."

"Go on."

"Did you ever know his real name?"

Taylor shoots out a little laugh, taps his fingers on the porch railing and looks into the darkening sky. "No."

"Are you lying?"

"I'm not fucking lying. What would be the point of lying? What would I be protecting?"

"Your company? Your factory?"

"You know what, lady? Fuck this." He's about to walk back into the house.

"He gave me a code." Taylor stops to listen, so I finish. "He never said what it was for, but he said if I lost him, I should use it. He didn't say what to do with it, where to put it, or who might know what it means."

"What is it?"

"You don't have such a code?"

"No."

I can see the question annoys him, and maybe that's a good thing. I want him to be a little on edge. I hand him the code handwritten on a yellow Post-It. He takes it.

"Seventeen digits. Alphanumeric." He cracks his neck and looks at it again. "I have a list of shit it isn't. Not octal. Not hex. Obviously not ASCII."

"Obviously."

"Where did you get it? Did it come up to the top of your bowl of alphabet soup?"

"Keaton gave it to me. He didn't say what it was. Maybe it's a path to Keyser. Maybe it's a map to buried treasure."

He thinks, pressing his lips together, casting his eyes downward as he wrestles with a question I cannot imagine. "You know who you need to talk to? And I'm not really enthusiastic about suggesting this, but I promised Keaton that if you ever needed anything, I would give it to you."

To me, that's just another hint that he always knew he was going to have to disappear.

"I need this," I say. "Whatever you can do, I need—"

"You need to talk to Harper. If there's anyone who can figure out what a random string of numbers is supposed to be, it's her. But you have to promise me that you won't bring her any trouble. If anything happens to her…"

"No one outside of the bureau will know that she and I spoke."

He nods. "If you find anything out about Keaton that you can tell me, let me know. Because some days I feel like I never even knew the guy."

"You may have not known his name, but you knew who he was." I tap my sternum.

Taylor clears his throat. "Are you sure you don't want something to eat?"

"No, thank you. I've been transferred to San Francisco. I think I might take a trip to California to find an apartment."

"Good luck. You're going to need it."

CHAPTER 55.

CASSIE

I see a couple of apartments, and they are utterly, ridiculously expensive. Especially because I constantly have to think about my grandmother moving in eventually, which requires space. I also have a nagging hope that there will be a six-foot-four British male in the house.

I meet with my new boss at Cyber Crime. She's tall and graceful, with a long curl of lavender hair and ears full of silver piercings. She gives me my assignment.

I give myself my own assignment. Find Keaton before I go undercover.

After the meeting, I take the train and slip into crowds so that I'm harder to follow. I don't know where Keyser is. I don't know if he's after me, but I did promise Taylor I wouldn't put Harper in danger. So when I get to Stanford, I'm pretty sure I'm alone. I check freshman classes for computer science majors, peeking my head into the lectures. She's not there. I check the second-year classes. Finally, I find her in a huge auditorium, learning a version of math I will never understand.

She's sitting in the center, away from the goof-offs in the back and the brownnoses at the front. I sit next to her, taking out a little notebook as if I'm a student late for class.

When she sees me, she seems a little startled; I'm out of context. I flip to a page in my notebook with Keaton's code written in the center and tap it as the professor runs through math functions well beyond my capacity.

She takes the book, putting it in front of her, thinking. She slides it back to me without a word, and I wait. I don't get up, and I don't give up.

The class goes on for another hour. There's a shuffle, a shouted assignment, and we're out in the hallway. I walk beside her.

"Your eye looks better." She flew out to Barrington after the accident to be with Taylor, and we saw each other briefly.

"Time's the best doctor in the business."

"What's the code?" she says, flicking my notebook.

"I was going to ask you."

"It's nonsense. Did you dream it? Did it appear in your alphabet soup?"

"Taylor didn't tell you?"

We're outside now. Harper doesn't slow down to talk, or turn, or do anything. She walks as if she's running a race.

"Taylor told me, but he doesn't know much. He said Keaton gave it to you, but he didn't tell me the circumstances. You know that's important, right?"

"He was fucking me and he made me memorize it before he let me come. Happy now?"

She doesn't slow down to be shocked. But she should be. I would be. She just laughs and shakes her head.

"All right," she says. "That means this is personal. I'm happy to help." She makes a sharp turn through a narrower campus alley. "Let's go back to my place. The fucking computers in the lab have more leaks and holes than…" She waves as if her mind is on other things. "They're not secure."

The alley spits us out into a parking lot. She bloops the alarm on a black Tesla.

"Thank you." I say.

"You kidding? Keaton was the most mysterious guy on the planet. I'm going to figure this out if it's the last thing I do."

CHAPTER 56.

CASSIE

I order in for Harper and pay cash. She barely eats. She types as if she's trying to break her keyboard. She asks me to get her some white tape from the bathroom drawer. I almost ask her which drawer, but each of her bathroom drawers has tape.

She loops it around her knuckles and types faster.

Her apartment is a massive loft overlooking the Bay. The rest of the loft has such an underused, untouched feel that I can't even tell if she lives in the whole thing, or if she just lives in the path between the front door and this room. It is banked with computers on shelves that line three walls with wires and circuits and soldering irons everywhere. She has flatscreen monitors ranging in size from "I'd like to watch an action movie," to "I think I need glasses."

"Okay," she says. "From what you told me, I had to open up a tunnel through an allied nation with bad monitoring and use the protocol to—"

"I'm sorry, Harper. I know you work hard to understand all this stuff, but I don't care. Just give it to me."

"I got into an MI6 cache, and I found him."

I leap from the couch to her desk and look over her shoulder.

I found pictures of him on Google, mostly from his time with QI4, but I looked at them so much, trying to spear him into my memory, that they wore thin. This one is new. It isn't recent, or candid, but every time I see a new picture of him, my heart opens up a little wider.

Harper's not as impressed. She flicks to the next page. "It's all stuff we already know, more or less. I don't know what to do anymore"

"There has to be something. He wouldn't have given me the code for kicks."

"Have you considered it was just a sex game?"

"No. He kept mentioning it. He said it was important, and if he says it was important, then it was important."

She scrolls, and on the left, a word becomes visible. It's an evil word, rendered in bold all-caps type, as red as a bloody lip.

DECEASED

I pretend I don't see it. "His parents' names are here. Charlie and Anna Bridge."

"Hang on," Harper says.

She works on another screen. Pulls up Charlie Bridge's name, does some other crap I don't understand. A blank blue screen comes up with a white field. Nothing else. Just a white box with a blinking cursor on the left.

"What's this?"

"It's up a level of security. You can't get in without a password or a hack that's beyond me at the moment."

I lean over her and type Keaton's code, slapping Enter without pause.

The life of a family stretches before me.

A name. A place. A reason for a split-second decision to move across an ocean. It's all in front of me, including David Webber's death, which has a date.

"He's dead but the file's active?" I say.

"I have no idea if that's normal. Let me check."

"I only have a few days."

"I have less than that." She covers my hand with hers, looking at me with an expression of sharp-edged sincerity. "We'll find him." She squeezes my hand, and I believe her.

CHAPTER 57.

CASSIE

We don't make it. MI6 is a dead end.

My despair lasts a few hours, but is replaced by hope. If I'm undercover, I can keep looking, I just can't expose myself. I have a week before I start, and I know I have what I need in that file. I just have to figure out where the clue is.

I'm meeting up with another agent three hours outside San Francisco. He's briefing me on the case, and we're leaving for Scotland on Tuesday to track Keyser's last known whereabouts.

I'm nervous. Nervous about starting a new job, a new city, a new life with the man I love still missing and potentially a target of the criminal I was chasing.

Trusting he could handle himself was as good as trusting he hadn't left me.

It's foggy here, just west of Yosemite. I wonder if that's intentional. A signal that I'm close.

The address here was all I had that I could use, except their real names and the real name of their only child.

I take it slow up the mountain. Redwood trees slash the sky on each side of me. The sun is just about rising over them. I'm a three-hour drive out of San Francisco.

I wonder if that's intentional too.

The location was more of a suggestion, a piece of land with a lot number, a purchase date, and a shell company as an owner.

My palms slip against the steering wheel. I'm so nervous I'm sweating. There's a driveway into the forest, and a wrought-iron gate that's locked. I pull over to the side and walk to the small opening big enough for a person. I walk a good quarter-mile on gravel winding through the trees. Finally, the house appears.

Modern. Large windows. Lights still on upstairs.

A dog barks, then another. I get nervous for a second. I'm not prepared for Rottweilers or guard dogs. But when they appear, one after the other, they're sheepdogs and they seem happy to see me.

Sheepdogs. Why sheepdogs?

Could it be?

I pick up the pace. The house seems so far away. I don't know what I'm going to do when I get there. Knock or bang on the window? Sit and wait? No way. I'm bursting through my skin. I'm like an over-full water balloon about to spill all over the Sequoia Mountains.

The dogs reach me, and I stop to pet them.

A whistle echoes over the mountains. The dogs spin and run in the opposite direction toward a man in jeans and a pale blue shirt.

He's tall.

He's as handsome as the devil himself.

The dimples in his cheeks are a promise. The smile lines are a joy. His voice, his looks, the leathery scent that precedes him as he runs toward me; all of it belongs to the only man in the world I'd lay down my heart for.

The distance between us seems miles. I'll walk it, I'll run it, I'll fly to this man.

I leap for him, arms around his neck, legs wrapped around his waist as he holds me up, lips meeting and speaking without words.

He snaps away, eye to eye with me. We're both made of breath and fog mingling in the air around us.

"Cassie, you came."

"David," I say.

"For now, until we catch or kill anyone who wants to hurt us, I'm still Keaton."

"I knew you wouldn't leave me."

"I tried to move back to London and couldn't. I had to be near you."

The dogs circle us, whipping into a barking frenzy.

I push him a little, but with the same motion, I grab his jacket in my fists. "You made me come and find you. What if I hadn't?"

He takes my wrists in his hands but doesn't pull them away. "That's why you're my partner now."

My eyes must have gone wide, because the muscles around them hurt.

"Given the choice, I would have taken care of it myself and saved you the trouble. But I needed to go back to MI6 and by then—"

"I'd been put on the case." I jerk him to me then away. I want to shake him, but he's too big.

"It's a cakewalk. Once we get him, you and I are going to get married and have babies."

"How long have you been planning this? Since the code?"

His lips curl into mischief, and his dimples are a promise that he's going to keep if only I believe in him. "The code was so you'd know what happened. I was going to become my old self, my real self, and live a normal life. This?" He puts his arm around me and extends his arm toward the house and the forest. "I changed plans after my death went so well."

"You gave up your dream in order to be with me?"

"If I'm going to be my real self, I want to be my real self with you."

One of the dogs jumps, putting his front paws on David's thighs. He loses his balance and we fall together into the grass, kissing, laughing, loving.

He's everything. I love him, and more than anything, to the ends of the earth and the end of time—I trust him.

EPILOGUE

CASSIE

Chris is having a panic attack, and Keaton is trying to soothe him in the middle of a windstorm of people. They're both in tuxedos, standing in front of the mantelpiece at the Barrington mansion, not that anyone could see the mantelpiece past the 744 roses it's layered with. Apparently there are supposed to be 749. It's five short.

I said Keaton. His name is David. I'm slowly getting used to his real name. Patiently acclimating to his real, gentle, giving self. He's been showing me the places he grew up, the people he knew. I met his parents, and the extended family he hasn't seen for years.

It's been a year since I found him in a house in the Sequoias. A year since he decided to live his life and commit to a place and a person. Been a few months since we nailed Keyser. But that's a story for a different book.

"I'm thinking of paper roses," Harper says from beside me. "Or just lying and telling her there are 749."

People arrive in pairs and family sets, all dressed in their best. The young pastor sets up a makeshift altar in front of the rose display.

"What's his deal with having an exact number?"

"Sentimentality. But there's not another rose in the state. So sentiment's gonna have to take a bow to math."

Chris and Catherine are finally getting married, a banner day when you consider they were high school sweethearts separated for thirteen years. Keaton glances at me and winks ever so slightly. His smirk still drives me wild, and his dimples are Morse code for happiness.

Taylor joins the two men, pointing at the rose garden in the back. I know what he's saying. You can pick five damn roses from there and none will be missed, but Chris's deal was that the rosebushes in the back stay intact. He's a stubborn guy. Handsome. Rich. Unbearably smart. And stubborn. But I guess waiting for someone that many years takes a certain kind of pigheadedness.

Keaton—no, David—peels away from the discussion and comes to me. "You need to be sitting."

"Oh God," Harper says. "I can't even think with you two arguing about this." She takes David's old place near Chris and Taylor.

I'm left alone with David putting his hand on my distended belly and saying, "Doctor's orders, Special Agent Grinstead."

"My ass gets tired sitting down all day."

"There'll be time enough to massage that arse later."

My pregnancy hasn't slowed us down at all. Not sexually, at least. He's become more gentle and sweet as the months have gone on, but I can't wait for the old roughness back.

Everything in its time. I'm having a baby boy in three weeks and getting married in two. Nana and his family are meeting us in Vegas for a big, splashy wedding. I had the choice to get married in a pregnancy-friendly wedding dress or get married with a baby in my arms. Nana put her foot down. She made no apologies or excuses for being a single mother, but insisted I break the cycle.

Harper stomps to the back of the house and slaps open the kitchen door. Keaton pulls a chair around for me until its seat hits the back of my thighs. I acquiesce and sit. He kneels on the floor next to me and takes my hands, flicking his thumbnail over my diamond engagement ring.

I love when he kneels next to me, puts his hand on my belly to feel our baby kick. It's the most dominant thing he does.

"Are you sure you want to wear these shoes?" he asks.

"It's not like you're gonna let me stand up."

The screen door slams open then shut again as Harper runs in with a handful of roses. "Look! These had just fallen right off the bush. Can you even believe it?"

She hands them to Taylor, who laughs.

"That's cheating," Chris exclaims. "The entire point was to leave the rose garden in the back exactly as it is."

"No," Harper says. "The whole point is that you have a good time at your own wedding, and if you're gonna freak out over five roses that no one can even see, then you need to take the roses from where you can get them."

"You should try getting married yourself," Chris replies, accepting the roses from Taylor.

"I'm still in school. Don't push me."

"Who's pushing?" Taylor asks.

Nana trundles in from the backyard in a sparkly sequined dress. She's holding five roses. "I heard you were short some flowers. You got a ton of them out in the back."

Chris throws his arms up as if surrendering to a mighty foe. I shift in my seat, sliding to the edge so I can get up. Keaton stands with me, bracing his arms against me as if I might tip forward, which actually, I might.

"Where do you think you're going, young lady?"

"I'm going to help them set up the roses… five of them. And the other five…" I had an idea about what to do with the extra five, but it flies out of my head when I feel liquid trickling down my leg.

"What's wrong?" Keaton asks.

"I think my water broke."

I kick my foot out a little while Keaton holds me straight. My stockings are wet all the way down to the shoe.

I look at him. He looks at me.

"I don't want to ruin the wedding," I whisper. "We should just sneak out to the hospital."

He presses his lips between his teeth as if he's holding back his words.

"Just grab my bag," I say, pointing at it. "And we can—"

"Father Grady!" Keaton calls.

"Yes, yes," the pastor intones as he removes a silver chalice from a box.

"I need you to marry us right now."

"David!" I snap, using his real name without thinking for the first time.

"I'll tell Catherine!" Harper shouts before bolting up the stairs.

Grady doesn't look up from arranging the silver. "I have thirty-four minutes."

"We can wait," I hiss.

"Did you piss yourself?" Nana asks. "Or is the cake baked?"

"The cake is baked," Keaton says. "Father Grady!"

The handsome priest looks up for the first time, pushing his glasses up his nose.

"We need a quickie before this baby is born out of wedlock," Keaton says.

"Your parents," I whine. "And the party."

"We can still have the party. We need rings. Right?"

"Right," Grady answers, still looking a little flummoxed. "I think. Uh…"

"Use ours!" Catherine flies down the grand staircase with her wedding gown unhooked at the back and her veil waving behind her. "Chris! Give them the rings!"

Chris has his hand over his eyes. "I'm not looking at you!"

"Who has them?" Catherine shouts.

"The best man," Chris says from behind his hand. "Back upstairs, woman!"

I turn to face Keaton fully. He's David. He's real, and he's mine.

"It doesn't matter," I say. "Not really. Let's not take the wind out of their sails."

"We'll be gone before Catherine Barrington even walks down the aisle. And it does matter. It matters to your grandmother, for one, and it matters to me."

"I don't think you're going to leave me."

"I will never leave you. I hardly think even death can separate us." He leans his forehead on mine. "This child was created out of our love. Let's make sure he's a part of our commitment too."

He's looking out for me, and in his eyes, I see only love and care for me as a person, not the consequence of a wedding after a birth.

Chris has the rings. He hands the big one to me and the smaller one to Keaton.

Grady stands by us with an open book.

"The short version," Keaton says.

"Do you have vows? Could be quicker that way."

"No," I say.

"Yes," Keaton says at the same time. "I'll go first." He takes my left hand and isolates the ring finger.

"Make it quick," I whisper. "I'm leaking onto the carpet."

"Cassandra Grinstead. You are the partner to my real self. More than a name. More than a title. You are more than family. You are the flesh of my heart and the reason it beats." He slips the ring on my finger until it nestles next to the diamond.

"That was nice." I sniffle, running my fingers across my cheeks, clearing the way for fresh tears.

"Come on, come on!" Nana shouts. "You're going to drop it in the car."

I hold up the larger ring and isolate David's finger. In a room full of people, half of whom don't even know there's a second wedding happening, I can only see his seven o'clock eyes.

"David Webber. I don't… I can't…" Words leave me. I want to get out my notepad and read off the stupid, flowery vows I'd written, but we don't have time, and they express nothing that needs saying. I can walk right into hell alone because I know he will follow me. He can run straight into oblivion and I will be right behind him.

What I need to say can be said in six words.

"I love you." I slip the ring on his finger. "I trust you."

"By the power vested in me," Grady interjects. I'd forgotten he was there. I'd forgotten everyone in the room was there, but the volume in my head gets turned up ever so slowly. "I now pronounce you man and wife. You may kiss the bride."

David smashes his lips against mine.

That's when the first contraction hits. It's more of a twist than a pain. But still, I say, "Ow."

Nana puts my bag on my shoulder. "Get moving!"

"It'll be hours, Nana," I protest. "Take it easy!"

"So you say. My mother dropped me so quick, my father barely had time to grab his hat on the way out."

"Let's just be safe." David hoists me into his arms and carries me to the door. He navigates the crowd in the living room, the porch, and to the car without taking his face off mine.

He gently puts me in the passenger seat and buckles me in.

"I have the music all picked out." I tap the screen on his stereo as he closes the door, crossing to the driver's side. When he gets in, I finish my sentence. "It's all in English too."

"It begins, my dodger. Stealing my stereo and stealing my heart."

He pulls onto the road, smiling all the while. I can't keep my eyes off his jaw and the curve of his neck. I want the baby to grow up to be just like him, with a soul so deep and layered, a lifetime isn't long enough to figure him out.

A man worthy of a woman's trust.

I'm embarking on an adventure that's been written by generations of women before me, and yet it's a story that's never been told. It's our story.

THE END

ACKNOWLEDGMENTS

My family won't let me write on weekends. It's absolutely infuriating, and completely necessary. Those mandated two days of brain rest always leave me with more and better ideas. So, thank you, Reiss family, for being the pains in my arse you are.

I'm so blessed to have people to call on to read my work before it goes out. They work fast, too. In particular, Jx read an unedited mess early on, gave story notes and corrected my British usage. My thanks go out to her. Any idiomatic mistakes probably happened after the first edit, so don't give her a hard time.

Angela Marshall Smith, my developmental editor, is always there for me. She tells me stories of her life or things in the news that clarify what the book needs, or digs deep into my circumstance to shake up my patterns and expectations. She's an emotional mentor.

These acknowledgments are unedited, because I finished this book so close to deadline I'm nervous many of you won't even have the right book. But for those of you who do, thank my editor Cassie Cox, who dove in with a schedule opening, allowing Keaton to be unleashed early in the new year.

I know I seem like some kind of badass ninja online, but that's because I hate burdening people with my insecurities, but trust me, I get really nervous about releasing books. I work hard and the odds that they can flop are pretty good. Sometimes it's the book, sometimes it's concurrent releases, or the world at large. The only thing I have control over is the book, and Serena and Michelle read an early draft and gave me the confidence to release. It was such a gift.

Jenn can kiss my butt, because that's how much I love her.

Jana Aston gives the most amazing beta notes. Seriously. She will never, ever, let me give anything less than my best. Friends like that are the best friends to have.

Jean Siska is my right hand and legal eagle. I look forward to the day I lose her to her own writing career, and dread it at the same time. My Drazen World writers. I. Am. So. Proud. Of. The. Work. You. Do.

This is the year I consolidate the tasks I do and don't do. I'm focusing on writing and hiring the rest out. You have no idea how hard this is. Maybe you do. It's hard.

Hillary cleans up dictation and Cameron keeps my world alive. Sarah F helps me whenever I get lost in my complexities. Anthony manages my business. Laird at memphismckay.com keeps my website humming along with Jay at techsurgeons. Glorya puts on the best signing in Los Angeles. Ashley does beautiful emails and Sandy does data analysis. I bet you didn't know a writer needed a data analyst, did you? This one does. Andi's gonna put together a smashing audio-book. Kayti McGee performs a service for me I cannot discuss in polite company.

If you're starting out as a writer, the first thing you should do is make smart friends. I'm blessed with too many. It's the mentorship of other writers that keeps the lights on.

In particular, Lauren Blakely and Laurelin Paige.

Is it too much to say I'd be nothing without these women?

Maybe.

Draw a line between here and "too much." Mark a spot about 3/4 of the way in, and that's what these women mean to me.

On that, I leave you with a reminder to be kind to each other. Assume the best of people, whether they're in your tribe or not. Get past the gotcha. Listen without fear. Love without expectation.

I always end with a sales pitch, because we have to eat. Stay tuned for Catherine and Chris in *White Knight*, and if you want to know how Taylor and Harper got together, give *King of Code* a try.

I have a killer series queued up for 2018. Another married couple. I don't have a title, but good-golly-holy-smoking-kindles. I don't know how I created anything this dark and hot, but I did. Now I just have to write it and give it to you.

Stay tuned.

ALSO BY CD REISS

HACKERS AND CODERS
Meet the new Silicon Valley royalty.
Prince Charming | Prince Roman
King of Code | White Knight

THE CORRUPTION SERIES
Theresa Drazen and Antonio Spinelli are combustible. Their passion
will set the Los Angeles mafia on fire if it doesn't get them killed first.
SPIN | RUIN | RULE

THE SUBMISSION SERIES
Jonathan Drazen is rich, Dominant, and hopelessly empty, until he
meets Monica Faulkner and brings out her natural submissive.
Submission | Domination | Connection

THE FORBIDDEN SERIES
Fiona Drazen, celebutante and sex-addict, has 72 hours
to prove she isn't insane. Her therapist has to get through
three days without falling for her.
KICK | USE | BREAK

THE GAMES DUET
Adam Steinbeck will give his wife a divorce on one condition. She join
him in a remote cabin for 30 days, submitting to his sexual dominance.
Marriage Games | Separation Games

CONTEMPORARY ROMANCES
Shuttergirl | Hardball
Bombshell | Bodyguard

FIC REISS

Reiss, CD
Prince Charming

04/11/18